RIDING THE CENTIPEDE

JOHN CLAUDE SMITH

Praise for *Riding the Centipede*

"A master storyteller who infuses his work with a poet's vision and a madman's eerie gaze at horrible things."

– Joe Pulver,
Shirley Jackson award winning editor and author of *A House of Hollow Wounds* and *Blood Will Have Its Season*

"Even if you set aside the rich beauty of John Claude Smith's descriptions and the dense atmosphere he builds into this tale of horror both cosmic and man made, it's a joy to observe how he brings all of his marvelous and monstrous creatures together. A poetic sensibility and the cynicism of a classic California private eye meld with the spirit of William Burroughs informing/infecting countless details. And over all, Smith extends the deep shadow of something incomprehensible threatening to overtake the boundaries of detective fiction and its implied logic. Beautiful, crazy, poetic, and strange..."

– S.P. Miskowski,
author of *The Worst is Yet to Come* and *The Skillute Cycle*

"The breadth of his references— from Frida Kahlo to Celtic Frost (Are You Morbid?), Johnny Cash to Lena Olin, from "The Wounded Table" to Marilyn Monroe—sloshes together to concoct a hallucinogenic broth that's equal parts surreal, horrific, and compelling. This isn't a brew to be sipped by the easily offended— the folks within Smith's debut novel are hardscrabble, amoral, desperate druggies (Burroughs' preferred term over "junkies") willing to drag themselves through Hubert Selby-esque levels of depravity to attain their mind altering sustenance. The novel immerses the reader in a world where a P.I. hunts down an elusive target, we experience tragic Hollywood scandals, wallow in deep dark secrets, and witness a villain whose reign of chilling brutality brings to mind a mutant cousin of Anton Chigurh. Smith's prose is gruff noir, never tumbling over into camp, shot through with veins of luminous poetry."

– Christopher Slatsky,
Alectryomancer and Other Weird Tales and *The Immeasurable Corpse of Nature*

"*Riding the Centipede* by John Claude Smith is an impressive, hallucinatory and dynamically written novel that entertains, and provokes depth of thought with visceral prose and poetic hum. More than an ode to the Beat generation, this mythical, psychedelic drug trip mirrors the complexity of unorthodox language, uncommon perspective and nonconforming communicative style made famous by Henry Miller, Jack Kerouac, and Charles Bukowski, yet stands on its own with the very heavyweights it pays homage to. Smith masterfully anchors his story in lush description, cleverly crafted analogy and metaphor, and a twisted and darkly imaginative narrative. Highly recommended."
–Taylor Grant,
Bram Stoker Award ® nominated author, *The Dark at the End of the Tunnel*

"Fans of Burroughs and PK Dick will find a lot to like in John Claude Smith. *Riding the Centipede* is an intense trip into Bizarro Land."
– Laird Barron,
author of *Swift to Chase*, *The Croning* and *Not A Speck of Light: Stories*

"RIDING THE CENTIPEDE is an intense, crazy, brilliant and inspired work of imagination. Totally-gonzo-Beat-horror-experimental-noir-bizarro insanity. I give extra credit to artists who capable of doing something nobody else could do, and this is definitely that."
– Michael Griffin,
author of *The Lure of Devouring Light* and *The Human Alchemy*

For my love, Alessandra Bava, as well as the writers of the #weirdrenaissance, whose words inspire always.

Thank you to my family, friends, and the readers who've spent time with my previous tales. Much appreciation for your feedback and encouragement.

Special thanks to Kate Jonez for her editing prowess. The book in your hands would not be what it is without her assistance.

Special thanks to David Dodd for all his exemplary help in getting this reissue ready to roll and out to you, the readers, again.

"Desperation is the raw material of drastic change. Only those who can leave behind everything they have ever believed in can hope to escape. "

— William S. Burroughs

"A willing vein is a cause for celebration. A willing vein opens many doors."

— California Myers

"Sometimes we have the absolute certainty there's something inside us that's so hideous and monstrous that if we ever search it out we won't be able to stand looking at it. But it's when we're willing to come face to face with that demon that we face the angel."

— Hubert Selby Jr., *Last Exit to Brooklyn 7*

CHAPTER 1

BLAKE

...as the current pulled the child away, he reached toward her with his damaged right hand. The current pushed back; it wanted its prize. He yelled and water filled his mouth. He tried again, desperate to save the child, his daughter, Claire. The frothing tide pushed against his fingers, intent on bending them all the way back to his wrist, flattened out as a stump sculpted from futility. "Daddy..." He watched his daughter's shocked expression as she lost her grip on the car seat she should have been strapped into and was sucked out of the splintered halo of glass where the passenger side window should be. Jagged glass sliced into clothing and flesh, but the eyes moments ago filled with joy were now nothing more than dull buttons on the rag doll that remained. He yelled again, a stream of bubbles flowing from the inside roof of the car and out the crack in the driver's side window. He pushed against the stick shift with strong legs, his shoulder shattering the window. The sound was a muffled explosion. He watched the rag doll fade to black beyond the car's beams. He closed his eyes, fighting back tears as he swam up, or somewhere, this watery oblivion, his personal hell...

Chirping sounds clamored for his attention, a physical force pulling him up from the harsh realm of the dream-lands, grabbing his hand and winning the battle over the cloying mental quicksand that is Morpheus, not that this was a victory for Terrance Blake. The sound was akin to beetles picking at the remains of his dead past or the dregs of his present so-called life…or possibly of a future draped in shadows and secrecy and the same old, same old. Along with pain, the ever-present calendar wrought in his bones, his soul, every breath.

The promises spewed by the world of his hardscrabble youth, counterfeited and further cheapened by the accumulation of years. Endurance—the pin plucked from the grenade, while he waited for the explosion that never came. Endurance, the true meaning of life.

The squalid five-dollar-a-fuck hotel room smelled of smoke, the cut glass ashtray overflowing with lipstick-stained cigarette butts even before he'd lit up his first Marlboro. Remnants of passionless couplings.

The stale stench of the room was infused with the ghosts of those who had passed through before him: transients and junkies and one-night lovers, nomads and madmen and private investigators like him, getting by on somebody else's dime, dismantling somebody else's broken dreams.

The chirping continued; his cell phone the culprit. He reached over in the dark thinking it couldn't be time to be awake yet as shadows held conference in the room, his eyes. A glance toward the digital clock adjacent to the television confirmed his suspicions: 3:36 a.m. Scooping the phone into his thick, gnarled fingers, the light from the screen corralled motes of dust lifted by his clumsy maneuver. Dust he hadn't noticed last night when he placed the bottle of whiskey there, the now two-thirds-empty bottle.

He wondered how long he'd been in this room, sleeping like Rip Van Winkle or dying with every stale inhalation, exhalation, and long pause to consider the prospect of terminating this bleak routine before carrying on, carrying on.

He realized it was not the alarm that has inspired the insect revolution. It was a phone call. The name on the screen registered as familiar but not one he'd used often.

"Mr. Blake, I've found evidence of Marlon's whereabouts."

No matter how many times he had told her nobody called him Mr. Blake, it's just Blake, she persisted. He let the miscue slide. The voice was unmistakably that of Jane Teagarden, a voice braided with iron and perseverance, something he could relate to.

Jane Teagarden was the only daughter of successful Hollywood producers, Warren and Stella Teagarden. A production team made rich beyond filthy, producing a slew of action movies starring Stallone, Schwarzenegger, Snipes and Van Damme. All good things must come to an end, though, and with a glut of bombs, the freewheeling excess that had dominated their lives simmered cold and hard until rumors arose of Warren having affairs with some of the help; "affairs" being a polite take on the harsh underbelly of what often happens when the rich are overtaken by failures and/or their eccentricities.

One of the maids made headlines with allegations of rape.

One of the mechanics on the premises quit in a huff, suggesting Mr. Teagarden was a sexual deviant. A hush-hush payment altered his initial statements, casually sloughed off as a mistake of perception.

The tabloids ran with it all, going so far as to suggest Stella Teagarden, fifteen years younger than Warren, subsisted on over-the-counter and extracurricular drugs that induced supportive silence, a sheep in fox's clothing. The fox wired for the depraved transactions of the flesh of which her husband allegedly catered.

Rumors, all rumors, erased with the remains of their dwindling bank account, until their only son, Marlon, two years Jane's junior, ran away when he was fourteen, hitting the streets while hitting the newspapers with torrid accounts of sexual abuse nonpareil.

The ruination such an incident would suggest disappeared as swiftly as Marlon had when Jane, dressed as one might imagine a modern-day fairy-tale princess—a formula façade worthy of Disney—made a televised statement to the contrary.

I think it's time I spoke up on my parents' behalf. Over the last few years, rumors created by those seeking financial gain have cast my parents as monsters. She glanced down, considering her words. Her voice grew steady. *I'm here to tell you nothing could be further from the truth. Two more loving and generous people one could never know. With the recent developments involving my brother, I must say, I do not know what world he lives in. Our lives are special and we are treated as special. We are shown love in…so many ways. But Marlon has always been a bit aloof. I am saddened by his disappearance and look forward to his return, so we can be the family you all know we are. And we can give him the help and love he needs.* She smiled, her slim lips stretched tight, mouth unopened. *Please leave us be while we deal with our sorrow and the authorities help us find him. Thank you.*

Blake remembered watching this little scene with curdled curiosity, thinking it an Oscar-worthy performance jammed into a B-movie steeped in melodrama and deception. Because there was nothing in sixteen-year-old Jane Teagarden's tone or expression that rang true. *(Claire would have been sixteen, had she lived…)* He hedged his bets on hollow and scripted. Yet the public ate it up. Her glassy, tear-stained eyes drew support from the legions whose bible was *National Enquirer*-style rags and who gave a flying-squirrel-fuck-all like-minded media manipulated television programs such as Entertainment Tonight. A month before her nineteenth birthday, her parents died in a suspicious house fire that turned any evidence within the scrubbed-clean and lie-imbued walls to ash. Blake thought it a perfect obliteration of the crime scene; investigators always missed *something*. Speculation may be the trigger to the gun his instinct wielded, but he knew deep down he was right.

Because the false sympathy the search for Marlon elicited lasted less than the usual run for most sub-blockbuster movies, the Teagardens had taken refuge as phantoms in their own lives, their chilly castle. They became non-existent to those they used to call friends. Those not willing to believe in them, perhaps knowledgeable of the accusations prior to Marlon's leaving. Perhaps protecting their own high-profile asses in attempting to avoid the harsh, accusatory bleat of "accomplice" or "participant."

Jane Teagarden inherited what most thought must have been meager financial remains, only to be proven wrong. The latest version of the will contained the updates and restructured profits for the DVD and burgeoning Blu-ray contracts—restructured a mere two months prior to the fire—that set her up for life.

When Blake heard her voice on the phone, the muffled ringing of *the truth* he never heard in any of her statements at grief-stricken appearances traipsed into his migraine infused cranium. Nine months after the fire, her voice had gone from Hollywood-practiced and Hollywood-refined grief, to the voice he knew now on the phone. Strength tinged with desperation; iron braided with perseverance. She really wanted to find her brother.

"You, well...you and your family have had others looking for—what is it now?—almost three years? What makes you think I will have any better luck?"

"Mr. Blake, you have a reputation of getting your hands dirty. I want those dirty fingers digging into the dark corners for the sake of my brother. I still believe he is alive. I need to know for sure. I want to help him."

"What if he doesn't want to be helped? He's not come out of hiding as of yet, and with your parents gone, you might think he would have, if it mattered to him." He said this with a smattering of thought that Marlon may have been the one behind the suspicious fire that killed them; then again, with the timing so close to the restructured will...

"It doesn't matter what he wants..." She paused.

Blake sensed her rearranging her thoughts.

"I just need to know he's okay, Mr. Blake. I need to know he's okay."

The connection crackled, slackened then tightened as a noose, as if words were about to follow. It went slack again.

Blake felt himself being drawn into a mystery he had no desire to explore. Though his home base was in Los Angeles, much of how people conducted themselves in the City of Angels left him dry. Rampaging egos and decaying ethics suffocated humanity, then molded it into media-prescribed perfection with plastic surgery. The prevalent smog was the perfect statement for it all, a black cloud corroding a moral compass that spun with relentless disdain out of true. Yet despite everything, his instincts told him she was telling the truth, even though something he couldn't quite define bothered him.

"I'll pay you triple your usual fee, as well as all expenses."

Well, no dilly-dallying now, he did have his priorities. He'd made just enough money to eke by for the previous two years. Questions of how she'd found him—who had suggested him—what rumor of him getting his fingers dirty had been passed around, dissipated into dust, motes captured in light, only to fade when drifting into shadow.

Just as everything faded to dust, eventually.

He put his all into the case for the following year, with no results. There was usually something, at least a trace he, and only he, could discover or decipher. It was as if Marlon Teagarden truly had disappeared. Even with no results of any sort, Jane Teagarden still kept him on retainer, yet he expected minimal contact.

This was only the third call in five years. Wild goose chases and dead ends had been the result of the previous two. He expected the same from this one. He sensed Marlon was dead and her belief was simply propped up by denial.

"Miss Teagarden. Good early morning." He said this more for himself than for her, her voice, the wake-up call he did not expect on this dreary day. "What can I do for you?"

"I have evidence of Marlon's whereabouts," she said again, her tone rimmed with annoyance.

Direct and to the point: "Continue."

"I've had not one but two sources inform me of Marlon being sighted in San Francisco's North Beach. I need you to head there immediately, to confirm it is him and to make contact."

"As in the beginning, Miss Teagarden, perhaps, quite obviously, he does not want contact. Perhaps—"

"Perhaps you should do as you're told, Mr. Blake. I don't pay you good money to question my motives."

She was right, of course. Yet the desperation increased from haloing her tone to wrapping around it as a cloak.

"If a couple sources have alleged to have spotted him in San Francisco, might I suggest getting photos to confirm—"

"I want to speak to him."

Again she cut him off. He felt his blood rise.

"I want to see him face-to-face. I want to know…all he knows. I need you to finish the job."

Why Blake? Why did it have to be him to finish *this* job?

The stale air grew electric. Or perhaps it was his blood's pace picking up exponentially amid her desperation and oblique comment: "I want to know…all he knows." Smoke burned in his lungs, at the back of his throat. He exhaled sharply.

He popped four generic aspirin he'd purchased at the airport, downing it with the rest of the whiskey.

"I'm presently in Portland, Maine, wrapping up a case. I will be finished in a couple days, then heading out to San Francisco."

"Leave now and I will quadruple your fee."
The line crackled taut — tauter still — the static noose strangling him.

He made the airport in time to catch an early morning flight to San Francisco, attempting to clean himself in the small restroom and failing. His clothes needed a wash and masking his sweat in cologne only magnified this problem. He stared out the window toward the top layer of clouds that seemed to go on forever and half-heartedly wished the plane would go down in a fireball of screaming metal and charred bodies. Half-heartedly, because he knew that was not his destiny, if one were to believe in such a thing. His instincts, a psychic gift or an eternal curse, let him know this much.

He tilted the black cowboy hat he'd bought in San Antonio, Texas, many years ago—bought on a whim while running around with a woman whose name evaded recollection—over his eyes, and thought it still a better option than this misguided excuse for a life.

CHAPTER 2

CHERNOBYL

The only light in the room came from the man's glowing, mismatched eyes. The left pupil was a black ink stain abyss, a swirling wasteland devoid even of the promise of starlight. The right pupil was gray as ash, the remnants of hope long dashed. Riding the rim of each pupil, flares worthy of the Sun writhed with furious intensity. The veined white of each eye illuminated the room in a blinding brilliance that ebbed into a sickly, jaundiced hue, depending on his focus, until the man closed the lids and the room went dark.

The eyes may be the windows to the soul. These windows were pitted with cracks, as if pebbles had been tossed for attentions never attained. Furthermore, what resonated within the man in no way resembled what paltry beings usually defined as "soul." His allegiance was to a higher force bereft of humanity. At least in its purest distillation.

He rubbed his thumb, pointer and middle fingers together, an instinctive practice he used when conjuring the past. Sparks crackled at the tips of his callused fingers.

As he concentrated, he pried the memories from the clutches of time, refurbished as if recent. The initial stage of the ritual delved into the few minutes *prior* to his conception and included details about the participants as if he were jacked into *their* thoughts and memories. The room smelled of burned plastic and animal musk, of damp, aged ruins and electrical currents that tweaked the mind as well as the nostrils.

The fragmented mind-field was a flurry of clipped imagery: gagged and bound, a thin woman, flesh stretched taut over a blade-like pelvis, the hollow between her tiny breasts. A man carved out of the same tainted material, though a wiry strength accentuated the muscles of his back, his buttocks. Hours of physical exertion defined by semen, sweat, excrement, misery, torture. The genetic material each contributed the product of generations mired in futility and rife with mental deficiencies. The man in particular spawned from a long, corrupted squiggle of a line of nefarious design, his father and the fathers before him: cruel, sadistic, evil. Though they were all infused with deep intelligence, they were all psychologically broken—a Ming vase shattered into thousands of tiny pieces, chips and shards and miniscule slivers, with no desire or means to mend what's bred in the bone.

The seated man tilted his head back, remembering the annihilation of the ovum, the vile, dissonant echo that accompanied his conception. A reverberant pulse filled his resting body as water fills a balloon. His core stiffened. His penis stiffened. Passions wrought in immorality were at the root of his being.

It was 4:27 a.m., 26 April, 1986.

He salivated as he pictured the man starring in the mad play in his head stuffing a urine saturated rag into the woman's mouth. He didn't delight in the thought of the foul taste, but he thrilled at the depth of sadism he assimilated from the man.

The woman was simply a means to an end, a born victim, human refuge, a whore, a junky. The man was a junky as well, but he was a functioning addict. He could fit into society without notice. Nobody ever thought much about him as he worked the swing shift janitorial job at the plant. Though he understood much more about how things worked within the plant, he chose to immerse himself in his insidious lusts rather than the higher aspirations his intellectual gifts would have allowed him to pursue.

He didn't aspire to be human. He fixated on the black malignancy that corroded his every ideal.

As the seated man with the sparking fingertips continued along the diseased path of his origin, his memories splintered, as they always did.

Loudspeakers filtered into the womb, voices tonally different than the harsh tones of the man, or the muffled grunts of disapproval from the woman. Those voices he *felt* as much as heard. The other sounds were surging floodwaters and fluttering jackhammers and a flailing salmon pawed by a grizzly bear — the body in revolt — and then silence. Days of silence.

During this time, he sensed something within the speck of fleshy self, the idea of his being: radiation.

Some moments roam outside the realm of possibility, outside the laws of nature — what a comical assumption, nature adhering to any arbitrary laws — and miracles that join those moments as they roam.

A smile illuminated the darkness.

What meager aspirations and understanding humans had when it came to the immeasurable potential that was life.

Humans believed they understood it, but they constructed their theories within a limited mindscape. Their egotistical certainty disgusted him. They were rather pathetic.

This much the seated man knew. He was evidence of what a concoction of radiation, region — hence, nature — human potential and unyielding desire could be. He was a hybrid of flesh and foible: radiation infused with radical intent; with whim and impossibility.

He was a miracle.

Behind his sealed lids, the luminosity from his smile creamed the black to orange, a distant fire. He tamped it all back, pulling on the reins. After years of training, it was easy to control that which resided inside him. Easy, yet necessary, for his existence relied on restraining the chaos within, only tapping into it when required.

Radiation with a sentient foundation. Radiation with a nuclear heritage. Radiation acclimating to *its* birth with a whisper of phantom consciousness and a dream of life as melded with the fertilized egg.

Converging on a moment, crystalline and clear as the immaculate merging of sea and sky into a lush, electric blue horizon.

Not a radiation to destroy, but one to create, to carry on with *his* and, hence, *its* creation.

In the now dead womb of the woman, radiation blanketed him with soothing, tingling warmth, and a desire for improbable survival.

For life.

The radiation accelerated his formation. Neurons and electrons bristled impatiently while axons and dendrites jolted into corporeal conspiracies, into a jitterbugging frenzy. Hot-wired channels within the sticky web of fresh tissue that was his being prompted a profound topographical transformation fused by revolutionary synaptic hardware, enhanced muscularity and heightened gray matter development.

Yet, within, his roots—demons cackling for attention, strapped with subversive, generational binds—would always play tag with his potential.

Bony, talon-like fingers scratched at the viscera as he took it into his toothless maw and absorbed all he needed from it, and then continued on, until he tore a hole out of the womb, out of the stiffening carcass.

He didn't cry as the stale, infected air entered his lungs for the first time. He only yearned for more.

It was dark but his vision glowed much as it does now, in the vast art gallery that covered the walls around him, only with less control.

All of the fundamental elements of the third and most prominent participant in his creation had taken hold. The man and woman of flesh were only a means. Radiation from the exploded fourth reactor at the power plant nearby served as the most vital ingredient. The itchy trigger finger squeezed hard, prompting mischief of an inconceivable audacity.

He survived by sheer will, living on the remains of the mother, then gumming insects and rats, suckling them as surrogate breasts in his eager mouth; and sucking on torn wires and cables, draining them of whatever was left to fuel his being.

After a time the splintered pictures glued together again; even if fragmented, they were clear enough.

He was taken from the desolation by a big man—Dmitry Ramazanov—part of a final reconnaissance crew sweeping the area before it was turned into the Exclusion Zone.

Dmitry was astonished a baby could have lived without food or water for the five days since the evacuation, and six days since the decimation of Pripyat.

As he clutched Dmitry's large finger, the big man said in Russian, "Strong grip. I fear he's not long for this world, though."

During the decontamination process, the radiation coiled into his heart, disguised itself with efficiency. Much to the shock of all involved he lived. His accelerated growth slowed down, back to a semblance of normal. He was only six days old, yet he passed for six months No one would ever know, or believe, the nine months gestation that zipped by in the wink of a blind eye.

When Dmitry got back to his home in Tolyatti, his wife, Tatiana, took the baby into her soft, eager hands and showered him with affection. She'd never been able to conceive which had been an issue between Dmitry and her in an otherwise loving relationship.

The years that followed were filled with their love as they showered him with affection and what little they could afford, nurturing his love of art by spending money best set aside for food on art books that he would immerse himself in for hours at a time. But there were also the stark truths delineated by death as Dmitry succumbed to the cancer his lone trip to Pripyat had inspired…and how he was pleased to have this message from his true father, the radiation that lived in a symbiotic state within him. A message of power. A message of means. Not the threat of cancer when contained, as much as the gift of radiation that he knew he needed to explore. It was his birthright.

Despite Tatiana's unwavering love for him, soon after Dmitry's death, with her health failing as well—similar cancers had taken roost in her, though she'd never stepped foot in Pripyat—she sent him off to her brother, Ivan, who lived in America. Her overwhelming grief had crippled her spirit and exacerbated her condition. The terminal kiss lingered within her; she lasted three more years on the steep downward slope to death.

At this time he was ten years old and had already filed her in his memory banks as nothing more than a stepping stone across a wide ocean.

Time simmered as he grew up in America, "the land of opportunity." The years accumulated without much fanfare.

His Uncle Ivan recruited him into the family business when he was seventeen and big enough, strong enough, imposing enough, to lend a menacing presence in situations requiring such appearances.

Acne scars littered his otherwise handsome, sharp-chiseled face; acne, born in those moments when his control had slipped. Moments when anger moved beyond simmer and boiled over. Moments when spontaneity unleashed the beast within. Moments he avoided as best as he could.

He remained stoic, a sponge for all that transpired around him, while Uncle Ivan's Russian underworld connections thrived in small pockets around America, taking advantage of the opportunity America flaunted and abusing it unmercifully.

The man whose fingers sparked brighter as he climbed through the muck of thoughts and memories, now purely his own, cherished the depravity that swelled in his head. Thoughts of murder, mayhem and deeds done quite dirt cheap with value besides financial gain and sadistic glee filled him with a feeling like hunger. With his special tastes, he had to feed regularly.

He opened his mismatched eyes and the room was momentarily lit as with a fire. He smiled and his whole body reacted with rare pleasure.

He pulled hard on the reins, not allowing himself to get lost in the joy of such experiences. His breath heavy, he regained control.

He remembered Tatiana telling Dmitry they would name him Rudolf, after her father.

He liked the name Rudolf, though when he was thirteen and a kid in the neighborhood made jokes about a reindeer with a red nose, he'd lost control, for the span of a minute, perhaps two. He'd experienced the first concentrated distillation of his power, surging with tingling efficiency as he squeezed the boy's neck in his already large hands, pulverizing the vertebra as he did. It was his first taste of murder on a personal level. Sure, he might have played a part in the deaths of Dmitry and, more so, Tatiana, his mere presence and what frolicked within seeping out on occasion, but this was hands on, and he liked that, loved the feel of life bending to his will, his strength.

No one caught him. He left the body slumped next to a homeless man drinking and sleeping away his life. Nobody ever made fun of his name again.

By the time he was eighteen, he was six foot three, a stone-faced mountain of brute force topped with a shock of slicked, spiky, white hair. He'd garnered a reputation for delving into the deepest gorges of pain distribution for Uncle Ivan and his cohorts in crime. He was ready to freelance, move beyond the constrictions of Uncle Ivan's rule. It was time for him to cater to his own whims amid the mayhem he promoted. For this he needed an appropriate surname.

Though Ramazanov had been the name he'd used since Dmitry had taken him from his birthplace, he finally could acknowledge his origin, no matter the curious looks he got from others.

He finally could acknowledge his only true father:

Chernobyl.

CHAPTER 3

TEAGARDEN

"What are you fucking looking at?"

The woman cowers, as if disgusted. Shields her baby from my glare, as if I will bring her or the drooling tyke harm. As if they amount to anything within the world I live in. As if they matter.

She does not understand me. How could she? She's one of the boring. Those trapped in conformity's clutches. The normals.

Can you think of anything more revolting than them, dear sister? Well, perhaps you can, you've never joined me here. Perhaps you've become one of them, a blob never to be shaped into anything of worth.

You see, dear sister, it's like this, my life. It's like an oily, black glacier slowly melting, new revelations gleaned from the process. Years spent opening the synaptic channels, rewiring the corrupted neural circuitry, has culminated with a new purpose, a new revelation. This purpose is derived from all that has come before it via experience and memory and my excursions in the dark frontier. Memory is altered by time. Time is of no consequence in the life of the enigma. Therefore memory is of no consequence. Melting away.

The trick is not to alter the truth, to allow the passage of time to sheer the edges off of memory and soften the impact of the truth. The trick is not to manipulate anything. Simply let it be, as is, without enhancement or embellishment or contemplative distortion. The knot is incorporated into the weave, the tongue within the mind's faculties. The teller of each tale, each autobiographic recitation, must adhere to the experience in its purest form.

The teller is God. Yet God is a fantasy, an illusion. Therefore, the teller's words are only worth the spit it takes to tell them.

Believe what you will. I deal in truths.

After ten years, time is irrelevant, The life I've lived in the margins and ephemeral black holes dug out of ragtag tenements and garbage-strewn alleys, out of shards of broken mirror is coming to an end now that the promise of the green limousine is on the horizon. I've finally found what I was looking for, even if I had no idea what it was until I found it.

"Fucking hell, all of you, march on your petty way."

I split my lips to show them my chipped, decayed grimace and let my tongue loll like a dead toad to send them on their way. They have no idea what it means to live. I disgust them because I am different, yet my difference is negligible in the scope of things, because I live a true life.

You're always with me, you know? Yes, you're always with me. I wonder if we have a psychic link. I've never felt you, sensed you, but perhaps you are a receiver. Not many of them in my world. Only those who take.

When was the—

I make a face at man in a thousand-dollar suit and his broomstick skinny woman in her short, snug, red dress, teetering and about to topple, unaccustomed to her too high heels. She's hanging on his arm and hiding behind the pinstriped limb. What the fuck are they doing in this part of town anyway? Strip clubs and slice-of-pizza joints, a few Beatnik bookstores.

"Oh, tell me to fuck off, will you? Slumming might get you closer to living if you just let go of your ideals. You wouldn't understand living if it bit you on the ass."

I trod in their direction, lanky me and my ragged attire, worth a buck fifty, perhaps.

"That's right. Listen to your woman, just leave me be. I'm fucking *crazy*, man."

Laughing now. Lunatic laughing. There is joy in watching them awkwardly avoid our dance. Wallflowers. The normals.

Where was I? When was the last time we were together? Perhaps you are a distant memory made concrete by my insistence and nothing more. I could let you go, but this was always our plan. What came before in our time together lingers as rumor as much as truth. Because out here, where living is truly experienced, I know of truths that blur the past. Out here life is lived uncorrupted by the media-manipulated mentality of the average human, the normals. Overstimulated expectations stunt dreams with the avid assistance of glitch-in-the-machine technology. Our parents literary decadence is part of the inspiration obliterated as they crumbled into sexual obsessions. Yet I often wonder, with all this madness, why you've never made the trek out here yourself, joining me in the bliss of experiences without restrictions. Away from the world we hated.

Why did you not come with me, dear sister?

I wonder if these words that constantly roar in my head are even for you.

I've been to San Francisco so many times you'd have thought I would have heard about the Centipede before, and of Riding the Centipede. It infuriates me my slow learning. My different learning in the dark frontier. It infuriates me.

I repeat myself as a means of refining all I have learned. I will get to the Centipede soon enough. Here and in the limitless world I live in.

I live. What are you doing?

Rumors are the hobgoblins of any true reality. Equal parts imaginary imp and soldier of substance.

Allow me to enlighten you, as I often do, with some of what I have learned:

1. Reality is objective.
   A. My reality is not your reality.
      i. Not yet
      ii. But soon
      iii. I hope
*Define soon.
2. Time is irrelevant.
3. Rumors are the hobgoblins of…
*I said this already.
   Expand:
      A. Rumors court truths within the psychic realm.
      B. Lies constructed from truths usually get lost in limbo.
      C. Rumors have their fangs set in the throat of reality.

"Fuck."

I spit and stick my fingers into my mouth, scraping out the vile condiment. How could anybody ruin a perfectly fine burger with this yellow shit? Must be why they dumped what's left in the garbage.

"Watch all you want. I'm not here long. I got people to see, meetings to attend, drugs to ingest, rides to take. Watch all you fucking want."

Back to you, dear sister.

4. Memories are psychic lies and nothing more.
   A. The past—what's known as the past—is inconsequential to the ideals forged in the Now.
   B. Memories wallow in the swirling undertow of the past.

        i. Therefore, memories have no bearing on my life.

    C. There is only ever the present. Now. Which dies with every passing second.

        ii. What is essential one moment is parchment the next.

5. Drugs are the trains we use to travel along the rails of the metaphysical world.

    A. Only full immersion allows the sensory expansion inspired by full immersion.

        i. In your world full immersion is a fantasy.

        ii. In my world it is a way of living.

The word metaphysical has a different meaning in my world because it is just an acceptance of the totality of reality, not a splitting of the known and the unknown, the undefined. I separate them above so you can understand. That is all.

The drugs of the world you live in serve purpose as pain killers, pleasure derivatives, and means of mind expansion.In my world the drugs are different. Different. The word different is paramount for understanding in my world. I know it is different here and better at least for those who wish to experience spiritual and physical sensory overload. For those who wish to experience. I've done time with heroin, cocaine, et cetera. They bore me now that I have experienced the drugs only those such as myself and a few who really engage in the polished-to-gleaming gist of living life as if they mean it.

6. Literature is truth.

7. Imagination is freedom.

Enough of this. I will infuse more insight as I go along but now I've spotted my connection. My rig with the first and perhaps last ride to the place where Burroughs awaits his followers.

Yes, William S. Burroughs. He is not dead. The literary translator of languages and drug-infused visions from inner and outer space, William S. Burroughs, waits in a tomb of sorts somewhere, I don't know where yet.

He is alive. In a way.

The ticket comes as it always has via hypodermic syringe. Specifics still need fleshing out but apparently one is to inject a full syringe of their own blood into him. The blood courses through his body, hot-wiring his brain, and after a couple hours one is made to draw out the blood and inject it into one's self. This is meant to show you what he saw *and felt*. Without inhibitions. Complete and uncensored. True sight. True experience.

You do know the original text for *Naked Lunch* was twenty-seven thousand words longer, right? No of course you would not know this. A portion of it was even written in the language of insects, best considered simply as "the language of insects," as any attempts to define it with our meager alphabet are rendered futile and even in some cases have left those who have attempted mentally scarred. It is the most prevalent language in my world, though the language of reptiles—see the previous note on "the language of insects," add ten, subtract millennium—is also widespread. English and Spanish and some obscure and mostly dead African languages are also spoken by most. I've learned some but not enough. Yet. Latin was apparently a joke that took foothold in the old world. The insects still find amusement in this.

"Riding the Centipede" is supposed to be the ultimate experience for any living being. All living beings. Human. Insect. Animal. Alien. As well as those of other dimensions.

(I must clarify: when saying "insect." I do not mean the minimal percentage known in of your world. I mean insects that only the imagination of those in sync with the dark frontier can even fathom. Thus goes defining animal, alien, and those of other dimensions. I've only made acquaintance with a few of each but must confess their repulsive beauty or beautiful difference enamors me. So different. So different.)

I must experience this.

I've only now gotten this much information. I had heard of it on the hot winds in southern California before. Along beaches in Oregon and alleys everywhere. It was only when Grimes, one of my regular suppliers, detailed the most concise refinement of information beyond whispers and cacophonous dreams, that I realized it was real.

Real in my world.

Hence, as I talk to you here, in my head, where you might be a receiver picking up on my messages, I make way to the green limousine parked in front of the Beat Museum, to take the first step into total illumination.

Hold my hand, dear sister. We're on our way.

CHAPTER 4

BLAKE

San Francisco was always one of Blake's favorite cities, despite his less than cheerful history within its crisp, cool borders. He'd even thought of moving there after the last job that led him to the City by the Bay, sinking into the more relaxed vibe.

He knew it was all a masquerade, though. The true personalities of all cities were revealed by what lives in the dark spaces between. The core, the essence, of any city was mired in parchment promises and dreams eroded by tears, grist for hope to chew up and spit out. Nothing more.

Though he'd taken many trips to San Francisco, he'd only had a couple of North Beach experiences. They left him wary of the task at hand. The crux of his existence was wariness. It was woven into his flesh, holding him together. Pain of memory; pain of the physical type. Pain, his ubiquitous god.

The first North Beach incident had occurred almost thirty years ago, when he was on the edge of adulthood, still feeling his way through a world he did not understand. He'd spent a summer in town, a nomad in need of money, and his six-foot-four-inch frame allowed him to provide bouncer services for a couple of the clubs.

After the rough upbringing he endured with his army father, it seemed the only logical path. His meat and muscles, and especially his mind, never refreshed with a word of encouragement or any words at all really, made this kind of work ideal.

He'd also done some on-the-sly detective work for one of the club owners. It led to a metal pipe pummeling that shattered the bones in his right hand. He also got a message to move on, big fella, move on, from guys not as big as he was but more experienced. The message was punctuated with one sharp crack to the skull, a fracturing exclamation point. He woke up hours later in a hospital, head and hand wrapped in gauze. Before the nurse made her second pass, he slipped out. Pain and humiliation had prompted his swift exit. It reminded him of home, the one he'd left after barely graduating high school, so he left San Francisco, burying another body in the already stuffed coffin of his past, this one still fresh.

The second time he came to North Beach was ten years ago, having graduated to official private eye status, his diploma wrought by-rote experience. Time may have healed the head and hand on the outside, though every chilly night was a merciless reminder that magnified the pain to unbearable levels inspiring his alcohol intake to push into the red, but it did not matter. Anything to alleviate the initial pain, and the harsh memories it inspired. The memories couched in events from a few years after the damage had been done...(*Claire*...)

Pain reminded him he was alive.

He was on the trail of a wayward husband of a rich socialite from down south. Cheating seemed as popular as shopping to those with money to spare and time to waste. For most of his time on surveillance he had been on stakeout outside of Vesuvio, a famous, poet-friendly bar where the husband made regular connections. With the strategically installed mini-cam Blake ended up snapping a few less than flattering shots of the man in a dank hotel room in the Tenderloin while he was getting anally reamed with everything and the kitchen sink. A couple of the local denizens, a poet of minor ilk—Blake had never understood the attraction of poetry, his tastes veering toward men's adventure tales and pulp fiction, Doc Savage and the like—and a former hot-shot player for the local baseball team who'd succumbed to steroids misuse and a rumored propensity for bleaching his anus, watched in dimly lit revelry.

He'd drifted for a few days after sending the photos to the wife. The information she received inspired a smoke and shifting mirrors sleight-of-hand campaign that somehow kept the illusion of their marriage intact. While the couples' carnival act played out, he took in North Beach's cafes finding a brief moment of fresh air before the place lifted its veil again, showing him things one would rather ignore, Disillusioned, he headed back to his home base.

When he got to San Francisco, he contacted Derek Potters, an old boxing buddy from his two-year stint in the army, a like-minded private eye based in the area, to secure Potters' beaten-up dog-shit brown sofa for his stay, acclimating to the task at hand: the search for Marlon Teagarden. One he was sure would lead nowhere. He's already had Potters scope out the street-laden rumor mill via his informants, to no avail. He slipped as discreetly as a man his size could, into the margins, asking questions himself, to similar futility.

After living on double slices of pizza for three days, he stepped out of Molinari's Delicatessen chewing on an Italian sandwich—prosciutto and provolone, straight up, no trimmings—ready to call Jane Teagarden with the insubstantial news, when one of the street vermin he'd spoken to the previous day sauntered up to him and said, "You'll know it when you see it."

"See what?"

"The Ano-anomaly."

What the fuck was that supposed to mean?

Dozens of flies buzzed feverishly about this wiry person's unkempt, dirt-crusted head, like some mud-packed pigmy. The smell hit him next, the heavy stench of excrement. The man's pants sagged obscenely.

"You've already seen it, you know?"

The grimy man twitched uncontrollably, guffawed sharply. He was an obvious meth zombie, the place was crawling with them, cockroaches dressed in soiled human flesh. Razorblades sliced through his skittering eyes.

Though he classified this man as street vermin, scum, he also knew he could be like him within a week or three of giving up and giving in to the painkillers and alcohol. Chances were he'd find purchase in harder drugs, ones made of diamond and meant to slice cleanly into the soul, dump the spirit, purge it as one would sour milk or fish gone fishy.

Blake started to verbalize the thought—"What the fuck's that supposed to mean?"—but the man was off, loping like a sick gazelle, finally turning toward the dark seam between two buildings and disappearing.

Blake followed with curious detachment. The message meant nothing to him. The scum—he remembered him from the previous days' paltry encounters, had said his name was Joe, "but my friends call me Skinny J," so Blake called him Joe and moved on with haste at his lack of anything important to say. When Blake observed the slim seam between buildings, there was no sign of Joe, but also no signs of exits, no doorways, no nothing. Where had he disappeared to?

Blake backed into the bustling midday street-life, contemplating the derelict's words, finding nothing to hold on to.

Then it hit him. *An Ano-anomaly. You'll know it when you see it.* A flicker from twenty minutes previous, before he'd strolled into Molinari's—a green limousine.

Parked on Broadway, across from an array of strip clubs, an oddly shaped and more oddly colored neon green limousine had caught his eye. So out of place. So out of place.

An anomaly.

He dumped the last third of the sandwich into an already overflowing garbage receptacle and raced toward the corner of Columbus and Broadway, glancing to his left the whole way. Barely acknowledging the flapping books artwork above his head or the various words stamped into the sidewalk he stomped on.

What if this green limousine had something to do with the whereabouts of Marlon Teagarden?

His instincts kicked up a notch, triggered by the odd statement from the derelict. Receptors on high, he didn't just sense this might mean something more, he knew it.

But when he made the corner, his pace slowed. The green limousine was gone.

He cursed his folly, and then cursed his uncertainty.

Never doubt your instincts, they've always been good up to now.

He shrugged his heavy, black trench coat snug to his big frame, the chill of something besides the weather weaving through the clothing to address his flesh with the faint kiss of discomfort.

Wandering back to the space between buildings the derelict had slipped into, he lit a cigarette, dragged deep, and measured the whole space with his eyes. Even though Joe had been skinny—Skinny J—it seemed impossible he could fit into this space. Perhaps this fella walked through brick walls. He chuckled unenthusiastically as he regained a foothold in the here and now, though still unsteady. Tracery remnants of shit tickled his nostrils.

That's when he realized the prevalent buzz of flies that accompanied all this, just as it had accompanied the filthy man. He swatted at the flies as they hurried with intent over a section of the brick wall.

Perhaps the man *had* the talent for walking through walls?

Either way, in the six years since Jane Teagarden had initially called him, he felt like some sort of progress had been made for the first time. Not that anything here pointed to that much, or even to the whereabouts of Marlon Teagarden, but the surreal quality to the episode touched his instincts with this impression. His instincts: the only thing he really trusted.

CHAPTER 5

TEAGARDEN

Tiny dents like acne scars are littered across the grungy neon-green skin of the limousine. Greasy fingerprints, not mine, smudge the door handle. A long, lean arm the color of a dung beetle's carapace or perhaps petrified shit with the veins wending over it push the door open and it squeaks, this door, and it reminds me of another language I need to learn. My mind wanders, a stray cat in need of a midnight hump, juiced by the language of desire.

Everything speaks in my world. Everything has its own language.

I'm drawn back to the car, the open door, the gateway to an abyss about to swallow me and the woman inside smiles with leering intensity.

"My name is Alice. Welcome to Wonderland." She snickers, the sound akin to a cage door being unlocked. There is cruelty in her tone but I skip past that because of what I need. I don't listen to my instinct when my mind and body yearn for experience at all costs.

Thoughts scatter:

I wonder what pills Wonderland's Alice was really taking. Specifically what pills or drugs was her creator Lewis Carroll taking? Was he one of those opium hounds from way back when?

If Lewis Carroll was privy to the world I travel in, he most certainly ingested drugs outside of the homogenized norm. With his proclivities for young girls, he was already wired for deviance. No, not exactly deviance though in the limited views of your world, the domain of those afraid to tap into their true selves, it might seem that way. What those people might consider as a perversion, I, and those like me, consider simply different.

It took me a while to learn this, the depth of this. Circuits open to evolve without restriction. Naturally. Leading into the dark frontier

I'm still learning now. It is constant. The influx of information. Of understanding.

I still want our father and his cohorts to die slow and painful and fully experienced deaths. There are some things I can never change…

Alice sits across from me, heavy breasts encased in a filthy yellow tank top, but not mustard yellow, so I don't chew on it just to spit it out. Upon further inspection, watching a spider dance on her shoulder, I realize the tank top might once have been white. Might once have been silk. The spider might be her tailor.

Denim short shorts, frayed edges caressing her brown thighs, smoother than the arm, her arms, no cracks to scar the surface. Sweat and the raw stench of her unclean womanhood clogs my nostrils. I'm hypersensitive already. I know it's the anticipation of the needle taking over. Of the drug I've only recently heard about. Of the drug meant to enhance my journey. Get me to the point. Make a point. Sharpen perceptions.

Open unseen doorways.

They're everywhere these doorways. But only those with the proper mindset and different eyes can see them. Travel through them.

I've never traveled this way before. I may be nervous but am also eager to undertake this new experience. Life demands as much.

Beyond the tinted windows, I view the faceless minions; truly faceless, putty to be molded, but molded by what? By whom?

Or squished beneath my thumb for their conformist rituals.

It took me a while to learn the depth of the possibilities that render this world relevant, even if wired properly.

Alice speaks, her rough cadence scratching at my eager veins:

"I am the way. The will and the sacrifice burn through my veins, man."

She can't mean literally, though the promise of doorways opened and more importantly information attained causes my pores to gasp on the fever sweat of anticipation. I don't care what she says or does. Whatever is necessary is always the path as long as she gives me what I need.

I must assure myself of her intentions.

"Burroughs. The Centipede"

"The Centipede. Burroughs, yes, Burroughs. The first step is...in here," she says, nodding to the syringe and the thick green liquid within. Something or some *things* swim in the liquid. Clawing for escape. For a willing vein. Pulsing to the tip of the needle. "The Centipede is yours...soon. I need one thing from you." She hands me some pliers and opens her chapped lips wide, the maw teeming with teeth and more teeth.

In my world, currency comes in many forms. Fetishes, objects of desire, are the most commonly bartered items. One's murkiest transgressions are polished to crystal clarity without the shadow speculations of your world. Here, there are no boundaries.

Perversion blows hot air with regularity up the ass of the addict.

My loose grip signifies I'm at a loss. Alice, sweet Alice, and her mouthful of filed, sharp teeth, jabs a thin knife into one of the blackened sections of gum in her mouth. Blood beads and drips.

She rudely slides filthy fingers into my mouth. Caressing teeth. Pulling on what's left. I gag from the force of her intent. More likely from the years of disreputable transactions coating her fingers like a glove, etched in the lines, never to be washed off.

I've only got half my teeth left since dental care is not a big deal in my world.

She grunts. Words are not necessary but I know what she wants. One of my teeth to join her enamel colony, her bartered collection.

She beams, her face in the shady confines of the green limousine, a black-light horror. Her point is made.

My hand trembles but I am not sure if it's with fear of the pain yanking a tooth out will instill in my already pain-wracked body or if its adrenaline amping up. I need the Centipede now.

No matter. I stick the slimy pliers into my mouth, taste the sticky fingerprints and residual fear leftover by those who have succumbed to Alice's proffered addiction before me, as well as the tangy, bitter taint of rusted metal, and let the snapping jaws make their choice. Halfway down the left side of my jaw their jaw clamps down on a loose tooth and I assist by squeezing with all my might to make the acquisition of the tooth as swift as possible. My eyes close and I hear only Alice's rapid breath as if on the verge of orgasm.

Anticipation has her in its slippery grips.

A harsh groan accompanies the task. The tooth refuses to come easily. My muscles, what muscles I have left, tend to the battle at hand.

Alice's long bony fingers wrap around mine as a spider to the cocooned fly—not her pet, her tailor, another arachnid imposter—but I shove them away.

Her breath only grows more hurried.

Finally, twisting as I pull, the sucking pop narrows the pain that inhabits the whole of my body, the nerves stripped bare and gnawed on by life, to this one point, the intersection of tooth and gum, and the deed is done. Blood spills on the crinkled fast-food bags and empty cigarette packs strewn across the floor of the green limousine and my shoes. My fingers ache from the mighty grip and are still shaking. Tears of pain varnish my face. I see my reflection in the metallic void of her eyes. An unhealthy gleam. A tortured repose.

Alice pries my fingers from her pliers and takes her prize. She pushes the tooth into the recently excavated hole and uses the closed pliers to hammer it into place.

"Now," I say. "Now. Give me the Centipede."

I watch her teeth vibrate and a sound like a chainsaw emanates from her mouth. Laughter. Satisfaction.

She hands me the syringe and I do as Grimes told me I must do before commencing with this trek. He didn't know much, but knew this much. After getting the register, I jam the needle into my neck. It burrows into the soft flesh, into the hungry artery. I let out a scream as the sensation is like nothing ever experienced. I've known the itch and scrabble of insects on my flesh, under the skin, countless times before. Though the sensation relates, this…this was atypical.

I feel many—hundreds, thousands—of tiny feet scrambling for purchase in my artery, my veins, branching out as I relieve the syringe of all its contents. My eyes bug out and I see differently. Wider. Deeper. Broader. More honestly? I don't know, but Alice's already monstrous smile seems even more inhuman, like slivers of glass spilling drool in slimy waterfalls upon her chin. She's hungry, too, and I wonder what she is hungry for.

I don't know what more she wants. I gave her what she *needed* in order to acquire the Centipede, the first step of Riding the Centipede. That's all that is required of me, at least as far as I know. But she's salivating with obscene, mesmerizing intensity, dripping into her dark cleavage, and my tongue hangs limp as a wet noodle as uncertainty makes the experience elusive. Perhaps it's just the understanding that a step is being taken. Yet that never hindered me before. Perhaps the experience is to feel the Centipede in my veins. And to let this green liquid and its insect inhabitants do whatever magic they must do to get me where I need to go. But the discomfort is mounting as they seem uncertain as well. Their trek is slow to kick in. Hemorrhaging at my throat, my breathing clipped. Worry hovers as a vulture about to swoop down and scavenge my soul.

That's when I realize it's not just my artery and adjacent veins being clogged. It is the visceral machinations of me. My body. Hordes famished and pecking at me, drilling into me. Into the sweet meat within, the sweetbreads, the blood a la mode dessert of my organs. I don't enjoy this part of it. Yet. Will I? Has Alice duped me? Does she want to use those glistening teeth to devour me?

She would not be the first to resort to cannibalism as a means of sustenance in the dark frontier.

All manner of food is undertaken here…

Yet Alice goes on.

"Let the centipede free. Let it roam within. Let it take control."

"I can't…"

"You must. That's what the voice told me to tell you. His voice."

Lack of control in this case makes me wary. Why am I going against the grain of the usual experience? Swimming in mud. Stuck. Uncertainty meant to disappear, but it's not. Hanging like an empty noose. Waiting to kiss a neck, hug it.

She foams as a rabid boar, the hot white tide coating my mind. Is she in there? Has she lied to me? Liars run rampant in the dark frontier. No repercussions mean no fucking rules. No nothing.

But then her words ride the gray matter railways with furious intent. I watch the space expand even more. Sucking me into the G-force vacuum of surrender.

Shadows shuffle within the confines of the green limousine. Alice pants as she chews on them. She squirms as she slurps them up with unhinged glee. She spreads her legs open, no shame in this expansion of her addiction. The abundant teeth, the swallowing of shadows, and the yawning, churning chasm between her legs.

Sighs reverberate, slick as tongues around a tasty morsel. I hear a cacophonous din of breathing, just breathing. Wind from Hell. Exhalation of demons or perhaps poets, literary explorers. Whores who babble-on…

Broken bone chimes dully decorate the plane of sound. It all flutters on wings of sandpaper.

I'm not sure what Alice is riding, and I don't care. She's getting what she needs. As I am getting what I need.

The Centipede crackles in my veins.

The Centipede fills me to bursting. Will I? And into what, I am not sure. Into where, I don't know. All I know for sure is I am on my way.

I am on my way.

Are you still holding my hand, dear sister?

CHAPTER 6

BLAKE

B lake liked it bloody or not at all.

"You might want them to kill it next time," Derek Potters said, as he did his T-bone steak no justice, dousing it in A-1 sauce.

"I prefer it red over dead. Gotta feed the beast within." Blake sliced off a chunk of the barely seared meat and shoved it into his greedy maw. His teeth ground the meat into mush as blood trickled out of the corner of his mouth. Potters pointed toward the escaping juice; Blake eagerly dabbed it with his tongue.

"You must be getting in touch with your atavistic side, my friend."

"When haven't I been in touch with my atavistic side?" Blake swallowed and sliced off another pink chunk. He was more meat and potatoes, while Potters, who had been meat and potatoes when they first met, had moved on to meat, potatoes, and perhaps caviar. San Francisco and its sometimes-snobbish demeanor had added frilly edges to his man's man repertoire, though Blake considered Potters more asexual than gay, as he'd never seen any outward signs of the latter, except when an occasional lover would drop by while he was hanging out and feign jealousy at Blake's presence.

Blake's years in Los Angeles only added indigestion and disposable women to his repertoire, so who was he to judge. Potters was a good egg.

They'd decided to meet up on Blake's presumed last night in San Francisco, though Blake felt his plans altered by the scenario from earlier in the afternoon: street vermin spewing curious clues before vanishing into the seams between two buildings, leaving only his stench and a head-scratching revelation.

"True, true. You've always willfully exhibited your Neanderthal roots. Hunter-killer. Bloodlust."

"Pussy."

"I'm sure in ancient times, bent over and taking whatever they wanted, Neanderthal man probably wasn't too picky as to what hole he was filling."

"Well, I still prefer mine to come slick and with a pair of tits."

"You are such an icon of class, my friend."

Blake raised his bottle of Heineken to Potters' raised glass of wine. He thought about the ridiculousness of the conversation. Hell, he hadn't been with a woman in over a year. All bragging rights or phony mano-a-mano posturing aside, he had a moment to contemplate Potters' cheerful manner and the possibility of following in his path, only to find himself gagging on his beer.

"Smooth, eh?" Potters said.

"As a baby's behind."

"Too bad. I prefer mine hairy," Potters said, winking at Blake, inspiring a squirm of disapproval.

Switching lanes without signaling: "Any signs of Marlon Teagarden?"

"No real signs, but something for me ponder." He shook the Heineken bottle toward the waitress, a sleek number with wide hips, just as Blake liked them. They'd had a glimmer of flirtation that turned to ash when a younger, more virile specimen showed up at the bar.

"Ponder away, Sherlock," Potters said, as the waitress set two bottles on the table, realized she'd brought one too many as Potters was drinking wine, went to pick up the extra, but Blake grunted, "All fine," as he pressed the icy mouth to his lips.

Sufficiently fueled, he said: "Had a run in with one of the local scum, one I'd talked to yesterday and left me cold. Hinted at something odd, as if this odd thing meant anything to me. I went on a brief chase to follow up his misconstrued hint. It led to nothing, and then I couldn't find the scum to question further. The whole thing, perhaps five minutes from the day, played out as a Keystone Kops comedy skit, as if somebody was funnin' me."

"What was the something odd?"

"Mention of an *ano-anomaly*. Me working the ano-anomaly into a just viewed green limousine that—"

"A green limousine?" Potters set his fork and knife down with a hard metallic clunk that turned heads in the restaurant.

Blake set his utensils down with less drama, leaned back and said, "Yeah, a green limousine. Is there something I should know about a green limousine?"

Potters relaxed his shoulders, the weight of surprise lifted. "No, well…"

"Don't fudge, get on with it."

"Have you ever heard of the urban legend about the green limousine?"

Blake shook his head as he picked up his fork and dug into the sour cream and butter drenched baked potato, though his eyes never left Potters.'

"The legend is, whenever somebody enters the green limousine, it's meant as a sign of one's fate, of one's final destination moving to the front of the line in the queue. Though it doesn't completely reveal if death is the final step, or if something else is in the cards. Something like that."

"Wouldn't intimations of a final destination point toward death?"

"Because of the source material, it's left open-ended."

"Just the way you like them."

"Asshole," Potters said, shaking his head in amusement at his crude friend.

"Cheerful," Blake said, tipping his ever-present black hat. "Source material. Give."

"I first read of the legend in one of the experimental short stories written by Peter Solon."

"Never heard of him."

"You wouldn't. Most people haven't. Anyway, he was cut from a similar mold as William Burroughs, California Myers, Hubert Selby, Jr., and any number of lesser-known writers who cut their teeth on words as though they're laced with drugs."

"Never much liked Burroughs. Don't get him. The others pull up blank slates." Blake remembered a couple of watch-tapping, time-filling "relationships" he'd had with women into the likes of Burroughs. He tried to read his work, thought it might be good to get into what the women were into—always a failed concept within his love life—but there was nothing there to hold on to. Too perverse, though some of the wild imagery touched something within his eager to learn mind. But not enough to sink in and push for more. When the relationships petered out, he left Burroughs behind as well.

"So, I'm on my last legs…"

"No, actually, the reference is for those who enter the green limousine. You saw it and did not enter. But seeing it under the circumstances you saw it…I don't remember, but I believe there's a like-minded take on simply seeing it if one has a connection, however loosely, to it—yours being the person who informed you of the anomaly…and how this might relate to Marlon Teagarden, yet…" Potters shook his head, perhaps trying to jostle the memory, but it seemed to remain lodged in a crack in one hemisphere or the other, unobtainable.

"Well, I've no use for urban legends or experimental fiction." But what did he prefer? Men's adventure fiction and occasional porn, both bound to let him know how empty his life was. Life had led him nowhere on a trail to nowhere in the middle of nowhere—all rather inconsequential, this fair maiden, Oblivion. What good was it all? Perhaps the green limousine would be a welcome addition to his life or a chauffeur-driven ride to his grave.

"Well, in Solon's fiction, the urban legend is something we know he made up, yet many urban legends have a foundation in our world." Potters swished the wine in his mouth, looking much like a puffer fish as he did.

"So, who's to say it was simply something he made up, then? Perhaps it's one passed down from when he was a child."

"Right. Though the nature of Solon's writing was so—how do I put it?—different. I mean, the use of an urban legend was as close as he ever got to something that might even make sense in our world."

"Our world?"

"Solon dealt mostly with an imaginary world in which insects and reptiles and the likes ruled, and humans were low on the totem pole. He even incorporated elements that might be indicative of how those in this imaginary world would speak. I remember reading a copy of his first book—never got the second one; he only published two—and that stuff was just hard to comprehend."

"Like reading A Clockwork Orange without the glossary of made-up words, eh?" Blake remembered reading the book and tossing it across the room before finishing it, so put off by the gibberish. He dug the movie, though.

"Kind of, but much different and way more extreme. Anyway, it was not easy reading. It made me think and really stuck with me for quite a while afterwards, but somewhere between twenty or so years ago and now, the book must have been lost in a move, or stolen."

Blake's thoughts were dogpaddling to the edge of understanding, but never getting to the shore.

"None of this makes any sense. We're speculating on the impossible, on the meeting of circumstance and a strange tale as influenced by too much beer. And wine. Can't mean anything," Blake said, though his stomach roiled as if the dogpaddling were being conducted from within.

"I...I would be careful, Terr. Not liking the vibe of this one."

They sat in silence for a few minutes, taking it in, letting it roll over in their minds. Potters poured himself another glass of wine while Blake acquainted himself with the extra bottle of beer the waitress had left behind.

Blake flirted lightly with the waitress as they paid the bill, though her flirtations, already diverted, were bandied about with formula calculation. With the tip in mind and nothing of substance beyond that.

They stepped outside into the always chilly San Francisco night.

"I wasn't kidding, pal. You've never found any evidence of Marlon Teagarden up to now. This isn't evidence of anything but weirdness. Not a good weirdness—"

"Is there a good weirdness," Blake said, lighting up. Dessert: smoke to distract the indigestion.

"Look. Sometimes things are meant to show us something. Sometimes whatever it's meant to show us is a warning."

"A warning?

Potters harrumphed. "A warning. Time to make a choice and move on. Ignore this day or, more aptly, avoid what it suggests, what is already playing ping pong in your over-used noggin'" Potters knuckles wrapped lightly against the black hat upon Blake's head. Blake sensed a migraine stumbling around the periphery and already wanted another beer. Or something stronger.

Back at Potters' apartment, more beer and something stronger were ingested, to deal with the clusterfuck of nonsensical thoughts. Or perhaps to shut up the ping pong paddles that sounded like mortar being shot into a brain not prepared to deal with the possibility that Potters had touched on more than a nerve. He'd yanked it out and stomped on it. A handful of aspirin and more scotch blotted it all out, his usual path to sleep. Or at least to Morpheus, waiting patiently and ready to have his usual fun with Blake.

CHAPTER 7

CHERNOBYL

Rudolf Chernobyl, sharp angles and stiff composure, posture rigid as he sat in a wooden hardback chair, focus narrowed—thin as a paper cut—was mesmerized by one of the many paintings peppering the sunset, yellow walls in the sprawling den.

He did this often, a call to meditation. A means of grounding himself before the game commenced.

Two lamps adorned in tin lampshades shaded bronze and copper illuminated the visual wonder of oils and imagination that so intrigued him. He sipped from a Bloody Mary, stabbing a green olive with a toothpick, chewing with fervor.

He knew this would be the last calm instant for him until his latest job was completed, so he cherished it all as he waited. But the impatience inherent in the act of waiting disallowed the pure joy he usually got from immersing himself in Frida Kahlo's masterful painting, *The Wounded Table*.

There were other paintings in the long room, some famous, though most were frivolous exercises from his own hand. But *The Wounded Table* was the centerpiece, all two hundred forty-four by one hundred twenty-two centimeters of it, and it was his.

A knock from behind attracted his attention, derailing his already brittle concentration.

"Yes," he said, the Russian enunciation barely touching the words, his voice cavern-deep, yet stiff as his back.

"We've got her," a voice replied, muffled by the door, but the words were clear. A grunt followed, signifying physical exertion, as well as a female voice: "Let me go, goddamnit. Let me go."

"Show her in," Rudolf said, still taking in the painting, not wanting to give in to obligations quite yet.

The large oak door pressed open, shifting the dry air in the room. Dodgy shadows did a cryptic dance. The owner of the voice tossed a tiny woman into the room. She hit the floor hard, yet bounced up, fists clenched, turned to the shadows as if she were ready to rumble, though her attitude was a façade, and, anyway, the door slammed shut in her face.

"Welcome to my humble abode."

"Let me out of here," she said, turning from the locked door—the knob filled her fist, unmoving—eyes skittish as the surrounding colors flooded into them.

Rudolf Chernobyl sipped again from the square glass, set it on a thin-legged table apparently made for holding a single drink upon it, and stood. As he rounded the table, he said, "Come, Alice Seniyro. We have business to discuss."

Rudolf saw in her spooked eyes a woman who lived in a perpetual state of wariness.

"Fuck you and your fucking goons. I got no business with you," she said, arms crossing over her abundant bosom.

She reminded Rudolf of the table upon which his Bloody Mary sat: skinny, yet large where it counted. It was a sexist thought. It reminded him of his human father. He wondered what it would feel like to destroy this woman.

But that wasn't why she was here.

Rudolf walked toward her, the flat click of his polished black Bruno Maglis sounding like brass knuckles kissing a cheekbone, a rib.

Alice Seniyro's arms dropped to her side, birthing fists at the end of the bony appendages.

Rudolf extended his hand to her. He smiled benignly.

She cautiously opened her hand and reached toward him. He took her whole hand in his, completely engulfing it in the hungry palm. He could tell by the glass-eyed repose that settled over her countenance, she understood he meant business.

"Try to escape, Alice Seniyro, and I will break you in half." He clenched tighter; her breath ceased, then leaked slow as a nail-punctured tire. She was set to sprint, but there was nowhere to run. "I will turn you into ash," he said, as if breaking her in half as accompanied by the oppressive vibe and grip wasn't enough of a threat.

"Do you understand?" he said, he smiled as if in cahoots with the Grimmest of Reapers.

Alice Seniyro nodded as a broken bobblehead doll. Rudolf released her hand and she pulled it swiftly away, massaging the fingers, the wrist, as blood surged into compressed veins.

"What do you want from me?" she asked.

"Information, my dear Alice," he said, and moved to her right, large hand to her shoulder like a sleeping python.

"How do you know my name?"

"Does it really matter?"

His gaze drifted toward Kahlo's *The Wounded Table*, not wanting to move onward yet.

"Lovely, isn't it?" he said.

"Sure," she said, though Rudolf noticed she wasn't really looking at the painting as much as gauging the situation.

This annoyed Rudolf.

He squeezed her shoulder as if squeezing lemon over salmon or swordfish, drowning the fish in the sour liquid. Alice Seniyro said, "Ouch," bending forward, almost buckling to her knees. But he held onto her shoulder, held her up. Didn't allow such leniency.

"Don't just give me a *sure* without considering the painting and all its metaphors, its meanings. Its beauty. Take a look, a real look, and tell me what you make of it, Alice." His insistence was steeped in a menace that came naturally.

"L-Look. I don't know what you want with me. What business we have. You want I should suck your dick, that's how I make my money. But I don't get you want that from me. And paintings. I got no eye for paintings. Metaphor, whatever the fuck that is."

"Initial responses to the painting compared it to da Vinci's *The Last Supper*. An interesting interpretation, but one that fails beyond Kahlo sitting front and center, a Christ-like figure"—his free hand gesticulated wildly, as if wind allayed the strong fingers to dance, to play—"because in her world, one where God was absent and pain took the reins, no mercy from this reminder hoisted her into the surreal realm of existence where she understood, even with Diego, her husband, or even in crowds, she was alone. Yet her solitude of mind, something I can relate to, honed the image within and expressed by so much of her art as God as self. We all should consider ourselves God-like. No, *The Last Supper* is the easy way out for scholars and art critics. Those who know Kahlo's body of work realize she only persevered out of a sheer will to create. Yet her autobiographical art, in which she was always the focus, self-portraits steeped in experiences most of us would shove away as too painful, confirmed the assumption that she knew, completely, who her God was. Crippling pain could not hold her back. It might be the one she bowed to, but she did not allow it full reign. She reigned as her own queen, her own God."

The room fell silent as Rudolf stared at the painting. He pressed on.

"This is the original, you know? Stolen in 1955, swept underground, shuffled between a handful of aficionados of Kahlo's work, those with the knowledge and means to acquire it and appreciate, with awe and respect, its beauty, but here it is, in my possession. Mine."

After fifteen solid seconds, he glanced down at the woman. She was oblivious to any of his observations, yet surprised him with a question.

"How'd you get 'hold of it?'"

Rudolf's hand lightly pulsed on her shoulder.

"I deal in destinies, my dear Alice. Altering destinies. I'm paid quite well for my services. My interests veer toward art, as you can see. Even rock stars like Madonna, the former owner, have a price," he said, turning his head to take in the room as her head swiveled along with his, taking in paintings that surely meant nothing to her.

"Madonna? The Madonna?"

"The Madonna of our era, though there are many more substantial Madonnas throughout the history of art," Rudolf said, pointing to the opposite end of the large room where Raphael's *Sistine Madonna* reigned.

He glanced down at Alice Seniyro's blank expression, sighed lightly and said, "Which brings me to you, my dear Alice. You have something I need. More so, you have something my employer needs. Information."

"Does this have to do with Rummy? I told him I wasn't working for him no more."

"Such a small mind you have," Rudolf said, his lips stretched wide, canines glistening.

"Fucking…just…what the fuck do you want from me? Insults don't help, man." Alice feigned toughness, but Rudolf expected she was whittled from shit and desperation.

He glared into her eyes, her face. The hand on her shoulder settled into a vice-like squeeze, the mouth of the python opening wide to swallow her whole, and brought her to her knees.

"What I fucking want, fucking fuck *fuck*—God, your vocabulary repulses me, you *fucking* feeble excuse for a living being—is to know where Marlon Teagarden is? You were the last to see him. I need to know where he is. Where he is off to. Tell me and you might get out of here with nothing more than a faint kiss upon your chapped lips and a thank you, my dear." Rudolf realized he had to tamp it down, though those like her, those who catered to addictions in a way that destroyed the gift of life, brought out his bad side.

Simmer. Simmer…

"Marlon…Marlon Teagarden? That was not my deal, man. I just did as I was told."

The look in her eyes traversed the same dimly lit empty house Rudolf had registered when talking about *The Wounded Table*.

"You saw him yesterday. This much my employer knows. My employer apparently has his eyes on Marlon." Rudolf found it curious that, if his employer knew this much, why hadn't he snagged Teagarden then and there, but it was not his place to question motives. "What I need to know is where he is off to. Anything you can divulge would be appreciated."

"Look. I gave him what I was supposed to give him. Got a phone call and weird shit followed. Did the deal in a dirty green limousine. Got what I was meant to get. He got what he was meant to get. I watched him shoot up and fucking disappear—"

Rudolf abruptly cut her off, pulling her within licking distance, both hands gripping her biceps, accentuating the already bruised arms in ways that brought tears to her eyes.

"I don't appreciate lies, my dear Alice. Disappearing is not a part of the deal."

"You don't gotta believe me, but that's what happened. He shot up and disappeared. It was the first leg of a thing called Riding the Centipede."

Rudolf released his grip, dropped his arms to his sides, though Alice remained stone still, fear sculpting her into a statue.

When his current employer "Mr. Smith"—a name many of his employers used—had contacted him, he only gave lean information. A price well over seven figures. The name of the one to be tracked and found: Marlon Teagarden. As well as mention of something called *Riding the Centipede*. This last item was outside of Rudolf's knowledge. Though for the money and with the name, that was all he really needed.

Until now.

"What is Riding the Centipede?"

"How the fuck should I know? I just know it had something to do with the drug."

Rudolf furrowed his brow. So, this was a wild goose chase for a person that would lead his employer to…a drug? What a steep price to pay for what must be a really good high.

He mulled over the situation, when it hit him the obvious path to finding Marlon Teagarden.

"What did you receive from Marlon Teagarden?"

Alice shrugged her shoulders, looked away.

"Come now, Alice. Don't irritate me as you've done so far. Just tell me what you got from Marlon."

"I got what's mine. What I had coming to me," she said, lips creased as a wound. Teeth, plentiful and haphazardly jutting to and fro, peeking out from behind chapped, bleeding lips.

Rudolf grabbed her hard and pulled her close. Alice's thin, large mouth gaped open as she gasped. Rudolf took a gander at the abundant mouthful and overflowing enamel congregation, and asked, "What did you receive from Marlon Teagarden?" when it came to him, so obvious.

Some people's obsessions reached deep into the weird. This much he knew from experience.

Alice only shook her head. There was no way she was going to give up her prize.

Rudolf brusquely pried open her mouth even wider than it seemed possible. Tears stained Alice's cheeks. Fresh blood trickled from the corners and chapped seams of her lips. He ran his large fingers over the rows and jagged hills of teeth, some hers, some from others.

Lifting her off the ground, pulling her face to his: "Which one is his, my dear Alice?"

She still refused, recoiled in fear. But with her mouth up close and stinking of rot and cock and the bubbling acid cauldron of her stomach, Rudolf noticed the black blood caked around a tooth to the left of three canines.

He ran his fingers over them again, closed his eyes and sensed the wayward life this woman has lived, and the equally as depressing and wasted lives of those who had contributed to her horrible smile. If she wasn't going to tell him which one, he'd figure it out himself.

He had his ways.

He was right: as he touched the freshly procured tooth, he allowed his finger to linger, to pull up a snapshot image. Marlon Teagarden. Along with a man, and a woman breast-feeding a baby. A foul scene steeped in disarray, confusion. Most of all, though, it brought up a location and a soft blip in his mind's ear. A soft blip to escalate to harsh gong when his prey was in range.

"You must understand, my dear Alice," he said, a sneer in his deep rumble of a voice, "Rudolf Chernobyl always gets what he wants."

She shook her head and he nodded, oh yes I do, and pinched the tooth between two fingers. With minimal effort but much pain to her, he plucked it from its diseased, gummy nest.

Letting go of her, she stumbled backward, banged into the spindly table, sloshing the Bloody Mary to the rim of the glass, though not over the top.

"Careful, careful," Rudolf said, shaking a finger at her, though his focus was on the tooth.

"Fucking freak," she said, hand covering her mouth, her gums throbbing. Blood streamed out of the freshly excavated wound.

Rudolf grabbed the neckline of her rancid, ragged, yellow tank top and pulled her close again. "You've no room to speak of fucking freaks, Alice. But I thank you for your help. Whether you wanted to help or not."

"Let me go, then. You got what you want. Fuck," she said, looking into the bloodied palm of her hand. Red rivers filled the lines.

Rudolf beamed so wide the room lit up: a lighthouse, a crematorium furnace.

"But I promised you a kiss as reward for your cooperation. A thank you, my dear, sweet Alice." The name was a hiss spat by a cobra upon striking.

He forced his mouth over hers, tasting blood, relishing the coppery tang, sensing the bile rising in her gorge but unable to seek release, relishing her struggle. Go ahead, struggle now, there's not much left for you in this life anyway. His tongue swirled deep into her mouth, tasting her fear, a sensation of gagging, of wanting free of him, Rudolf Chernobyl. Pity her loss, but not the loss of a life wasted.

When he slowly disengaged, her lips were sealed as if glued, as if mummy stitched. Alice's eyes grew wide.

"A kiss, yes, a kiss. A moment to cherish, my dear Alice. Your final moment of bliss, kissing Rudolf Chernobyl. What a way to go!" He laughed, licked his fingers, and pinched her nostrils; they remained pinched close when he pulled his fingers away.

"Now, you and your fetish for teeth can be put to the test. I mean…why else would one want more teeth than to eat more, to be able to really eat into or out of something? I suggest you get to chewing on your lips, your cheeks—anywhere will do—if you expect to live beyond the next few minutes. My dear, sweet, loathsome Alice. Thank you. Thank you."

He dropped her to the floor where she started to flail, tearing without much success at her mouth with fingernails chewed to the nub. Her oral obsessions, as exemplified by her patchwork smile, useless against Rudolf's insidious handiwork.

Rudolf took the tooth and mashed it between his strong fingers into a thin powder, which he snorted up his left nostril, laughing at the irony. Him, sniffing as one would cocaine or any other drugs that only dulled the mind, the senses—life.

Alice's feet started to drum a disjointed rhythm, black scuffs tattooing the hardwood floor.

"Better hurry, Alice. Better masticate like you mean it."

Her grunts and other muffled sounds associated with the desperate exercise she was ensnared in ricocheted with abandon, futility.

"Better fuck off you fucking freak," Rudolf said, his tones drenched in a cruelty Alice had never experienced, with all her bad experiences. This one by far the worst as she pounded the floor with her fists, a percussive release signifying imminent death.

As Rudolf approached the door, he opened it and said to the shadows, "When she's done, eat her. Don't leave a trace. And wax the floor afterward."

A grunt of understanding followed, bordering on pleasure.

Rudolf exited with a vision of Marlon Teagarden in his mind's eye, while Alice's drum solo reached a furious crescendo before falling silent. Her last performance quite spectacular, but there definitely would be no encore.

Chapter 8

Teagarden

I did not know what to expect, dear sister. Vertigo? Somehow that seemed the obvious choice, but this was nothing like vertigo. Because the stretchability of time, of the now and the Now, makes me feel brittle. As if the molecular foundation of my self has passed through a cheese grater and has only now reclaimed my original shape, body, mask. Mashed together by the clumsy hands of an uncaring god into a blob of me.

I have no sense of how many seconds, minutes, hours or days have passed since I took the first step of the Centipede. Though my journey has officially begun, I've no measure of where I am along the path.

Though I do know where I am.

The dank, fetid apartment reeking of weed, the flame to light the joint, the unclean diapers clumped together, stacked as a pile of skulls—this was not the green limousine. The smell was ubiquitous, an aromatic shithouse ambience that bruised the nostrils upon inhalation.

Then again, I understood implicitly when Grimes had mentioned the green limousine what it meant. Which is why I was so anxious to get a move on. So many years on the fringes, finally my purpose aligned. We seek meaning when experience *is* the meaning. The ultimate experience, a rumor to be made concrete. My destiny, as noted in Peter Solon's masterful, narcotic short story, "The Chattering Vein," that included the history of the green limousine, set in motion. This story, all of his stories, despite the mad, hallucinatory circumstances that imbued them, attempted to address the language of insects on terms most humans might understand, yet most distinguished as gibberish. Those who got the gist, peeled beneath the flaking surface, acquainting themselves with a reality beyond comprehension, yet their willingness to keep peeling, layer upon layer, brought a form of transcendence. All of this threaded into fiction that might not have been fiction at all. Hence, the fantastical reality of the world Solon knew. Of the world beneath, that Solon lived in, even if trespassing in ours.

Solon, a journalist, not a fiction writer.

Peter Solon, one we read with perplexed fascination. Yet as with most of those in your world, back when I was there and more so, now—Solon's mark fades to invisible, if not already gone—you shrugged and set his two books aside without in-depth analysis, or conjecture beyond the shrug.

I immersed myself in his words, made way through the forest of inconceivable sequences, finding purchase on a ledge in my mind, teetering, but somehow connecting. Peter Solon, who five years ago I learned was a major literary force in the dark frontier. Two lone publications in your world, a dozen more here, all written in the language of insects. Completely. A language I am still learning to translate, but the snippets I've uncovered confirm his mastery of journalistic reportage.

Write what you know, the experts say. The fools who read Solon's work and distinguished it as nothing more than gibberish, the rambling of a drug-inspired lunatic. I know otherwise. He wrote what he knew, oh yes, dear sister. Nothing more, no frills. A literary genius because he was the only one willing to fully confirm the veracity of the dark frontier. He reported to your world twice. His first short story collection, *Dawn of the Insects*, published in 1952, received a confused reception, often relegated to the horror genre for the disturbing, impactful imagery, yet only disturbing to those of your world. To the feeble minions who did not "get" it.

It had nothing to do with horror.

His second collection published thirty years later, *The Insect Revolution*, a slim volume, six stories total, was met with revulsion by the few who claimed to have gotten their hands on it. The print run being a mere forty-five copies, the only book published by the tiny press, Black Carapace. Here for a moment of brilliance, than gone. It was one of the rarest items father had in his collection. I'm sure he never read it. All those books and the art as well, all for appearances. But we read it and you were fascinated but unwilling to give yourself to the words, hence, a shrug posited as a lack of desire, much as you were with James Joyce's writing, while I was bowled over by the audacity of the stories. Even if they made no sense to us, the language often culled from what I now know is the language of insects, I pored over those stories one summer, my mind set free. More willing, yet not understanding how those words, those letters, the sequence of symbols and such, somehow slithered into my skull and shaped something within me.

I know, despite your front, you had to be intrigued. I still wonder how, after all we'd read—Burroughs and Myers and Selby, Jr. and so many more and including Solon—you could choose never to venture into my world, into the dark frontier.

Nonetheless, the note of revulsion at Solon's words, misunderstanding mutating within the minds of the few who'd read the stories, triggered something in others as well. The death of a few of the more well-known writers, a reviewer. The "sordid" influence acknowledged by a few writers. Pity they didn't all take it for what it was and allow the words, the letters, the symbols, goddamnit, to take the putty of their mind and perhaps set them on a similar path as mine, as I had and I thought you might—wishful thinking: a palm full of steaming shit.

Not the path to the Centipede, though. This is my trip.

Now. Here. Coming to wakefulness on a hardwood floor littered with toys for toddlers that squeaked and rattled, presently stoic in silence. My brain a flood of contemplation derived from thoughts of Solon and Burroughs and all the Gods of the Word. My vision spiraled outward from the cranial cinema, my spotlight eyes brightening the dim room.

A familiar sofa decorated with flowers in hues of sienna and gold materializes firmly in front of me, with a figure perched against one arm. Flickering into permanence. No, two figures. A mother and child. The mother bone skinny. The child latched onto a sagging, stretch-marked breast. The tattooed words arching above the sucking maw: Trey's Honey, wrapped in roses that look more liked squished ladybugs, Trey no longer in the picture.

The mother's name is Tricia. Her glazed eyes settle on me.

"Daryl," she yells.

"Daryl," again, and I hear my buddy, Daryl's, clipped reply as he unfolds from the nowhere into shape on the opposite end of the sofa from her.

"I told you this was gonna happen. Let me fuckin' deal wit' it."

A tectonic sound like mountains groaning into a vast gunmetal gray sky fills my ears. I sit up, left hand a kickstand propping me up, and say something that I cannot make out, yet it's met with a response from Daryl.

Your lips move but I can't hear what you're saying.

I laugh, though not sure why, feeling uncomfortably numb, body hitching but still no sound or real sensation. I watch him tap his cigarette into a beige ash tray with red and black trimmed stenciled letters signifying Holiday Inn stamped on the side. Sunlight pulses like orange neon from between the slits of the cat-clawed, drab, pea-green curtains and I sit up all the way, vertigo finally making an appearance, bouncing me to this position. I feel my gorge rise, yet nothing comes up.

I think.

"Fuckin' get him a towel, Tricia," Daryl says, and I am aware of the warmth on my chin, my ratty The Doors T-shirt, and his voice, sucked through a straw through the black hole hologram solidifying—me solidifying—and I smile as he shakes his head. He doesn't look too pleased.

By the way, Jim Morrison is not the Lizard King. I've met the Lizard King, and it is not Jim Morrison. Anyway, it's the Reptile Queen who has all the power, as I break on through to the other side, sensations and sound finally zooming into prominence…

"We're gonna make this as quick as possible, Marlon, so's you can get on your way and we can get on wit' our fuckin' lives"—me rudely thinking, this is living?—"and no one's the worse for wear."

I've known Daryl Jackson since I left dear old Dad's place. You remember Daryl, toward the end of my stay, don't you, dear sister? The son of one of father's accomplices.

Daryl has always epitomized cool, never one to let the deteriorating world he lived in—like yours, but trimmed in mine—sway this always eminent air of cool, until now. It was probably the hours and days spent in a pot haze, sure, though here he taps just a cigarette again as he watches Tricia, still with the kid clamped to her breast, lean down to me and start to wipe the mess up.

"He's not my fucking baby," she says, dropping the already stained Mickey Mouse hand towel to my lap.

"Thanks," I say, as Daryl stands and hovers with pissed-off orangutan aggression at her. She doesn't back down. She stares right back, her intensity a fist brandishing a clawhammer. The stare beneath drawn on eyebrows lights her olive skin, so he turns back to me, to the task at hand.

Their heat and psychic struggle makes the walls shake. Then I realize it's not them, it's the music, the four-by-four rhythmic thump of Rap music squeezing the walls, every one.

Something old school by Public Enemy stands out, marches to the forefront of the brutal, decibel crushing volume that surrounds me.

Turn it up! Bring the noise! Turn it up! Bring the noise!

"The Centipede. I don't know what the fuck it is. I don't know nothin' and don't wanna know nothin.' But I got a call—"

"A call?" I say, wiping the rest of the bile from my chin, my shirt. As I glance at Mickey, his smile almost brings up more.

"I got a call. Not the kind of call you can fuckin' ignore."

"The Godfather?" I smirk.

Daryl's stare could cut steel.

"A call? Who was it?"

If this was the next step of the Centipede, I didn't know what the hell was going down. I just had to pay attention, take it in. I feel the blood in my veins or perhaps the drugs that share the confined space throttle up a couple notches, as if circling the extravagant NASCAR race course within my body.

"Look. I don't know who the fuck it was, I just know by what they said, I was to give you some info and this rig. So's that's all I'm gonna do. Then you can get the fuck outta here and leave us be."

A fully loaded syringe lays next to his thigh on that grubby sofa, nudging an empty baby bottle next to him. Dried milk collected along the curved angles at the bottom of the bottle, white tinted green.

Rising up, I stretch my legs and kick a rattle that plays a percussive rainfall tune for the extent of its lazy tumble. Public Enemy has given way to Tupac. More old school jams. *I live the life like a thug nigga, until the day I die.* Another gem, damn prophetic: *All Eyez On Me.* I may dig classic rock the most, but Rap's got balls enough to leave an impression I don't mind.

Especially when it's cranked to brain scrambling volume. But you already know this, dear sister. You know I dig it.

"Why are you so on edge, man?"

He snickers, a cough of derision.

"You do know you just materialized out of thick, smoky fuckin' air, on the fuckin' floor of our livin' room, don't cha?"

He had a point. It was weird. But his brusque attitude seems more a product of—

"And I don't know about you, but receivin' phone calls like the one I fuckin' received an hour ago, with specific, bizarre fuckin' info to relay to you and only you, and made to understand the imperative nature of makin' sure I got this info to you ASA—fuckin'—P, so you'd be dropped into the lap of shithouse luxury here," he mockingly opened his palm and swept his arm with a flourish to the disarray that is their apartment, "and we'd get you on your way with real urgency 'cause that's what the fuckin' voice said. That's what it *impressed* upon my wee drug-addled mind made sober by the tone, the words, the implications, the fuckin' threats."

The stale air in the room crackles as if struck by lightning. Daryl barely looked at me as he spoke. Tricia seems chiseled from a hole in the hollow, the baby still sucking on her depleted breast. Her cheeks deflate even more as it feeds.

"Everybody's gonna want somethin' from you for their services."

"What?"

"Just pay the fuck attention, wouldja? Everybody, along each leg of your trip along the Centipede, to the ultimate experience of Ridin' the Centipede, is gonna want somethin' for their fuckin' services."

"If this voice is so threatening, why would anybody want to mess with it with idle requests? I'd think those along the path—"

"Leg. The voice said leg. Each leg o' the Centipede."

"Leg. Path. Does it matter? Alice called it the first step. Does it matter?"

"The voice said leg. So leg it fuckin' is."

Daryl fidgets, unsure of what to do with his hands, his body, before finally looking up at me.

"I think everythin' the voice said matters."

He turns to Tricia, who looks as though she might fade away if she keeps feeding the baby and, really, what more could the baby be getting from that drained tit?

"Get me a beer, baby."

"Get your own beer," she says, as her too red lips stretch thinner.

"Fuckin' get me a beer and take the fuckin' baby and your skinny fuckin' ass to 'nother room. I got business to deal wit' and I don't think you really wanna know any more than what I told you already. I will deal wit' it. Let me deal wit' it and get it done. *So, get me a fuckin' beer.*"

"Asshole. Piece of shit. Limp dick motherfucking loser," Tricia says, as she gets up on cranes' legs to wobble into the kitchen, grunting something about the dirty dishes, I do everything here, don't know why I stay with such a limp dick loser, before coming back, handing Daryl a beer.

"Thank you."

"Fuck you very much." She grabs the packet of cigarettes, peeks inside, and crumples it in her thin fingers. "Fuck."

Daryl wags his tongue at her, a strange reaction, before he sticks the bottle top into his mouth and uncaps it with his teeth. A quick twist, spitting the cap to the floor. It rolls in circles as we watch it before it deflects off a pacifier and rolls all the way to the hibernating heater.

He takes a long swig, the bottle almost completely drained, just like Tricia.

"Down to biz'ness. Down to biz'ness," he says, belching.

"I don't really know what the fuck this is," he says, holding up the syringe. "I normally would have taken a hit, y'know? But not of this. Not after that phone call and you poppin' up here just as the voice said you would." He finishes the beer, lights up another cigarette, one he had tucked behind his ear. His hands are shaking. Cool Daryl is really freaked out.

"Fuckin' Alice, that decrepit bitch, whoever the fuck she is, she was supposed to relay this info. The voice told me this. Made my skin crawl, the owner of that voice, man. So that greedy fuck gave into her kinks above what the voice had told her to do."

He shakes his head hard, eyes focused somewhere else. Somewhere beyond the assaulting smells and sounds and clutter of this place.

"I can only imagine what grim fate awaits her for divertin' from the path the voice laid out. Anyway, here's the lowdown."

He hunkers down, set to divulge information and set me on my way. Me, sure, I know the info is necessary, but the twinkle of a sunbeam shimmering off the syringe has my deepest attention, so Daryl snaps his fingers in front of my face.

"I don't wanna have to repeat any of this. Pay the fuck attention."

My attention is his, though my veins chatter much as I expect the unnamed narrator of Solon's explorative tale chattered to him, though mine have yet to find their tongue. Solon's did, in telling the story.

"First, as I've said repeatedly and you just gotta understand, everybody is gonna want somethin' from you, as payment for their services. For being a leg of your journey. The voice told me this much. Even if they don't want to take somethin' from you, they will. Payment. It's human nature, the voice said. The voice demanded."

I notice, even with the cigarette in tow, as much a bad habit as a calming crutch, his hand is still shaking.

"We're all to give you the rig, but…but the voice insisted on playin' on both our needs, as if we need somethin', though I suppose the voice understands what type of individuals it is dealin' wit,' as well as what it demands. If the others are like me, they will simply want it done and get you gone and never have to hear the voice again. Services rendered, connection clipped off like a fuckin' hangnail. But I expect some are more…I expect some are more deeply entrenched in this wretched lifestyle."

I think of Alice and her acquisition of my tooth.

"Don't question, just give and receive."

The ash from his cigarette glows red as he inhales, and breaks off, crumbling onto his lap. His fingers have somewhat steadied, now that he is passing on the info. He wipes the ash off his lap nonchalantly. As if it is a regular thing which, with the burn marks scattered throughout his clothing—one on the hem of his shirt; one higher up and larger; another burned all the way through the pocket of his jeans to the flesh beneath, a still raw scab filling the hole—it's obviously true.

Daryl is primarily into pot. He's dabbled with harder stuff, but pot is what he and Tricia live on. Though with her present skinny bitch condition, I expect she has moved up the self-destruction ladder, unless it was the baby's addiction, its need for milk, which was drying her up.

She just doesn't know how to handle her drugs, like me.

I'd been over here countless times, crashed on that stinking sofa after we all vegged out and dropped with lit joints or cigarettes clipped between fingers set like a vice to hold them.

Hence, the burns. The holes. The hope draining away in those holes, except for those like me, who dug deeper and found our true paths. Something more. Not wallowing, moving forward.

"So, how many steps…how many legs, to my journey?"

"How the fuck should I know? As many as it takes. Perhaps it's a twelve-step course to oblivion."

Fine. Though I know it's not oblivion I am headed for. Riding the Centipede promises so much more.

"Each leg, each passage through an invisible doorway, like you did here, droppin' into the apartment as you did, is triggered by the drug in the syringe you are to receive at each leg."

"The drug itself creates the doorway." I kind of know this from what I've heard on the dark frontier grapevine. When Grimes legitimized Riding the Centipede, he only told me it was real, and how to get it rolling. Daryl confirmed what he implied.

"Look. Don't ask me questions. I have no clue. I am only the fuckin' messenger."

He drags hard on the cigarette. I think he might inhale the whole thing as more ash flakes onto his shirt.

"Along with triggerin' the doorway, each leg's drug is…different."

"Different?"

I almost ask how, but he doesn't know anything. His angry piranha stare at my question lets me know that much. He is on a mission. Let him get on with his mission. It is food for me to mentally masticate later.

"Each leg takes what the previous leg has done to your blood and enhances it."

Building blocks, that's what it makes me think of. How you set a few down, and then start building up. All pieces needed to construct the whole.

"Therefore, this ride, somethin' only set in motion once a year, is your ride and only your fuckin' ride. Nobody else can take it. Burroughs allows only one Ride on the Centipede a year and whoop-dee-do you're the lucky bastard this year."

His eyes are rimmed red, but the blue core is brilliant and piercing as he stares at me.

A lot to think about. Why only one ride a year? Why am I allowed to be the one this year? How was I chosen? Who is the voice? Is it Burroughs? How does this person, the voice, fit into the whole picture and what is he or she getting out of this? On and on, I'm sure there will be more questions, but at this moment, I do not care. I don't want to waste any more time.

"What am I supposed to give to you as payment?"

I expect he wants money for pot, or money for cigarettes, not that I have much on me, but one learns how to get by on little when living in the margins. Sleight of the empty hand and a purloined wallet to fill it.

He looks confused.

"Haven't had time to think about it. The call only came through about an hour ago."

"What day is it? I ask, before realizing it doesn't matter. Time does not matter. It is later, that is all."

"Today," he says, laughing as he scopes out the room.

"What do you want as payment?"

His focus slows down, narrows. His head hangs loose as if he is thinking hard. Rodin's *The Thinker*, without the fist as prop.

"Tie my shoe."

The white shoelace of his right shoe, a knock-off black Nike with an illegible basketball player's name stamped in cursive on it, dangles to both sides of the shoe. One tip kisses a rainbow-colored ball.

"Tie your shoe?"

A ridiculous request. I'd actually rather give him a couple bucks for whatever he really needs. Pot, cigarettes, perhaps food. Mickey D's or something from the taco truck that usually sets up roost in the parking lot next to the Liquor store around the corner.

"Gimme a break, I'm not your bitch."

He stands up and spews saliva with shotgun force.

"Tie my shoe. Tie my fuckin' shoe. Tie it so's you can get your fuckin' drug and that voice will never intrude on my life again. Tie my fuckin' shoe, you son of a bitch. Tie it."

His reaction shocks me. Cool Daryl spilling completely over the top into Angry Daryl. A side I have never seen. Even his attitude toward Tricia, until today, has always been more aloof, not knotted with such ferocity.

He is shaking again, not just his hands but his whole body. The Rap pummeling the walls has nothing on him.

So, what am I to do, dear sister?

I kneel forward as he stands there staring down at me, take the shoelace into my unsteady fingers and twist and lace it, knotting it tight, all the while thinking, what voice could inspire such fear? Whose voice could bring a man like Daryl to his proverbial knees while I rested on mine in front of him.

I stand up, had to ask the question again, this time more directly.

"Did the voice say who he or she was?"

All Daryl did was sigh as if the weight of our world and perhaps Mars, Venus, and Mercury, has been lifted from his shoulders. He slumps to the sofa and holds up the rig.

"Here. Do it. Take this and do it. Use the bathroom. I don't want to ever fuckin' see you again. Go. Do it. Now."

My question fizzles like a dead phone connection, passing down the back of my throat as I cough and snatch the rig from his hand. He sighs again and seems to droop, to melt. His eyes are moist.

I head to the bathroom, where Tricia is sitting on the toilet and wiping herself, that goddamned succubus of a baby still attached to her tit.

"Just a second, you shit."

"Such a wonderful and deep vocabulary." I wonder why Daryl sticks with her, then realize they are simply stuck with each other, stuck here in this motley apartment, dying a little more with every passing Now.

She pulls her frayed powder blue panties and skirt up and shuffles past me, pushing hard to be on her way to nowhere.

Me, I have plans.

Time to open the next doorway.

I hold the syringe up to my eyes. I smell ether, not stagnant like out there in the dying room, but with a tint of freshness. It is a natural occurrence when shooting up good shit. A welcome familiarity amid the already strange. Oddly enough, a wisp of smoke plumes from the tip of the needle. Perhaps not, perhaps it is my eyes playing tricks on me. It somehow makes me think the syringe had been set mere seconds ago (and anxious for *my* participation), but I saw it on the sofa for the duration of my unexpected visit to Daryl and Tricia's apartment. Home, Sweet Hell.

The thin hint of smoke takes shape as a praying mantis, a female dining on the male after copulation. I look away and the image still plays out on my corneas. I can hear the crunch of her kill as if she was chewing her way into my skull.

Doesn't matter. I notice something moving within the brown liquid. Something alive, but it also doesn't matter. I am already on my way and ready to continue. To find the next doorway, and an exit from this reeking bathroom in an apartment not fit for cockroaches.

I jam the needle into my neck and immediately feel my throat constrict, as if I'd missed the artery and had injected the liquid directly into the windpipe. Clogging the passageway as the liquid hardens into concrete. I gag, drop to the floor. My eyes settle on the open mouth of the toilet that Tricia has not flushed. Something swims in there as well, bobs up and stares at me. Leers at me...

CHAPTER 9

CHERNOBYL

Something was amiss. Rudolf Chernobyl's bloodhound skills wavered in an unexpected way. The signal from Marlon Teagarden's tooth, the piece of torn shirt sniffed to send the bloodhound on the hunt, had fluctuated.

After he had snorted the tooth, much as he had done with items before—a frayed edge of clothing, a hair in a comb, a scissor-snipped pinkie finger crushed to sticky powder (he ate that one, actually; different process, same results)—he was able to pull up a screen in his head, his own internal GPS, and note where Teagarden was presently located. An image, black and white yet quite distinct. He was able to take it all in, appropriate the necessary information in relation to Teagarden's surroundings, home in and be on his way.

It had never faltered before, until now. He'd flown to Oakland, California, across the bay from where he had had Alice Seniyro picked up in San Francisco—info acquired via his employer—the GPS delineating a path toward one of the darkest pockets of futility in that already dim place. Concentration narrowed the range and settled on Marlon Teagarden being in an apartment in a building that sagged as if defeated. The neighborhood seethed with disrepair, with lives beyond mending. It was filled with scraped-hollow husks of human beings who didn't think they were in need of mending, shadow people with tiny minds and tinier ambitions.

He did not like this place.

Parking along the curb, where oil stains and garbage and even shells from bullets, recently fired, littered the street, he stepped out and straightened his pristine white suit, finger-combed his lightning-streaked hair into spikes, and started on his way toward the apartment complex.

Bloodshot eyes peered from behind motley curtains. They prowled the spaces in between. Rap music blared from every hidden corner, every window, as if it was the word of God.

To these degenerates, it probably was. Rudolf did not belong here, not that it mattered to him. But to some of them, all of them, it did.

A huge man, skin the color of an avocado pit and bigger than Rudolf—no small feat—skulked out from behind a van propped up on bricks, the tires gone, the wheel wells rusted. His hair was in rainbow beaded cornrows. His wide-set eyes locked into the perpetual half-lidded guise of the eternally guilty. Of those who lived by fists above famine and drugs galore, sizzling in brain pans and in every burned bent spoon.

To any other, a swift turn around and exit would follow. No need to find out what this huge man wanted. To Rudolf, this man represented what he hated in this world, much as Alice, sweet Alice had. Lost souls. Space fillers. Human waste. He wanted to take out the trash, but that was never his purpose while on the hunt.

What Rudolf truly wanted couldn't be found in a place like this. He wanted more art, more beauty; more reason to be.

If his various employers required the trash taken out, though, he would gladly dispose of any and all who qualified.

Thankfully, the huge man, upon taking a closer look at Rudolf and being caught in Rudolf's drill bit gaze, decided to step aside, step back to his gibbering minions.

The murmur of confusion poked holes in the Rap music.

That's when the homing device, one of Rudolf's many special gifts, blipped then went silent, the sound sucked into the nebulous ether.

A woman stepped down the stairs, a plump baby pressed to her bosom, the only sign of meat upon her toothpick frame. She saw Rudolf, clutched the baby closer, her face a scowl, and turned to head back from whence she came.

"Daryl, you need to get me some ciggies. I just seen the whitest fucking devil, and you need to get me some ciggies," she said.

Her comment was met with a male voice bleating, "Get your own ciggies. Fuck the white devil, all devils. I'm tired of dealin' wit' devils."

The rest of the conversation evaded his ears, lost in the incessant thumping soundtrack and monotone delivery that droned on all around him.

It did not matter.

He was close, or seemed close, to finding Marlon Teagarden, but now…now he was at a loss.

He grumbled as he made his way back to the rental car, a generic Dodge something-or-other. His confusion inspired clenched fists. Rudolf Chernobyl did not enjoy failure. He exploited it in others, bringing down the hammer on many along his bloodstained path. But he rarely experienced anything remotely associated with failure himself. It was not a pleasant experience. Not something he knew how to handle with grace.

A wiry strip of a man, whose skin seemed like it had been dipped in the dark pools of oil on the blacktop, sauntered out from behind another rusted shell of a vehicle. Rudolf gauged that all these dead vehicles served a purpose as hiding places, shelter from the storm of violence that pricked at his neck.

"Dat right. Yo white motherfuckin' ass don't belong heah." His voice was filled with the same swagger as his gait. He cleared his throat, hacking with aplomb, before spitting a loogie near Rudolf's shiny, white, wingtip shoe.

Rudolf tilted his head to the side, cracking a vertebra in his neck with gunshot resonance.

The man ducked and pulled a pistol from his waistband.

The huge man from before yelled, "Deke, leave him be," which, though both Rudolf and Deke heard the warning, Deke ignored. His ignorance branched out as a tree hungry for sunlight.

"This be mah hood. Don't need no trespassin' motherfucker in they fancy duds be allowed t'leave they stink heah without payin' up."

Rudolf left the key dangling from the door and turned to face the man. Despite Deke holding a gun in jittery fingers, Rudolf did not hesitate to approach him. Though this man was much shorter and more daring—or more stupid—than the huge man from a couple minutes previous, his spine grew flagpole straight. He was ready for action. This was the life here, where Death loomed as a constant companion, nudging with glee.

"Unless you know where Marlon Teagarden is, I've no business with you. It's in your best interest to"—he grabbed the gun with whip-fast reflexes, tilting it up to Deke's now flushed face—"be polite enough to let me know where Mr. Teagarden is, or where he was off to"—Rudolf squeezed the hand and gun as one. A flicker of pain dented the portrait of aloof impudence Deke wore—"or die, for my pleasure and my entertainment." He grabbed the gun and pried it from the crumpled scorpion that was Deke's hand as the man moaned in agony. Rudolf squeezed the gun as Deke balefully watched. The gun bent to his strength, sparks crackling, squished into an indecipherable clump of metal. Rudolf dropped it and Deke fell to the filth-littered cement.

Anger rode Rudolf hard. The skin over his whole body crinkled and pimples bloomed and popped on his cheeks. He took a deep breath and reined it in.

Leaning forward, Rudolf peered at Deke with eyes aglow. "So, do you happen to know where Marlon Teagarden is?"

Deke shook his head, gripping his mangled hand, and scooted away on his bony rump. "What da fuck are ya, man?" Deke said, eyes wide and clear, more sober than he'd probably been in years.

With savage fluidity, Rudolf smirked and dropped to all fours, no matter the expensive white suit. He reared back and started to bark, bouncing on his knees and palms, toward the shadows, the buildings. Bodies scattered, trampling others.

He howled as Deke joined the frantic fray. Ten seconds and all music, all braggadocio, all courage, withered to sun-blasted weeds. He stood, brushed off his knees, and scanned the premises, this gangrenous limb of society. He thought about taking a break from his search, since he had the time—what with his inner GPS gone awry—and amputating it by offing the barely human inhabitants one by one, and how much bliss he would get from just such an exercise…but he wasn't a proponent of excising without reason. Death for death's sake, though there were times…

He unlocked the car door and slid into the seat.

He started the ignition and placed his hands at the ten and two position.

He wailed into the suffocating confines.

The windshield cracked, an invisible spider weaving a web.

With nowhere to go, his mission already in jeopardy, he screeched out of that pit stop in Hell with the intent to simply drive…

CHAPTER 10

BLAKE

B lake sat in a cushioned chair, calm as an old dog on the back porch in summer, casually observing the taxiing planes—Delta and Alitalia and Jet Blue and many more—contemplating what exactly to say to Jane Teagarden. His fingers drummed out an erratic rhythm on the metal armrests, two clamped around an e-cig, that handled most of the percussion. As an act of procrastination, he wondered about the validity of e-cigs. Would they satisfy his nicotine needs? Would experts find out in a few short years some sort of newfangled cancer they would breed? What kind of disease would this technological step forward create? Using technology to appease the addictions of smokers seemed problematic. Yet, he needed the fix.

He placed the fake cigarette between his lips and pulled his cell phone from the inside pocket of his black trench coat, stared at it, glanced over at a girl of perhaps five in a flowery watercolor pink dress that seemed too mature for such a young child as she bounced merrily around her seated parents. Both parents were distracted by their own technological addictions—the father with a laptop, the mother on an iPhone or some such contraption—their responses set on automatic. The girl finally stopped bouncing and looked Blake's way. Johnny Cash's somber, aching cover of Nine Inch Nails' "Hurt" flickered through his thoughts. At the margins of his mind images crept in—*a little girl, in denim shorts and a chocolate ice cream stained shirt with a goofy cartoon character stamped on front, beaming its toothy grin at him (a dagger, an accusation), the little girl's eyes bright,* Claire's eyes bright, *before the turbulent waters swept her to a place so dark, so dark (his soul).*

He smiled toward the little girl in the airport, not for her but for a past that clung to him, talons digging deep as always. As though terrified by the man in black, the little girl grabbed her mother's skirt and started to cry.

Her parents consoled her in a half-hearted manner, still hypnotized by their technological addictions.

As Blake looked down at his cell phone, it rang.

Though their correspondence had been sparse, he was not surprised to see it was Jane Teagarden interrupting his contemplative mood to hedge her bets, get some information or pass on another obscure bread crumb to set him on his path to who knows where. Grandma's house? No, that was Little Red Riding Hood. Hansel and Gretel, was the fairy tale with breadcrumbs, wasn't it? He shook his head, brain clunking solid as a boxer's fist in his cranium. No matter what the specifics were Jane Teagarden no doubt wanted an answer. She was probably hoping for something more than what Blake had for her.

"Hello, Mr. Blake," she said. "I'm in need of an update." Her voice sounded rough, as if she'd had a long night and too many drinks.

"I believe we've run into another dead end," he said, even though he wasn't certain of this.

Something about his tone must have tipped her off or perhaps her women's intuition told her that there should really be something of substance this time. "I find this impossible."

He laughed, no need to hide his chagrin, and said, "Impossible? What do you mean by that?"

"What kind of private eye are you, Mr. Blake? Those reports came to me via reliable sources—"

"Then, as I noted before, you should have had those reliable sources get you a photo of Marlon, something of substance. I've got nothing...nothing."

"Your nothing sounds like something, Mr. Blake."

Her mind-reading abilities had him at a loss. He took another drag on the e-cig, pulled it away, and glanced at his hand, looking for a possible response in the many lines there.

"Well..."

"I have no real news, Miss Teagarden. I had some curious experiences yesterday, but nothing..." Trailing off to a dead end; he was at a loss.

Jane paused for a long time.

Blake turned his head toward the couple and the young girl, who had been replaced by pod people of similar ilk. Another family disconnected by technology, though this time all three were victims of the exponentially corrosive disease. A young girl of perhaps twelve, in flower-rimmed bell-bottom jeans and pink shirt adorned with an Anime cartoon character was babysat by some handheld device that blipped and giggled electronically, like a conversation between R2-D2 and C-3PO, and reflected colors off her glassy eyes. She looked like an Anima character, almost alive.

"I'm paying good money for anything. I'm paying good money for everything. If there's anything, no matter how frivolous, I want to know."

"Fine. I had a run in with one of the local scum, a real skuzz, that led me to believe there was a possibility Marlon was in the area. Though when I followed up, when I looked to follow up on the possibility, there was...there was no sign of him." Or, at least, he could not verify anything, which was the point. Which made him wonder why this all settled like a piece of dying coal in his already rattled brain, burning still.

"Details," she said, speaking as he did: direct and to the point.

He watched a plane lift off. A bird, a gull of some sort, sprang into the sky from one of the portable stairs the airport cleaning crew used to get on and off the smaller planes. One took flight with such power, propulsion, such mechanical wizardry. The other took off naturally, a slight leap into grace.

There was no avoiding what he needed to say. "There was mention of a green limousine—"

"No!"

Jane Teagarden's response let him know all he needed to know.

"What next?" he asked. The cards were laid out, but the game was unknown to him. Perhaps with their upbringing—he remembered mention of a vast, extravagant and eclectic library in an article he'd read about the family, no reason to think she wouldn't know about Peter Solon and the green limousine—she might also have more insight into what he truly was getting into or, at least, what to do next.

"Mr. Blake," she said, more an exhalation that worked like the plane and not the bird, no grace present. "We've no time to waste."

"But we've got no leads as to where the green limousine or Marlon or any of this is headed." He almost laughed, scraping the bottom of the lunacy barrel.

"You actually saw the green limousine?"

"Yes. Initially. Before I knew there might be a connection."

"Hmmm…"

He heard this as he looked up and noticed a man in a hurriedly thrown together outfit carrying a suitcase, laptop case, cell phone and coffee. He looked Blake's way and approached with what seemed like urgency, but ended up being simply clumsiness. Within sparring distance, the man dropped the cardboard coffee cup, spattering the black pants Blake always wore.

Blake pulled the phone from his face and grumbled as he moved his boot from the spill.

The man, severe haircut seeming to pervade his tone, said, "Sorry. S-Sorry, I'm in a hurry. Sorry," and was gone just as Jane said, "The connection is between you and Marlon. But what can we do if he's already on his way?"

Of course he was on his way, but to where?

The man stumbled away. He glanced back at Blake, bumped into a woman with a stroller, begged pardon, glanced back again, and was gone around a corner.

Blake reached in his pocket and pulled out a leftover napkin from a muffin he'd eaten earlier—a muffin and a Corona, breakfast of champions—reached down to his pant leg, and spotted a piece of paper next to his shoe. Written in legible but legible enough cursive script it read: Roswell.

"The green limousine is a sign one's final destination is at hand," Jane said.

"Yes, I know."

"You know?" She sounded genuinely surprised.

"I know," was all he offered her again.

"But we don't know where it's taking Marlon. I cannot impress upon you the urgency of your quest, Mr. Blake. I know there may seem no leads, but I need you not only to get your hands dirty, but to dig down into the muck and find Marlon before it's too late."

Blake stared down at the piece of paper and took one long drag on the e-cig. It had to be for him.

"Roswell."

"What?"

"Roswell."

"New Mexico?"

"Why not?"

"Why?"

"If I told you…"

"Get the next flight to Roswell, Mr. Blake. I'll meet you there."

The connection died as he stared at the paper, wondering what the hell had he truly gotten himself into with this one. Wondering what Roswell, New Mexico, would show him: a green limousine? Aliens? Nothing but flat, gray terrain for miles and miles?

He'd never met Jane Teagarden in person. This was something new. He understood whatever was in motion would need to be played out.

He wondered if she had her own private jet, or if she'd hitch a ride on a UFO.

The way things were going, the latter made the most sense to him.

CHAPTER 11

TEAGARDEN

Waking in another room, another door opens and shuts. Should I think of it as waking? Perhaps it's just a shifting of consciousness that goes along with the shifting of locale. Perhaps it's just the way one travels when riding the Centipede.

The room is bright and clean. The ocher curtains are thin, dissuading the sun's blinding brilliance not the least. Everything seems stiff, as if starched. Two beds with tightly tucked, hospital corners. Behind me, an open door bleeds yellow to match the light outside: a bathroom. The walls are a hue somewhere between the ocher curtains and the piercing yellow bathroom.

I visually trace the wall, traipsing as a spider, and settle on a painting of a lone cactus amid a desert scene. The arid earth seeps into a white, polished bone sky. To the upper left, a pimple blooms, distracting me: somebody, a former occupant on the way from here to somewhere else, gathering a moment's respite, has hand-drawn in red ink a UFO. It's a sleek, old-school variation, something culled from *The Day the Earth Stood Still*. Though the alien here has bug eyes and two antennae as its head periscopes up out of the UFO.

Curious, my eyes hitch along with the imaginary spider and continue across the whole room, 360 degrees of nothing distinct. Bland on bland, a dull sheen coats it all.

There is an emptiness here that is absolute, which makes no sense. As the next leg of the Centipede, there is no promise here, no purpose. Yet.

"Hello," I call out, and the heat of the room turns my vocalization to cinder. There is no response.

I rise and stretch and my body feels different. I've not eaten in a while—how long, I don't remember. I'm not driven by eating, anyway. With the Centipede in motion, I couldn't care less, but it must be noted, my body feels different. Leaner and my arms hang with lankier abandon than usual. They seem to extend forever, as if I could drag my knuckles with Neanderthalian expertise. I close my eyes as my balance seems questionable, and open them to a sense of things passing. Unknown things, elements of me, of the Centipede's idle ministrations within me. Or perhaps this is just the way it works.

I feel mostly like myself again. Whether this is good or not is not the point. I expect to be affected. Part of the mystery of drugs is how they affect you.

I let my thoughts mist as I walk to the window. Through the thin curtains, I see squat buildings and not much more. Pulling the curtains aside, my focus crisp, I confirm the landscape is desolate: a few low-slung buildings, like an oriental woman's ass, sinking into the ground; cars for sale; another couple motels; a gas station. To the left: a desert. To the right: I cannot see beyond a row of motel rooms an extension of the building I'm in. I am in a motel. The check in time and room rates and fire escape info, laminated and thumbtacked to the door, confirm this.

Deeper observation draws my attention to the street lamps. They are shaped like the heads of aliens, E.T.s, little green men. I wonder if, when they are on, the illumination is tinted green as well.

Sweat beads and flattens out like an army of ants, the big, red suckers—you remember them, dear sister? The fascination stamped with pain as we watched them trample our flesh in search of a target then mark their territory with a sharp prick. "Ouch."

I am drenched, my shirt matted to my skin. The stench has a vinegar bite as it rises to mingle with the hairs in my nostrils. The hairs do more than mingle, trying to deter the intrusion.

I let the curtain drop, its meager shield unworthy of the moniker, and bump into the closer of two beds. The dull, brown blankets show signs of intrusion. No matter the stagnant façade, somebody has recently been here. The room, though clean, is not fresh.

There is a noise outside the door: a key being inserted into the lock. The knob turns, the door swings open, and a woman carrying a brown paper bag stuffed with who knows what, enters the room.

She is beautiful.

I am reminded of Marilyn Monroe, yet this woman has a dirt-cheap spin on her. The face shimmers with her charismatic allure, the body as well. Full, abundant tits. A sway in this woman's clumsiness that invites participation. But the clothes don't fit the movie star aspirations. Jean cut-offs, sandals that show off alternately red and black painted toenails, and a non-descript off white blouse, stained at the arm pits and matching the décor of the room, this place, tied off above her flat belly.

She smiles and the room brightens even more. The impression of Marilyn evaporates, shifts in a way. Confusing, yet now there's Rita Hayworth in a more defined countenance. The whole of the woman seems in flux.

Way back when the discovery of women meant something to my burgeoning hormones, Marilyn Monroe and Rita Hayworth, classic movie stars with real presence, were my first girlfriends. My first loves. Their photos decorated the entertainment den where their movies sat on shelves never to be watched by our parents.

All show, just like the library.

But I watched everything and took it all in. Marilyn in *Gentlemen Prefer Blondes, Niagara, Bus Stop*. Rita in *The Lady from Shanghai* and *Gilda*, fucking beautiful Gilda, capturing my heart and inspiring my youthful erections to explosive, uncontrollable orgasms again and again.

Despite what was happening behind closed doors with dear old dad, these women eased the pain and brought me pleasure amid the darkness that was my life.

But with *this* woman, her visual allegiance uncertain, Rita faded.

"Hello. My name is…" she says, and her name, something muffled and unclear, a loudspeaker tuned into distortion, turned down so as to not grate on one's last split-end nerve. Yet as I ask her to repeat it, the same indecipherable word is the result.

She sets the brown paper bag on the dresser, next to a remote control and a TV screwed into brackets attached to the wall.

"I was hoping you would be here when I got back," she says, her features caught in shadows without foundation. The tone of her voice suggests desperation. Desperation, the one true companion in my world. She is a part of my world, for sure.

Another familiar face rides her cheekbones, alters her eyes. This one less well-known, but one that had really set my burgeoning teenage sexuality on edge. Another old-time actress, Jacqueline Bisset. The bosom of the woman here seems to swell, the nipples jutting forth with enthusiasm. Her sweat makes her blouse cling to her figure, reminding me of Bisset in *The Deep*—her wet T-shirt a revelation that awakened my cock always—yet this woman does not even notice any of this. Does not seem to even sense what she is doing. Is she doing it? Or is it being done to her? She reaches into the paper bag and pulls out a generic soda, something orange.

"Thirsty?"

Again, there is something brittle in her tone. Something broken. Her elusive appearance, or to be precise, the illusive, contradictory allegiance of her appearance, seems a direct response to the crack in her voice, cracking her armor. Something within that rules her fragile roost, the ever-alternating façade, promotes this.

Two things become evident to me. Somehow, she is jacking into my mind, to my erstwhile buried memories, of the women from another lifetime who mattered most. Alternately, she is trying too hard to please me, to subtly connect with me, though subtleties are often lost on those at their wit's end, noose dangling as the mentally avaricious tendencies riddle their manner, their actions. Yet I also know whatever she is doing is a direct result of whatever *she* needs. Some kind of psychic necessity is unleashing this nebulous display with her body and face, both fascinating me and making me uncomfortable.

Her damaged qualities normally would be something I would take advantage of. In the dark frontier, one lives for one's needs at all times. Relationships are situational necessities and nothing more. Whatever she needs is expressed by what I am witnessing, yet, as with Alice and her enamel obsessions, it is still unclear.

Scaling the shadows between the lines, along the ridges, her face is amorphous and monstrous for the moment before another ex-girlfriend assumes her façade: Sean Young from Blade Runner, pristine, emotionally reaching, unable to fully grasp what it is to be human. The struggle lends Young's character — what was her name? — veracity, some amount of life beyond the automaton foundation. Perhaps this is relevant to what is going on with this woman.

She stands, condensation from the orange soda can collecting between her fingers, dripping to the floor. Her hand confirms my take on the desperation that is playing out. It trembles slightly, ever so slightly. I almost don't see it, yet wonder if it is physical evidence of her ever-shifting design.

"Thirsty?" she says again, this woman with a name lost between her teeth, or perhaps to the room's sharp geometry.

Doesn't matter. I'm not here to play games, to get to know anybody beyond the quest for the next rig. The next leg of the Centipede. What I thirst for is not contained in that orange aluminum can.

Her mouth opens, a sensuous invitation I once might have wanted to kiss. An invitation unspoken. Lena Olin from *The Unbearable Lightness of Being* stands before me, the woman seeming taller, and she's wearing a hat.

How she does this, I don't know, but this roll call of my past loves needs to cease.

"Stop," I say and she does. Lena Olin is here, but it's not her. Almost, but the woman's shapeshifting abilities quiver and roil beneath the skin.

The hat is gone. Too bad. I might have enjoyed Olin with the hat, as she was in the movie. But that's not why I am here. That's not why she is here.

"What do you want from me, so I can get what I need from you?"

She tilts her head and Rachel Ticotin from *Total Recall* emerges like a rising sun.

"Stop! Tell me what you need from me, so I can get what I need...now. No more masquerades."

Her features become tonally obscure, no distinction, blurred just like the sound lost in the muffled name. She is actually blurred, blurry, the quiver now a part of the vision. I turn away. The condition causes my eyes to ache, like too red print on a white background.

"I want to know what it means to be human," she says.

Like cement hardening, the blurriness surrenders to obscurity. She is somewhere in between, yet her eyes burn through. I would say she seems around my age, yet the wear and tear of shifting or the residual side effects of the lifestyle suggests an indeterminate age. Age perhaps is not even to be considered. This strange woman may not even be a woman for all I know. I've met many along my path in the dark frontier who far exceed her curious mutability.

"Shouldn't you learn what it means to be human by living life? You're doing that now, aren't you?"

Perhaps this will be easy. Perhaps logic will enlighten her. Perhaps I have no idea what it means to be human and don't want to fail in fulfilling her request.

"I need a normal day. Two people together. Partners. Being human." She licks her lips and Naomi Watts from *Mulholland Drive* streaks across her face.

I hated that movie until the audition scene where she kisses the old guy in ways that enhanced my arousal like rarely before. Thirteen years old, enjoying the rigors of masturbation, the heavy breeze insistence and ease of erections. Shaping my own sexuality with the fantasy of the actresses, my past loves. Blotting out the reality of father and his despicable tribe.

I realize my cock has been erect for longer than I can recall. This scene, with Watts, always set me on edge. I haven't seen it in ten years or so at this point. It is a reminder of something other than misery.

From what she's said, I expect it all comes down to sex. She just seems lonely. Her humanity seems embroidered with a sense of isolation, as though she doesn't feel, as though she doesn't fit in. Sex should do the trick. After all, that's the only real closeness I can give her, and it's distant in truth, yet for some, probably her, being physically entwined with another, getting fucked and tossing off a few kisses, that's all it takes to break the monotony. I'm not talking romance. She can't mean romance.

Another lesson to add to the list. In the dark frontier, sex is currency. Either as pain blotter or information retriever. The dog of sex barks loudest when it needs one or the other. The pleasure derived is ephemeral at best, even if potent. Pleasure is the true pain blotter. The mere act is the path. This is the primary motivation for existence in many people's lives in the world I live in.

Sure, in your world, it is currency of a sort as well, more counterfeit than real, yet the wicked wiles of admen and media manipulations do not dig as deep as in my world. In my world, there are no restrictions as to its use.

"I bought snacks: sandwiches, drinks. I thought we might have a picnic."

I laugh. An asphalt and scorching sun picnic seems ludicrous. And if we go the other way, away from the parking lot a stroll would lead us to the desert, which seems equally uninviting.

She shuffles her feet, her face a mass of shifting shadows. I cannot watch, so I look away.

"I'm not here to play house," I say, "even if this is just a motel room. How am I supposed to show you a normal and what it means to be human? What does that even mean?"

I've no clue as to the Muzak, middle-of-the-road cadences of normal. Hell, I tune out the normals as often as possible. I tune out all humanity…

But my thoughts swirl around and sex again comes to the forefront. She wants to know what it means to be partners, or perhaps something more. To be human. Whatever. I'll fuck her and tell her that's what it means to be human and she'll crawl back into her cracked shell and curl up and debate it all or die. I don't really care. Time's a-wastin' and I am both annoyed by this leg and anxious to move forward. Desperate.

I approach her, take the orange soda can from her fingers, and set it next to the brown paper bag. I pull her close and, though sex is not something I often engage in, what with drugs being my only true love and lover for years, kiss her hard on the lips.

Her mouth is stiff and dry, just like the room. I taste nothing but the vacuity of an abyss. Her tongue is a lifeless slug.

She pushes me away.

"What is this?"

Her face slants, as if sliding off. The abyss within her mouth is ready to suck her inside. Pinched and scrunching and quite ugly, this face.

"This is how people, couples, get as close as possible," I say. A lie dressed for the ball.

"This thing," she says—a kiss, I think; her naivety astounds me—"is what it means to be human?"

My hands rest on her hips and I lean back and without question, without hesitation, because time *is* a-wastin', say, "Yes," much to her chagrin, as expressed by that unsettled façade.

Her eyes dart about and a smile blooms. The ugly is washed away by Naomi Watts again. She picks up on my reaction. I stiffen, perhaps she understands, and take her.

But it's rough and fast, feels more like rape but that's negligible as this is the way of the dark frontier. It's not something meant for love, this is fucking for the sake of fucking. A means to an end, orgasm achieved, a split second in the void, dopamine Eden, like many drugs will trigger. I just want her to give me the goddamn rig. The furious melding ends as we merge at a point of climax, my climax as I watch all the women from before and many others flash across her face, like thin clouds being nudged by wind, the dragon's head into the shark into the roaring lion, constant movement, allegiance expressed, defined and polished by confusion as lava spills from within me to within her. The world magnified, amplified, cooling as ice dripping down the spine of God and down to His puckered anus and, hence, into the waiting, yawning mouths of His followers.

While Satan snorts a line and laughs at such mockery.

She pries my talons from her hips and screams, coughs, pushes me off her.

"What was that? Why would anybody do that? What of being human is this act?"

Such disdain slicking the faces as they bleed into one, then disintegrate into uncertainty.

"That was fucking. Many humans enjoy that. It's part of being normal. Just what you asked for."

I pull on my underwear, stuff my cunt-sticky cock inside, pull up my pants. She moves with such a lack of grace, arms akimbo, fingers clawing the headboard, the wall, legs askew and her skin, all of her, transparent in a way. I see her bones, symbols etched onto them, such a strange creature. Not the strangest, as I said, my dear sister. I wonder as to her true origin—perhaps she's a traveler of someplace besides the dark frontier—but my wonder is abridged. I need what I need, that is all.

"I do not believe that is what it means to be human. I cannot believe—"

"Your belief is not my worry. Perhaps I'm not the best one to show you what it means to be human," I say, realizing I cannot follow up, because if it is mandatory that some evidence of humanity in a positive or good way be applied to this exercise, I will be at a loss. I take a tact that cannot be disputed, no matter my lack of grace.

"Everyone does what they do in order to get what they need. In order for me to get the rig, the next step of the Centipede in my veins, I need to fulfill your aspirations to know what it means to be human."

The woman squirms uncomfortably, so human.

"To be human is many things. If you expected a feel-good experience, find your answers elsewhere."

She turns away, pouts, then turns back to me. Taking in her faux paramour.

"I live life in the margins, traipsing with wolves. My experiences of being human bring nothing but pain. I would rather not think about being human. I would rather not even be human. I would rather not share this with anybody. Why would you *want* this?" But this guise is what I have. Much as you do, whatever you are, whatever mask you deem appropriate to gather what you need."

Her transparent face, gnarled and throbbing, is a latticework of veins protruding, angry. Her skull is decorated with symbols that wander aimlessly beneath her skin.

If she were human, I'd expect tears would be shed. She simply vibrates, grows blurry again.

"Now where's my fucking rig?"

Niceties no longer needed, I've discarded them with the final dregs of interest I have for this woman; this thing. I no longer aspire to anything but success in my quest.

She points to the dresser. I yank the top drawer open and there, resting somberly next to a Gideon's bible, my goal.

Impatient and ready I prepare the syringe.

"If this is what it means to be human, why would anyone make that choice?"

Mind reader. Or just paying attention. Finally. She perplexes me, this one.

"Where I come from, it's not a choice. It's a curse. One I hope to remove."

I do not look deep into the tan liquid—of course, tan; no question, tan—as I thrust the needle into my neck and my eyes swell with tears. I sense the thick slither of worms within me...everywhere.

Screaming, I drop to my knees, the floor, drool slowly sliding from my lips, a string of it filled with worms. Worms that elude gravity and climb back up the wet rope. I close my mouth but they seek passage and success, filling my nostrils. I glance up, the room shaking, vibrating much as the woman was, but she's the only thing not vibrating now. She is still and stiff, this room an extension of her frustration, a psychic tsunami.

She smiles, a face like nothing human.

She's learned well. The value of distancing oneself from others. From feelings, emotional attachments. Humanity in a handbasket. Heading for Hell. The usual handbasket path.

Hang on...

CHAPTER 12

CHERNOBYL

Rudolf Chernobyl was irritated to no end. He made Interstate 880 and drove up and down the stretch between Oakland and San Jose for hours, with no destination at hand, perplexed by the loss of contact with Marlon Teagarden. Failure was rare for him. The crushed tooth, a cog slipping out of gear in his inner GPS, was a first. He wondered if this was evidence of his skills depleting, such an analytically human conceit. This thought disgusted him as much as the breakdown. He was a hamster spinning on a wheel, and this much was something he cared not the least for.

He eventually rented a hotel room just to the south of Oakland, a Motel 7 in Hayward. He wasn't ready to leave yet. After all, what if the radar within decided to slip its cogs back into place? Unable to sleep, he seethed as he flipped channels, not watching anything.

He knew what he was, how he worked. He knew what it took to fulfill each mission he was sent on. Though he detested mixing with those driven by their addictions, addled by a lack of willpower, struggling in the quicksand of futility, barely able to stave off death, he knew what it took. It wasn't just the class on par with flies who dined on shit who aggravated him as sandpaper to an eyeball. The upper class with their technological gadgets and frivolous follies wasting time and money on drugs and decadence, settled into the same pool of genetic muck. He understood it was all a part of the deal, of what this planet and its absent gods catered to. They were the grit he cleaned from beneath his well-manicured nails. But they also satiated his main lust, a love of art. As well as the other two heads of the Cerberus within: an opportunity to indulge in sadistic mayhem and the ability to mete out death.

The following morning, still awake, still seething, to the point he decided it best to reconvene to his headquarters, his private castle within the mountains east of Flagstaff, Arizona, his internal GPS blipped back to life with information he found impressive, thought-provoking.

Marlon Teagarden was in Roswell, New Mexico many hundreds of miles from Oakland, California, where he had last sensed his presence. This was not as farfetched as one might assume, but it still surprised him. Probably as much because his radar blipped back to life as anything else. Was it trustworthy?

Had the intermission been filled with Marlon getting on a plane and hastily making his way to Roswell? Had the lost time been triggered by something in that dreary apartment complex that deeper investigation would have revealed? This thought stirred a rage that caused him to crush the remote control in his fingers into melted plastic. He remembered something Alice had said as well, about Marlon disappearing because of a drug, a leg of the Centipede.

Rudolf rented a private plane, paid an exorbitant sum of money to make it to Roswell before Marlon Teagarden had a chance to evade his capture. The blip still strong, he paced the perimeter of the parking lot, a lion in a cage, before centering on room ten in the Crash Land-Inn motel. The sun was high in the sky, the heat, stifling. The motel was a bleak gray welcome mat on the outer edge of town. But the homing device that was Marlon's tooth had awakened with vengeance.

He was here. He had to be here.

As Rudolf raised his fist to the door, the blipping, which had ratcheted up to frantic rate, a drum solo worthy of Neil Peart of Rush, one of the few bands that brought pleasure to his ears — most music sounded like rubber squishing animals, roadkill serenades — ceased. Sudden and complete. Again. It was gone. He knew Marlon was gone as well.

Or was he? Was it simply a glitch in his machinery?

He gritted his teeth until he heard them crack. He pulled back and licked the teeth. They were as good as new again.

He knocked.

A female voice said, "Go away." She was sobbing.

He knocked again.

"Damn it. I said go away!" Adamant, the anger snuffed out her sobbing, and firmed the quiver in her voice.

Rudolf was also adamant, with frustration riding shotgun.

"I need to know if Marlon Teagarden is still here." Still. Already banking on failure.

"You just missed that jerk," the woman said.

"Let me in. I need to know where he's gone."

"Don't know. Don't care. Go away."

They'd reached a stalemate.

Rudolf Chernobyl was not good at stalemates.

He glanced both ways: one way a smattering of cars in the motel parking lot; the other a man getting a soda at a vending machine. He glanced up at the sun, drawing energy, his white suit feeding on the heat. With a concentrated push, the screws holding the lock in place popped out of the inside of the door, as well as the hinges, tearing at the frame. He gripped the sides of the door, finishing his grand entrance as the chains snapped in half.

"Hey," the woman said, leaping off the bed, her tiny, twitchy hands clenched. She was adorned in white panties stained wet at her crotch, and an off-white, unbuttoned blouse. The lower half of the blouse was crinkled, as if she'd been wearing it tied below her moderate bosom.

Rudolf set the door back in its shattered frame and scooted a large pastel yellow chair in front of it.

Tribal tattoos laddered up her arms, across her torso. Her legs were adorned in runes. Her figure was taut, fit, yet her face seemed a monument to indecision. Rudolf took this in and said, "He was just here? I didn't see him leave, and I've been outside, in this vicinity, the last few minutes. I would have seen him leave."

She laughed, slumped to the bed.

"He didn't leave by the usual means."

"He left by a magic doorway?"

The woman's undefined face seemed to morph, or at least the shadows that lived there dug deep into unseen crevasses did. Rudolf was intrigued, watching her emotions play out like this.

"How do you know that?" she asked.

"I'm also going to Ride the Centipede—"

"Ha! You've no clue as to what Riding the Centipede entails, do you, mister? One at a time, get in line." She seemed satisfied with her brash assumption, propped up a pillow behind her and lit a cigarette as though she didn't have a care in the world. Even though a strange man had broken down the door to enter her motel room. It was as if she did not care. Her life could be in peril—and was, truthfully—yet she was more intent on filling her lungs with smoke than realizing the full scope of what was in motion here.

Rudolf found this most displeasing, but had to rummage for more information.

"I'm…next in line," he said, wrangling for specifics.

"No, uh-huh. One a year, from what I was told. Marlon's it. I was tagged to get him along his way, get what I wanted from him. He didn't give me a very good spin on what I wanted."

"My name is Marlon. That other fella…he must have been an imposter. You know how…rare it is to Ride the Centipede, he must have heard I was on my way and…" Though his words fizzled as bubbles escaping atop a glass of champagne, the shadows in the woman's face brightened, the lines became less harsh, but no less indistinct.

"You're Marlon Teagarden? You're Marlon Teagarden?" She sat up taller, shaking her head. The face seemed a blur.

"That other guy. That jerk…" She pounded the bed with her tiny fist. Smoke cloaked her features. The shadows and blur, buried behind a thin fog. "No wonder he had no clue as to how to fulfill my request."

Rudolf slowly crossed the room to the bed, moved her legs gently, and sat down.

"I guess we were both duped, eh?" she said, her face no clearer up close. She was the epitome of average, nothing stood out, no real impressions to be gleaned.

"So the drug is what opens doorways?"

"Yeah, you know that. Isn't that how you got here?" she said.

Rudolf noticed as she scrunched her legs to her chest as if she finally felt vulnerable. He wondered if she was putting two and two together and finally getting four. After all, he had materialized *outside* the door…

"Kinda got eyes like David Bowie, don't you?"

"Sure. Bowie."

Tension sawed at Rudolf like razor wire slicing into a neck. Blood prayed for release.

"You like…you like Bowie?"

"He's one of my favorites," Rudolf said, but still, the tension cut deeper.

This tedious woman had nothing more for him. Teagarden was gone, but at least he had confirmation of his method of travel.

There was no time to waste. The chase was on, and it was different than any other he had encountered before. He would have to find a way to tap into the missing time between destinations. He would have to mull over it all, and follow up once Teagarden blipped to life in his head again.

Chasing a phantom, he must be swift or fail.

Failure was not something he wished to experience ever again.

"What was your request?"

Her voice was a swirl of foam atop a cappuccino. "I just wanted to know what it really means to be human. I wanted a normal day, not one driven by the self-loathing demons that roost inside me." Her eyes glazed over.

"We've all got those demons to deal with. I have made friends with mine."

"You're lucky then, I guess. You can't know what it means to feel like this always. Like every breath is an exercise in endurance."

"You're tired of it all, aren't you?"

"Yes. I just want to feel human. Normal."

"I believe I can help you," he said, staring into her moist eyes.

The shadows of her features softened. "I wish," she said. She looked at him quizzically as if wondering if he could really show her happiness.

"I can show you what it means to be human," Rudolf said, moving closer to her. He raised his hand to her cheek, delicately stroking it.

She closed her eyes and leaned into his large hand, her smaller hand touching it as he caressed with care. "Yes, please. Yes."

"Wonderful," he said, his smile brightening. Magnificent and awe-inspiring. "This facet of what it means to be human is called dying."

He squeezed her malleable face in his palm, slamming her head into the wall above the headboard.

Her eyes bulged; her hands tried and failed to pry his from her face.

"Now, most all living creatures die"—most, he thought, acknowledging his designs on immortality—"but the cognizance that death is imminent, the sharp shock and adrenaline rush. The pure understanding that these are the last moments of your life and the realization as well that you've wasted the whole damn thing. These things are purely human."

Intrigued by the doughy condition of her features, the undefined allegiance to her own self, he kneaded as one would raw dough. He twisted and bones snapped and cracked.

Her face, the layout of eyes and nose and mouth, contorted with the force of his vehemence. Picasso would have been proud. Or perhaps Dali would have appreciated his handiwork. The reshaped face the perfect accompaniment to the often drooping, dripping, soft materials in his art. Soft. Like Putty. He felt like an artist for the first time, this woman's death wrought with such stylistic flair.

Perhaps he should explore sculpture, he thought, distracted not the least by the woman's screams.

The force of his sculpting prompted her already bulging eyes to burst from her eye sockets, dangling as piñatas awaiting the baseball bat. Her body twitched and spasmed to finality.

He released her, uncorking his fingers from within the putty-like flesh. She slumped sideways across the bed.

He stared at his masterpiece. Her face was realigned, the eye sockets with the dangling eyes aslant to the right side, the nose toward the forehead, the mouth stretched into a clown's grimace across the left. It all fell into the looping shape of a question mark. The swivel and swoop. The utter impossibility, yet here it was for him to admire.

"I cannot conceive why anybody would want to know anything more about what it means to be human, Miss. But I hope I've satisfied your request."

Piss and shit leaked out of her panties.

He wiped his blood and snot coated hands on the bedspread.

Rudolf moved the chair out of his way and pried the door open, turned and set it in place again. Not perfectly, but in this bleak outpost, good enough not to be noticed for a while.

As if it mattered.

Rudolf Chernobyl was not a man to be denied. Especially when he was a man on a mission.

CHAPTER 13

BLAKE

Forty-five minutes cruising back and forth and to every edge of Roswell, New Mexico, the no frills chit-chat that had accompanied Terrance Blake's and Jane Teagarden's first face to face meeting had fizzled to dead air in the furnace of the rental car, no matter the AC cranked to Antarctica. Sweat pooled at Blake's armpits, the back of his neck.

Blake had landed an hour and a half after Teagarden. His first impression of the woman he'd seen only on television ten years ago was dominated by her severe gray-on-gray skirt, with darker gray heels that teetered at a precarious height below gams to die for, and that there were no laugh lines on her face. Nary any lines at all. Perhaps her hair being pulled back into a tight pony tail had something to do with this, the skin skimming the skull — no wrinkles allowed. Only the surprising extravagance of too much makeup broke the rigid presentation, the whole cheerless demeanor.

They weaved through now familiar streets to the western perimeter of a town constructed with a wry sense of humor. Alien lampposts and alien-themed businesses abounded. One restaurant that served a brisk cup of coffee, had a flying saucer crashing through the ceiling.

The more they drove, the more Blake felt as if he'd made a mistake. He'd simply picked up a piece of paper a disheveled man had dropped and taken it to heart. Maybe it was not meant for him. His instincts, usually spot-on, could be slipping.

("Ano-anomaly.")

Breaking the silence, Jane pointed out a motel to her left, a flat collection of blocks shaped like a horseshoe that, as far as Blake cared, signified all the good luck leaking out.

"You would think the proprietors would cut down that palm tree blocking the sign...and add a UFO like the restaurant."

Blake mumbled, "Mm-hmmm," and smiled, though he looked past her face.

Teagarden remained stolid.

("Ano-anomaly.")

When he spotted the man.

"He doesn't belong. That man does not belong here. Turn around."

Jane Teagarden swung a U-turn in the middle of the four empty lanes and slowed down.

"That guy, the big guy in the white suit with the glaring sun-on-snow hair."

Jane stopped the car and said, "I don't see what you see. He's probably just a businessman, got a room and heading out for an early dinner."

Blake's curiosity prickled like a rash, with the tenacity of poison oak, or the unnerving presence of an impossible to reach itch beneath a cast, inspiring unbent hanger madness.

Blake watched as the man dawdled at the door to a room in a way that seemed unusual. Definitely no Joe Six-pack. Something did not gel right. From where Blake was sitting, the car parked next to the curb, outside of the parking lot for the motel, his instincts cranked up to nearly intolerable, needle pushing into the red.

He stepped out of the car and stamped out the butt of his cigarette on the hot asphalt.

"Blake."

"Stay here. Just…" He held up his hand, a crossing guard halting traffic.

As Blake headed toward the man and, more precisely, the room—could Marlon be there? What about this man made him think he had anything to do with Marlon?—Jane Teagarden exited the car and crossed in front of it, hesitated, then stopped. She watched Blake.

The man with the glaring sun-on-snow hair—bottled lightning bolt brilliance, more white than any hair Blake had ever seen—turned from the door and walked away from the room heading out to the parking lot. His car.

As Blake and the man's paths crossed, the man tipped an imaginary hat and smiled. Blake stopped dead in his tracks, a hinky vibe derailing his progress, as if he knew exactly what he was doing. As the man carried on with his odd pantomime, pointer finger extending as a gun barrel—bang, bang. Blake thought the lightning infused hair enhanced a mental suggestion that sparks danced off his fingertips.

The man slowed and turned, still walking, though backwards. He was no longer smiling.

Jane Teagarden crossed her arms as the scene played out. Though she was desperate to get whatever information she could in order to find her brother, she looked unnerved by the presence of the man.

Blake and the man both stopped, gauging each other, a tango between lion and hyena. The man's eyes dug into Blake's—he could feel the glower burn through the back of his skull. His belly spiked as well, as if filled with battery acid.

Blake catalogued it all, everything about this "Ano-anomaly" in this small, desolate, comically nostalgic town in the middle of a heat-blasted stretch of nothing.

The man tilted his head down with purpose, reaching up for that imaginary hat again, tipping it before turning and swiftly making way to his car, a rental car of the same make as Blake's—Dodge—though painted white as a sheeted ghost.

How appropriate.

By the time Jane made it to Blake, they were both watching the man drive off, rubber left as a reminder of his urgency.

"What was that all about? Who was that?"

"I don't know. I don't know, but sense…"

They both turned toward the room he'd exited. Number 10.

"Is Marlon there?"

"No way of knowing until we make the trek across the parking lot and knock."

"Yes," Jane said, gripping Blake's bicep, which he did not mind at all. In most cases throughout his life, he'd ventured into bad situations alone. But with this one and the slippery manner in which it was all taking shape, company was welcome. He may have wanted her to remain in the car while the man with the lightning white hair was around, but now that he was gone—a glance down the road confirmed as much—her presence seemed necessary.

In some ways, it was. After all, it was her brother they were looking for. Yet Blake sensed within himself something that tilted the scales in a rarely experienced way. The world seemed to slow down. The rotation of the earth paused as unease burrowed within. Unease and even a nugget of fear.

Bad juju for sure.

No matter their urgency, time being an imperative and not something portioned out in dollops, it took them almost five minutes to make the door, their halting steps and curious pauses making it feel more like a game of hopscotch in Hell.

At the door, the matter of a key was rendered inconsequential. Jane knocked lightly; no response. Blake jiggled the doorknob, then ran his large fingers over splintered wood. Scaled the frame, nudged it firmly. The upper hinge was set in splintered wood.

"The door is not locked. It's set in place," he said. Jane nodded as Blake pushed it in. He was careful to grip it firmly so it wouldn't fall and draw unwanted attention as he had no idea what, if anything, they would find in the room.

As he held the door, his nostrils flared at the bad smell. Excrement, urine, perhaps even scorched flesh, and the corrosive underbelly that distended from it all: Death.

"I don't think you should enter, Jane," he said, but with the door occupying his hands, he couldn't stop her from slinking her lean body around his. He was quick to clumsily set the door into the frame.

"Oh, my god," she said, turning from the bed where a woman's body lay. If the eye-watering stench wasn't enough of an indication the unnatural position of her body made it completely clear that she was dead. Jane buried her face in his shoulder. An appropriate reaction to seeing a dead body. He was repulsed as well, no matter the years and many deaths he had witnessed, been participant in, or run across as result of the job.

"It's not Marlon, let's go," she said, both hands clenching his black trench coat, not wanting to pull her face from the security of darkness and see, smell, or acknowledge what slumped on the bed.

...a rare moment of security, something he'd faltered at so long ago...

(*"Daddy..."* washed away before she had the opportunity to say, *"Help me."*)

"It may not be Marlon," Blake said, "But I sense it...I sense she has something to do with Marlon."

Jane leaned back, still holding on to him. "What makes you think she has anything to do with Marlon?"

Her question fell into the mire of unanswered questions every case collects. Blake moved her gently aside and circled the bed. He took a white handkerchief threaded with monogrammed black letters—T.P.B., Terrance Patton Blake, Patton for General

Patton, a real man's hero to his life-long military father—from the breast pocket of his black shirt, and pressed it to his nose, his mouth.

Jane buried her face in the sleeve of her blouse as she watched him.

Blake reached up toward the dead woman's tilted askew face, the head at an odd angle. Something was wrong, something...

"Oh, dear god," he said, abruptly backing away. What he saw staggered him to the point of dizziness. He'd be fifty years old in a month. He'd dealt with the frailty and misfortunes of life and death in one form or another since he was a teenager, but he'd never seen anything like this.

The woman's face, her whole head, the flesh and bones—all of it—had been reshaped into a facsimile of a question mark. A question mark!

"Blake. Blake! What...?"

His composure went on reserve, came back as it always did, as it had to, no matter how his vision felt violated.

He turned and took in the brown paper bag, the slightly ajar drawer. A Gideon's bible.

A sensation.

"We should go. We should just go," Jane said, backing toward the broken door, bumping it, then moving away from it, as if feeling trapped.

"Wait," he said, shuffling to his left, not looking toward the woman any more, never again. Except in nightmares, where her mangled face would lurch out of the sleeping abyss, waking him to the shock of reality. All of the bad experiences and worse deaths tailored their attack to when he was weakest, which might explain why he rarely slept deep enough to dream anymore. (*All dreams led to Claire, anyway...*) He knelt down, not knowing why, but something drew him downward. Something whispered to him. Not a whisper of words, but one of knowing.

As abruptly as he'd backed away from the woman, he shot back up, standing tall, shadows shifting off the wall, inspired by his presence.

Or was it something else?

"Look," Jane said, as a snapshot shadow played out on the carpet. An undefined thing, with an improbable foundation.

Blake did not need her direction to look. He was right next to it, the shadow only there *within* his shadow, yet its movement separate from his, its shuddering not aligned with his firm stance.

What mad conference of reality and fantasy was being held in his presence? Was he finally losing his mind, too many blunt instrument concussions rendering him a hallucinating lunatic?

He knew it had something to do with Marlon. What? There was no way any of this would make much sense, what with the green limousine being a surreal starting point.

"Explanations are futile. I cannot tell you exactly how I know, but I know Marlon was here. That shadow. This woman—"

"I cannot imagine Marlon killed her," Jane said, her eyes glossy, polished silver. Still related to gray, but with a glimmer of something more.

"No. No, I don't think he did. That man with the lightning white hair may have. Either way, he's got information that could lead us to Marlon. It's fair to reckon his presence here was with purpose. We need to know the purpose. We need to find him and ask a few questions."

"How can you be so sure? Perhaps he's just a white-collar murderer, slumming on his way from one business convention to another, or home to his oblivious wife, his two point five children, a Dalmatian, white picket fence…"

Blake shook his head. He knew. He knew.

"Explanation is futile. I just know. He may very well be a white-collar murderer. But he also knows something, has something to do with Marlon."

"And he's gone. Long gone."

"The car was a rental. Perhaps…"

"Perhaps it would be best to head back to the airport."

"To inquire about him."

Jane glanced in the direction of the bed.

"Nothing we can do here, and we don't want to stall our quest. Best we make a hasty exit and be on our way," Blake said.

"Dear God," she said, turning her face from the taffy-pulled atrocity that used to be human, a woman.

"I don't think God has anything to do with what went down here," Blake said, as they maneuvered the door out of their way, and slipped through. They rushed to the car and sped away to the airport.

Seeking answers…but expecting only to find more questions…

Chapter 14

Teagarden

Violence. Most people in your world pray it passes them by, or they purposely avoid confrontation that might lead to its appearance.

While traveling in the dark frontier, the possibility of violence is always present. It is a possibility in your world as well, but here, every situation, no matter the levity or lackadaisical trance woven into the drug experience, is rife with the whip-snap shifting of...let's call it tonality, dear sister.

Something felt in the bones, inspiring adrenaline to rampage in the body, seek retribution for the intrusion, inflict a reaction wrought in flesh and muscle. At any moment, in any situation, it looms as a jackal, ready to pounce.

I'm not speaking of the cookie-cutter, cartoon violence displayed on movies and TV. Something experienced at a distance. Not the kind that inspires a vicarious thrill, followed by laughter and safety when the lights go up in a movie theater. Not the kind our parents coveted, bringing them wealth, this third member of their bloodshed ménage à trois.

I'm talking about the type of violence that is pure in intent. Has only one motive: a means to an end. Purity so intense it embellishes life. A primal urge meant to be tapped, not ignored and avoided. A reminder of where we came from and what it takes to continue to move forward, free of society's clipped-wing approval. Violence should be embraced.

So many in your world live to avoid its veracity. Cross the street and turn away. Crumble within and pray to God. Skulk home with their tail between their legs, justify cowardice with the lie of safety. Safe from bodily harm, when psychologically, the damage has been done by not entering the arena. It needles, it gnaws. You may think it wrong. When our primal origin revels in the occasional expression of sweat and blood, an expression of our true selves, wired into the limbic system. It may push us closer to death, the extremity of some experiences, but it is to be cherished.

That said, I'd never killed anybody until today. It was necessary for my quest, attainment of the next leg of the Centipede, but also a matter of vigilante justice.

Back when Grimes informed me of what Riding the Centipede entailed, as well as my status as the next chosen one, he divulged this information while we were at the junkyard he owned. A few of the ubiquitous junky stragglers were shuffling like zombies through the potholed mufflers, mangled car frames, and greasy rags. The ones lower on the totem pole than me. The lost souls.

One such strip of beef jerky was named Simon, a real tweaker. Always prying into everyone's business and wanting some of whatever one's business was. Always on the take, on the hunt, for whatever drug-fueled shenanigans he could get into. He circled like a scavenging vulture; his life spent forking through everybody else's leftovers. A taste of this, a taste of that. I'm sure you know the type, dear sister, even in your world.

I'd seen him a few other times, usually in Grimes' presence. He was annoying but easy to ignore. A few harsh words and he crawled into his shell of slime, smiling and chewing on a wiper blade or whatever was available. But this time, we volleyed harsh words; he ignored them and shouted something about, "I'ma gon get ta that green limousine afor you does."

It was instantaneous, as most violence is. Without warning. Necessary.

Without compunction, I pounded him to within a breath of his extinction.

Grimes just watched. He knew the rules of the dark frontier and all worlds, really.

As an exclamation point and final warning, I tossed Simon down the few steps leading out of the business shack, a wooden box held together with snot and a prayer.

"I see you anywhere along my path, I will kill you without looking back, fucker. You get my drift?"

Heard him moaning as I stepped over his pretzel-twisted body. Watched Grimes pick him up and already, even in pain, blood pooling on his ratty layers of clothing, Simon laughed.

"Whatcha got fer me?"

"Certainly not your integrity, shit stain," Grimes said, as always the perfect comeback for every situation.

He wished me luck with a nod and a look in his eyes that might have been envy, but was tamped down because he knew how things worked in the dark frontier.

I may look like easy prey, but living in the dark frontier toughens you up. Or it kills you. It's all a matter of choice: take action without hesitation or wait around to die. In the dark frontier every breath might be your last and you truly must accept this as your philosophy.

I am reminded of this continually. The time for necessary violence is inherent in every situation.

I wake in an aquarium, listless, floating to the surface. Brightly lit fishes of various colors and sizes circle around my groggy head. They swim along walls with patterns their passage does not define. I attain the surface, no life jacket on hand, only the ability to wave my arms. The water evaporates. A black mist and just the fish flying around the room. A small room.

A child's room.

I glance down to see a night light, the cover rotating. Fish dipped in every color of the rainbow.

To my right, eye level to me as I boost myself up on my knees, a bed. Star Wars sheets decorated with Luke Skywalker, Chewbacca, Han Solo and that princess, the one Carrie Fisher played—what was her name?—in animated form. And the child, a boy of perhaps ten. Perhaps. Sleeping, but not peacefully. A turbulent ocean plays out across his face. Beneath heavy eyelids, the orbs dart about, a hectic mamba with Morpheus in the lead. Morpheus in a sinister mood.

What am I supposed to do now? Everything feels wrong here. A child? Will a child have my next rig, be the proprietor of my next leg of the Centipede?

I lean forward and whisper, "Wake up." I do this again when there is no response. As my hand nears him, about to nudge him with all the delicacy I can muster, a voice behind causes me to almost leap out of my skin.

"He's not the one with what you want. Please do not wake him." The voice is soft in a way that would seem appropriate for the child. Perhaps it is this child's voice, but not spoken from his mouth.

Before turning, I sense the speaker's heat pour over me as a shroud made of lava. What I see is shocking even to me who's seen many bizarre things along the rails of the dark frontier. I tumble backward. I bump the bed hard. The boy continues to sleep.

"Careful." It crouches in the shadows, flesh glistening, defining its shape and girth in the abstract. It tenses, wary, tentative, and aware of my surprise as fish flash across it, dipping into crevices as if caressing stones. Saliva drips from yellow and black fangs, the tips along the teeth to each side ground flat, and grinding now — I hear them: bumblebees buzzing.

"We've not much time," it says, this monstrosity swathed in muscle that even in the darkness, even spattered with the colorful fish, is of a bruised hue that makes my stomach clench. The smell of something alive yet rotted through and through enhances my desire to faint. Yet I hold on, back against the bed, uncertain of whether I should listen to this nauseating creature or wake the boy and get to the truth. I notice in my coiled repose, my body feels different. I'm different than I was on my last leg of the Centipede. Transformation is definitely in progress. I am different, yet the dim, shifting lights in this room don't allow me to see anything beyond fragments.

Perhaps the monster is a product of this lighting and is simply another person as I am, hunched in the nook between door and dresser.

Perhaps the boy is a slug dreaming of a shell, protection.

No matter what, this leg, as I expect all legs of my journey will be, is sure to bring surprises.

A noise outside the door, another door slamming, causes the creature to stiffen. It reaches over to the nightlight, lifts the rotating cover off and the light brightens a section of the wall.

The revelation, filling in the blanks, forces me to shut my eyes. I need a moment to blot it away. When I open them again, I realize the creature wears no skin. The inner workings are on full display: muscles and shit and the arterial path the shit follows, veins, actual arteries; and scaly, spring-like things that weave within the anatomy, holding it together. Like some kind of living stitches in constant flux.

I have never witnessed such an orgy of obscenity.

Even with all I have seen, this creature takes the cake and frosts it with a liquid mixture of diarrhea and what smells like hot oil. With the light shining on it, the stench becomes intolerable. I mask my face with my hands, but it is futile. The stench simply burrows into my pores.

Am I to bargain with monsters now? Does it matter? No. I have a purpose here. Time to get to it. To move beyond my dread and get to it.

"The Centipede. Do you have what I need?"

"Of course we do. Why else would you be here?" The soft voice wavers. Plucked feathers seeking the history of their genesis, the ability to fly.

"Then what do you want from me?"

"We need you to kill the one who abuses."

Abuse. Child abuse. Murder as a response to abuse.

Necessary violence.

"As imposing as you are, why haven't you killed the one who abuses?"

My eyes scroll over the creature, citing talons twice the size of my hands, muscles striated across its body, abundant fangs filling the large mouth, much as Alice's makeshift fangs had cluttered hers.

"I roam the realm of his imagination," it says, pointing at the sleeping child, the length of the arm putting the talon near my face.

I flinch, then immediately steady myself.

"I can only administer help within the space between dreams and the waking world."

Fair enough.

"I kill this person—"

"Monster in human flesh. Monster more hideous than you find me."

"I kill this monster, you give me the syringe, and I'm on my way, right?"

Something outside the room, perhaps a fist pounding a wall, causes the room to tremble with earthquaking assertion.

I glance at the sleeping child. The turbulence tumbles out of his features, addresses his limbs as he curls deep into a fetal position.

"That's all. Just murder."

"Just murder. But swift."

The door presses open, condensing the room as a man steps inside. He is wearing white pajamas with blue and red stick figures frolicking about—as far as the odd light will permit my perusal, but at least there are no rainbow fishes clamoring for attention—or is it blue and red pajamas with white stick figures waltzing across the man's chest, his loins? Uncertainty distorts my perception as it often does. My eyes are playing tricks on me, or perhaps it is the three-ring circus in my head.

"Who the hell are you?" There is nothing of humanity in this being. It is a monster, driven by selfish, depraved desires and reeking of alcohol. Hungry for whatever it wants. Abuse. A battle...

I leap at it but am tossed off with ease. I land against a wooden toy box with a crunch and a groan as the corner jabs hard into my right kidney.

The man, the monster, knows violence well. He claws at me, hammers at my head with fists made of iron. I feel woozy, yet something blossoms in my belly.

My right arm, with elastic grace, strikes hard at his head, while my left arm wraps *around* his head, the fingers digging into his eyes. He screams at his impossible predicament.

I kick at his body, kick with kangaroo snapping swiftness and potency that surprises me. Whatever has blossomed within me has ratcheted up my physical capabilities. The wooziness has cleared. I smell his doubt. It is time to go in for the kill.

When violence escalates to this level, with death present and awaiting victory, every opponent becomes invincible...or at least thinks he or she or it is. The monster that is the man pulls a switchblade from thin air. He clutches it in a steady, experienced hand and jabs with flesh piercing precision. He is a surgeon, slicing the air with the expertise to keep me at a distance, while lunging twice with perfect aim. My stomach and shoulder suckle the blade, spitting blood at the intrusion.

"Don't know what you're made of. But we're gonna find out," he says, wiping sweat from his brow as he lunges again.

I grab his arm with both of my hands and jam the wrist against my knee. A knee festering with the blades of a saw. A diseased thing, the blades spin and rip through my flesh and pant leg.

Amputating the man's hand.

I scream as the man screams, shocked and delighted at the changes to my being, yet wary of the reality of it as I see my knee and pant leg are normal. I only have to question how I can be holding the man's dismembered hand in mine?

"Hurry," the sleeping child's monster yells, as another sound booms from the hallway. The sleeping child, less human and more a ball of putty being shaped by the events outside of its scope, seems embryonic now. A tiny ball of flesh, the putty made human.

The monster that is the man—father, dear father? Of course, aren't all fathers evil?—sensing defeat, lunges again, this time grasping my throat with his remaining hand, while finding the wherewithal, despite the obvious pain, to shove the stump of the other arm into my mouth.

I gag on blood and the serrated meat; on fractured bone and his desperation.

Desperation, again. As always, present in the dark frontier, no matter which corner of the dark frontier the drama is played out in.

Something shoves the door open, filling the frame. Cracking the entrance with its girth.

The sleeping child's monster cowers at the sight of this new shadow swelling at the doorframe.

My legs pull back, bent backward as an insects'. While my arms clutch the man's throat, my bony feet scale his body until they are perched on his clavicles, each one taking measure of the task at hand. With a concentrated push, the bones split and snap, puncture through the stick figures with the stick foundation of this man, this monster dressed in a man's flesh.

His high, tinny, screeching protestation is snuffed out by the humungous thumping sound a body makes when being thrust at a wall across a room. The lifeless meat slides down to the floor next to the sleeping child's bed. The sleeping child is a puddle of goo now, no distinction to be had. I only know it was him as he's not moved since I showed up.

The thing at the doorway blinks into nonexistence. The wood in the frame sighs in weary relief.

My breath is the only sound that follows. I look in my hands, my normal, human hands, my normal human body shaking as I stare into the dead eyes of the monster, the man, the abusive father, with both shock and envy for this boy. Finally rid of this encroachment on his childhood, his innocence.

I drop the head to the floor. Blood and viscera are smeared in arcing patterns over what looks to be blue walls with a trimming at the junction of wall and ceiling done in more Star Wars characters.

What a pleasant room for a child.

I stand, and, still shaking, say to the only monster that remains, "The Centipede. Now."

There is no time to rejoice in this victory. There is no time to delve into feelings I did not want to delve into, anyway. I have filled the request. I need to be on my way.

The monster opens the top drawer of the dresser, moving a bit of moist body part from the handle, reaches in and collects my syringe.

I take it and say, "Thank you."

The monster's smile is odd, but noticeably a smile.

"No reason to thank me. Circumstances present us with choices. You did what you thought necessary. We all do as we believe we need to, in order to get what we deem essential."

Rules of the game called life.

I turn to observe the destruction before heading on my way.

I have decimated a monster, or perhaps I have not. A man, not tall, not fierce—*not decapitated*—slumps lifeless next to the child's bed. Not even a faint trace of the smell of alcohol or the tang of blood bite my nostrils.

I run my hand along where the knife struck me, only to acknowledge there are no wounds, no blood.

I was at a loss.

"Be on your way, before you find out something that might shake you to your core," the monster says as it laughs, a sound like the rustling of the maggot-filled paper bag left to sit out in the sun and stew.

What the hell have I just participated in? I do not know and know it's best just to move on.

I take the syringe as the shade is placed over the nightlight and fish swim in my vision as something again swims in the syringe and it does not matter. Nothing matters but my destination.

I jam the needle into my neck and the maggots feel as though they've shifted from my ears to my throat, squirming, filling me, bloating the diseased flesh. Feasting on me. I am a toad pumped full of air and ready to explode. I open my mouth and something abhorrent coats my tongue with kisses from the void. Colorful fish breed colorful nightmares.

The sleeping child has awoken. I hear him say, "Did it work?"

Another voice, his voice but not, says, "Of course it did."

"You're one messed up genie," followed by twin peals of laughter cut with sadistic joy that reverberates off the walls of the aquarium.

The colors are so pretty, so pretty, as they fill me and I drown in them.

CHAPTER 15

BLAKE

Outside of the hotel room, Blake and Jane Teagarden spent a few seconds looking in each other's eyes, shaping their next move.

"The car the man was driving was a rental. Our first line of fire is to check the rental desks at the airport, see if he's turned it in. Get whatever info on him that's available." Blake drew a deep breath and watched Jane do the same, the fresh air outside needed to cleanse the lingering stench of the dead woman out of their nostrils. "If he's dropped it off, perhaps he's still there, waiting for a flight."

"It's imperative we find Marlon, Mr. Blake. Whatever it takes, we must get to him before he's gone forever."

Blake knew this, but added the two cents he'd been tumbling between his fingers in the back pocket of his thoughts. "What we've really got to do is get to Marlon before this guy does. I understand as well as can be expected, the deal with the green limousine, and fate. I just wonder if this guy is a part of the machinations of Marlon's fate." Blake mulled over what happened to the woman in the motel room. If this guy was also on Marlon's wayward trail, the end result would not be in Marlon's favor. Potters suggested fate might mean something besides death. In this man's hands, only death awaited. "I wonder if we can alter destiny, if this guy has intentions, well…"

"…they won't bode well for my brother."

They jogged back to the car, Blake insisting on the keys, and made for the airport posthaste. As he drove one-handed, weaving between traffic and pushing every yellow light to red, he called Potters, who had better connections than he did, with intelligence sources both well-known and covert.

"I need you to spin your magic web, get me some info."

"Is this about Teagarden?"

"Yes."

"I thought I told you to walk away from this one, my friend. The vibe's thick as congealing blood. Can't you sense it?"

Of course he could, but he was in too deep now. Three fingers raised above the waterline, but still hanging on.

"I know. But I need to see this one through. So, you going to help or should I look elsewhere?" He had other connections, but Potters was usually the most reliable, and quick to boot.

"What do you need?"

"Anything you can give me on a man we saw leaving a crime scene today."

"Crime scene? You are in deep, aren't you?"

"Deep enough. The guy was my height, about 6'3", 6'4", a solid 230-240, shock of white hair. Slavic cheekbones dotted with acne scars. Slight cleft in the chin." Blake glanced in the rearview mirror, half-heartedly expecting to see the man there. "Strange eyes, two different colored pupils. Black and gray. Lively eyes. An odd glimmer to the orbs. Thick lips. Like Cary, that fella you dated a few years ago."

Potters grunted, understanding.

"Cream colored, no, white suit, as if…as if it was a regular thing for him. Oh, the shock of white hair was trimmed short above the ears, yet jagged like lightning, all over the place. Spiky."

"Handsome," Potters said, though his tone indicated otherwise.

"He looked like a glam rock star, a degenerate glam rock star, or perhaps a gigolo with no preference as to what gender to please...or decimate. He radiated menace like a crown he wore proudly."

"Jeez, you got a good take on this guy. What did you do, have lunch with him?"

The thought made Blake's stomach tighten. He stared out the side window, at the alien landscape, the bogus alien landscape, prettied up to play up an incident from almost seventy years ago. It was comical, when a serious slant might be more honest. Especially with what he was learning of the world over the last few days.

"You still with me? Anything else?"

"Work with that. Make it as fast as possible. Time's running short." He glanced at Jane, before turning back to the potholed road. Perhaps UFOs had left those potholes, evidence of their skid-mark landings.

"Will do, Sherlock." Then, moving away from the faux joviality hinted at by the nickname, "And watch your back."

Blake had his wallet out and ready, having struck out at the rest of the rental desk clerks, flashing his private eye I.D. toward a petite blond wearing a snug lavender suit and a nametag that designated her as "Charlene."

"Charlene," Blake said, forced smile in tow, but his voice laced with authority. "A man should have turned in a white Dodge Dart within the last thirty, forty-five minutes. I need to know his name, any information you have on him."

"You know I can't do that without—"

"It's a matter of life or death, Miss." Playing it up, but not by much. "Charlene. Please."

Jane's timing was perfect as she made it to Blake's side, the look on her face etched with concern.

Blake had dealt with many situations in the southwest. One thing he could always bank on was the willingness of most people to help in any situation, no strings attached. Where those residing on the east coast thrived on the give and take help might garner, the advantage or upper hand built into the process, southwesterners flaunted good manners and willingness to assist, no matter the rules.

Charlene, though, shrugged her shoulders and said, "I wish I could help, but we've had no returns in almost two hours, Mr. Blake."

"What? How can that be?" Jane said, eyes shading darker.

"Are you sure, Charlene? Tall man, really white hair."

"No, Mr. Blake. My shift started two hours ago and I've only rented three cars, no returns. Wish I could help you, but..." Hands held up, palms empty. Her smile was a dagger into progress, though beneath the façade, the expression was laced with a sense of personal failure, as if it was her fault there was no information to be had.

As a cursory exercise in killing time, Blake suggested they drive around town, looking for the car, even though they both knew the car was probably many miles away. On the way to Marlon. While they floundered, beached and gasping for air.

After a pass along side streets seen a few times already, Jane—driving again, the pace more concentrated, yet no less imperative—pulled the car over on the outskirts of town at the opposite end, away from the palm-tree masked hotel, and said, "What now?"

Blake stepped out and lit a cigarette. Cranking up the machinery of his brain for the long haul. Telling her the truth would only irritate her further. Nonetheless, options were slim and none, with the possible exception of a pipedream.

"We wait. Potters is checking with his sources. We get that information, we might have something to move on."

"Wait? Marlon's path is fraught with negativity in every sense, and you expect us to wait? What if your buddy takes until tomorrow to get us anything of worth?" She stepped out and around to the front of the car. Her fingers did a jig along the hot hood.

"Then I suggest we get a hotel room or two and exercise our aptitude for patience."

"Fuck patience, Mr. Blake. Action is all that's necessary now."

Blake watched lizards scatter amid the cactus and smooth stones. Their trails were as random as the one he was stuck on right now.

"Miss Teagarden. Sometimes the only response is patience. That's the job. We've nothing to go on. We've exhausted our time here and now have to wait for whatever information Potters can find for us. Whether that takes an hour, a day, or a week, it's all we have. Besides that, I have no idea which direction to head," he said. Unless a businessman happened to stumble by like at SFO, dispensing with scribbled clues on torn paper.

"Fuck." She raised her hands, two scorpions about to strike, dug the long, thin fingers into her thick blond mane, pulling the hair in tangles, the scrunchie used to hold everything in place momentarily discarded, before pulling it all back, the shambles messy now, but regrouped in the squeeze of the scrunchie.

"I understand your worry, Jane. Abuse leads some down paths where the only people one meets along the way have bad intentions. Seems like the path—"

Abruptly, as if Blake's words carried the weight of his open palm across her face. "Abuse?"

"Child Abuse. The trigger for this whole mess, from my ringside seat."

"What are you talking about, you stupid man?" Jane said, furious as she stepped firmly toward him.

"Your parents. Child abuse." He snapped his fingers in her face. Wake up!

"I dispelled those allegations long ago—"

"And a fine performance that was. Meryl Streep would have been proud," Blake said, unable to keep it inside.

"You miserable piece of shit." Jane was all teeth, lipstick smeared on the two up front, like blood on fangs. "I told the truth. That so-called performance was by a child of sixteen trying to hold on to a life she understood while it fell apart all around her. Marlon was never abused in any way."

"You expect me to believe that?"

"I don't really care what you believe, that's your problem. Your prejudice. A product of years expecting only the worst of people. I am not innocent myself, but I can tell you, unequivocally, Marlon was never abused, sexually, mentally — in any way. He had his own issues…" She turned away, breath caught. Blake could tell this was not a regular topic of conversation for her.

"Then why? Why did he leave? What were these issues? Perhaps if you give me the lowdown. Perhaps…" He moved toward her, around the front right headlight, filling her vision unless she was to turn away.

She turned away.

"Look, I'm…I'm sorry about my misreading of the news conference, the whole thing, but my instincts are all I have in this meandering trek around the sun. Along with pain in my right hand, migraines that could knock down a stallion, and a desire to blot it all out with alcohol and painkillers on a regular basis." Blake clasped his black hat and removed it, ran his fingers through his hair as if combing it, only to put it back on, the action superfluous. "My experiences shape me and I am sure the shape is ugly. But if there was no abuse, what issues led Marlon to hit the streets and to virtually disappear, until now?"

After a long pause, Blake watching more lizards scatter, she said, "We had a loving household, Mr. Blake. But it was not your average home life." A smile slipped through, but Blake noted it was not a smile indicative of happiness. "Our parent's Hollywood connections led them away from us often. We immersed ourselves in the library, the entertainment center, with books and movies and whatever amused us. Many of the books were of a subversive nature." She tapped chipped nails on the hood, scratching the paint. "Our imaginations took it all in. We created our own world. We called the world the dark frontier. A trippy world where drugs and madness reigned."

"Why drugs and madness?"

"That was the focus of many of the books. Our parents, specifically father—mother was along for the ride, barely there when she was there—embraced all that was obscure or, again, subversive, while in the real world, he was a conformist to the T."

"Drugs...? Madness...?"

"The books, more for looks than to be read, something father collected for when he retired. He wanted to know all the weird and wonderful and strange things in the world. Our parents never read anything unless it was to be turned into a potential blockbuster. But his life was cut short"—emotions rising, then swiftly settling across her features—"before he had the opportunity to enjoy his collection. But Marlon and I, we explored those books. We were never limited in our quests, never told no, always open to anything. Father enjoyed our interest, wanted us to look at the world with original eyes, or at least not corrupted by what he created." She snickered, a sad, defeated sound. "Waiting for a time to join us and have us tell him what we had learned. A way of getting us to think outside the proverbial box, but he waited too long. When Marlon left, it threw him out of sorts. He never recovered. The fire ended his misery."

"I still do not understand why Marlon left."

Jane put her hands in her pockets, shuffled her feet. "Being... impressionable, he was more inclined to take the words in all those books as law. Our world was a game we played, to align the many ideas and ideals from the books. But...he was not a well boy. Always fighting this or that sickness, allergy...mental glitch."

"Mental glitch?"

"Funny, I have always assumed it was something genetic, handed down from our parents. Where father always wanted to know too much, push too much, never resting, never psychologically happy, what with the cage of producing those hit movies he had created, this measure of activity enforced long bouts of insomnia and sleep deprivation that flip-flopped into his daily life. He was brilliant, but flawed, as we all are. Flawed."

Blake noted that smile again, the one not born of happiness. He suspected the memory inspired it, perhaps a glimmer of joy, but nothing more than a glimmer.

"But Marlon was not brilliant. He was scarred, flawed, got all the flaws and none of the good. His mind stayed in the dark frontier more often once he'd made friends who dabbled in drugs and something there, something in the chemistry of his own madness and the drugs, as well as the books we indulged in, meshed as a kind of reality that ran parallel to ours, then took over for him." She slipped her hands out of her pockets, rubbed them together, then thrust them back. "He's been there ever since, I expect. Stuck somewhere in an imaginary realm made real. His life probably the life of a junky, in a way, but a junky with a high-octane imagination."

This was all a bit much for Blake. The aspects of reality and imagination that Marlon had dissolved in a glass of water and lapped up as if an elixir, preposterous. Yet Jane's words only once hesitated, and that had nothing to do with her spin on Marlon. More so, she seemed relieved to have gotten it all out. Furthermore, where exactly did this leave them? Because over the last few days, Blake's take on reality had been hit hard.

"What makes us think we have a hold on reality and this dark frontier is not as real as what we know?"

Jane lifted her eyes from their perusal of the ground, her shoes. Her eyes glassy, two marbles, polished and beautiful, but empty. "Did I say it wasn't real? I believe reality is what each of us makes of it. I think your take on reality is quite different than mine."

Blake banked on this, for sure. Though with their paths crossing, he was getting a sense for hers...

"As is Marlon's, though a seed of understanding, because of our upbringing, perhaps gives me a feel for his. Or perhaps I'm full of shit."

The moment lingered. Blake's cell phone chirped loudly, grabbed his attention.

"Talk."

"I've got something."

"That was swift."

Jane's posture firm, she crossed her arms over her now wrinkled blouse as if bracing herself for bad news.

"Only a tidbit. Passed on the info to a handful of people who should be able to give us more details soon, but when I got it to Kyle Sumners from the Agency"—one of the covert intelligence organizations, that's all Blake knew, not needing anything more than trust in Potters' connections—"his immediate reaction, well, if I said priceless, it was also bizarre. He said, and I quote, 'No way. That Russian slime.' He informed me of a handful of rumors he'd heard, stuff that puts any ideas on what you're dealing with to shame. Obvious fodder formulated to add, as you noted, menace to the mystique, but he said"—stopping, taking a deep breath, letting it all out in one fell swoop—"this guy, rumor has it he's a Russian thug, freelance assassin, yadda yadda yadda, but, dig this, was born the day of the Chernobyl disaster, crawled from the radiation and took shape as a man, lightning bolt hair, some kind of new breed of human and radiation, a blotch, an aberration, cancer with teeth. He went on and on in this vein. I had to stop him, his voice swinging between revulsion and almost giddy awe. I knew I had to get you this much, no matter the obvious illegitimacy of the info. Something about what you're dealing with—"

"Makes it less fantasy and possibly grim fact. No matter the outrageousness of it all."

"That's pretty much my thinking. Not that I believe any of this. A hybrid of human and radiation? He'd be dead for starters. Either that or a nuclear-powered Marvel Supervillain intent on taking down Batman, Superman, and any other worthy superheroes. You are no superhero, my friend. You ready to step away now?"

"Gotta push on, pal. No turning back." Though he wanted to, he wanted to. Every indicator, every iota of instinct suggested—*demanded*—and pretty much expected him to.

"Perhaps this will change your mind." With that, Potters told him the big guy's name. Blake heard it and as seconds lingered, Potters said, "You got that?"

"Yeah," he said, then folded the old school cell phone closed.

"What? What did he have for us?" Jane said.

Blake's eyes remained frosty, distant.

A glam rock star from the pit of a nuclear reactor. A gigolo with the intentions and means to fuck whatever it wanted to extinction. To annihilate whatever he—it—wanted.

Who else would call himself Rudolf Chernobyl, besides a madman, a mad being, the devil himself?

Shaking his head, Jane chattering in the background, he strolled away from her, to the dirt and cactus and abundant lizards skipping about, weaving their wiry paths in the dirt.

When his eyes dropped to his shoes, he noticed the trail of one lizard, a cursive scribble that looked like the name of another town.

Their next destination?

He continued to shake his head, taking in a monster named Rudolf Chernobyl, and a helpful lizard indicating a destination no longer unknown.

"Jane..."

CHAPTER 16

CHERNOBYL

Rudolf Chernobyl sat in the only chair ever to bring him comfort, in the only room ever to bring him joy, taking in another masterpiece: Gian Lorenzo Bernini's The Rape of Proserpina sculpture. Bernini was a man after his own cruel heart, what with his slashing of the face of Costanza Piccolomini, a married woman he was having an affair with, because of the possibility she'd had a liaison with his brother. Just the possibility. His control of the situation and the woman was something Rudolf could appreciate on many levels.

He ran his fingers over his face, displeased with his recent meltdowns, control stumbling and seeping out of his flesh.

As with many of the classic art pieces, for the proper price they could be obtained, as long as one had the sleight-of-hand skills necessary to acquire said piece of art, while leaving a close to perfect copy in its place. A copy so perfect, it might even be better than the original. With The Rape of Proserpina, he'd commissioned a fellow freelance mercenary artist, a covert, skilled sculptor known as Templeton—another shadow dweller dealing in the black market—to create the perfect copy of Bernini's sculpture. It was so perfect, those who dealt in the art underworld at the Galleria Borghese in Rome, Italy, wondered why he didn't just keep it and pocket the money he'd spend on obtaining the original, not that they minded his donation to their bank accounts.

Pity, he'd have thought earnest lovers of art would understand the reason why one wanted the one and only, no matter the number of copies that might be distributed throughout art galleries across the globe. To touch the marble that a great man, a great artist touched, is to be as close to a true god as Rudolf could imagine.

His purpose here was not to relish art, though.

He had a plan.

In most cases, when a snippet of self is taken and used as a homing device, Rudolf would jack in, get a location, then internally shift the homing device from the purely visual, to a topographical map of the location. A blip accompanied the process, escalating as he approached his quarry.

This time, he was not going to shift and move into hunter mode. He was going to settle in and observe everything as it happened. He was going to try and establish a link that would show him more, perhaps give him a clue as to the next stop along the precarious path. If there's a drug being used to engineer travel, perhaps if he remained locked into the visual, he could follow along, even as the blip fell silent. Staying connected.

Perhaps he could, at the very least, get a clue to the follow-up destination, glean something from within the process, and cut out precious minutes. Put himself face-to-face as opposed to just missing his mark. After all, he had just missed Marlon Teagarden at the last stop. Under the circumstances and not one to court frustration on a regular basis, it seemed a legitimate strategy.

One that might lead to him slipping into the oddest places imaginable.

The images from Marlon's world were hazy at best. Through Marlon's eyes, he saw fish and wondered if Teagarden was drowning. It went on and on, though, and Marlon didn't struggle. Until he saw a monster, something out of an H.R. Giger sketchbook. Or perhaps it was one of William Blake's muscled figures, yet it lacked something he could not define.

Rudolf saw a child floating in this dim realm.

He expected something he could latch on to, something familiar. Why were the images draped in the guise of the fantastical? The sense of it all was layered in nonsense, yet as the scene played out, another entered the fray. A man whose body seemed a playground for a menagerie of beings, alien and human.

What was going on?

A battle ensued—clumsy, amateurish—but within the sloppy struggle, the last one to enter the scene had tripped over his own feet and cracked his head on a dresser.

Afterward, the sketchbook monster and Marlon exchanged something: a syringe.

Through the mental mist Rudolf saw something swimming in the syringe, in the milky liquid: maggots. Something like maggots. Or was the milky liquid alive? He sensed as Marlon took the syringe and thrust the needle into his neck.

The sleeping child woke, eyes red as Hell's red light district, a sleazy invitation. No, something else he could not read.

Then—

A pooling darkness, ink stain fluidity. Blotch as beginning point, yet spreading. He heard buzzing. In the previous scene, he heard nothing; silence is usual. But here, a soft thrumming took him, a low, keening buzz.

He thought of blood flowing in one's body. Head to a pillow and the ability to hear it even more clearly. This felt like that, with no pillow. A metallic ting shimmering at the height of the sun-dappled wave. A blood wave. A blood tide. He did not know, yet he surfed in the dark place without fear.

Static pierced the thrumming, the metallic ting, a bleat of voices, music.

Rudolf's hands braced the arms of the wooden chair. Tiny slivers pricked his palms. He narrowed his focus, listened in.

"I only want to help," said one voice.

"Help yourself again, right?" said another.

One of Penderecki's ominous odes to suffering and terror slithered into the thrum, unnerving Rudolf.

"What are we supposed to do with him?" The first voice again.

"No," said the second voice, now screaming. A sensation as if being trapped, caged, ears plugged and no more sounds except what thrives within, the Penderecki snippet shoved aside by Jim Morrison's middle of the desert, back of the car warning from "Riders On The Storm," the rain coming down and splashing upon Ray Manzarek's delicate keyboard ministrations, winding into something by Dark Angel Asylum, Aleister Blut's corrosive wail threaded with anguish, lyrics from a song he did not know actually cut through, with intent—"No more rules and regulations/slaughtered here your destination/chiseled on the walls of time/no future here, not yours or mine"—slanting into Queen, Freddy Mercury ranting and railing about the "Great King Rat," and more, an avalanche of music and lyrics pouring through his ears, but not from the outside, it all clamored for cacophonous attention from within. From within Marlon Teagarden's mind.

The onslaught was unprecedented. Rudolf hung on as it all swirled with dreamscape lucidity, these sounds, as accompanied by images that veered from the source material—Morrison's visage, Aleister Blut, ear pressed to the Marshall Stack, Freddie Mercury with long hair and skin tight white body suit, along with images bathed in a degree of utter strangeness and perversion that included many nods to copulating insects, as well as an adult cartoon spin on Alice in Wonderland in which Alice was being fucked by the Mad Hatter while she orally pleasured the Caterpillar as the Queen of Hearts masturbated in the corner.

Morrison laughed in the background, somewhere unseen, but it was his voice: "I want whatever you're taking, Marlon."

What surprised Rudolf the most about this whole menagerie of madness was how he found himself thoroughly enjoying the ride. Never one for drugs, this one, whatever the Centipede was, was something he sensed he would enjoy.

Perhaps he'd get a nip, once he delivered Marlon to his employer. Perhaps he'd take what he wanted and skip on the formalities.

The momentary flutter of his own thought—of something beyond observation and riding along the psychic, psychedelic, psyche-bound roller coaster; a thought separate from the ride—loosened his grip. Yet before he was unceremoniously thrust back to his reality with all the whiplash abruptness of a slingshot, he registered one thing:

Movement. The experience had been accompanied by a sense of moving forward…to a next destination. This impression was curiously made relevant when Alice, face dripping with Caterpillar cum, said to him, "Follow the black tar-stained tunnel if you want to know where Marlon will end up next," before slurping up more of the green substance from the still groaning Caterpillar's penis.

Looking beyond the orgy of strange, the sensation as if on a boat. Floating forward at a casual pace. Allowing the water—the drug—to assimilate and show him what was next. Taking him to his next destination.

Thinking in the flurry before returning: *I see a light. A light. The next stop? So far ahead. What if I rush forward? What if I…*

But too late, the slingshot return slamming him into his own reality, the hardback chair turned to chips and ash all around him. His clothing also turned to ash, the fabric cinders at his feet.

Naked, he stood up, his body as white as his hair, a flare never to be extinguished. Beneath the skin, movement as well; a different kind of movement. He felt the heat swell, as well as his engorged penis, spewing as one would food poisoning, a paradox of two sensations he'd never felt at this heightened level before. The first one completely foreign, while the second one joined in only when he was at his worst: a dopesickness that made his head feel light, a balloon about to fly off into the deep blue, swirling as it did with dizziness and euphoria. He vomited out his pleasure, his seed, the spark and splat of liquid eating through the floor as he dropped to his knees. The first full-on lack of control he'd felt in years.

He pulled it all within, bringing the world into place again. Semen gushing from his still achingly erect penis.

The sensation ate brain cells and judgment for dinner, yet he welcomed the final jerk of semen, the surrender he had experienced.

Years of control, of utilizing his skills and the inherent justification to need this control, burned away in the sticky white liquid eating away at the hardwood floor. Sizzling with determination.

He cherished life, detested those who catered to experiences that blotted the living of life to nothing more than the passage of time. But with this experience, and only from the outside—he could not imagine the full effect—he knew, when he delivered Marlon to his employer he would also insist on a bit of this Centipede drug.

Insist.

Demand.

He needed just one fix. Just one *real* fix.

He was hooked, though he would never admit this to himself.

He took a deep breath, a deep controlled breath.

Something had changed.

CHAPTER 17

BLAKE

Switching his cell phone on as he exited the plane with Jane Teagarden in tow, Blake retrieved a message from Potters, confirming, at the very least, that Rudolf Chernobyl was for real, was bad news, and was an enigma, despite an appearance that would seem to make him stand out. The info was lean, the bone stripped bare.

Worse than the non-existent info, the sensation that the wild goose chase had taken a path into a forest without reason or rhyme to guide them left him with the niggling feeling it was all for naught. His instincts immediately told him Marlon Teagarden or Rudolf Chernobyl were not here.

So, why were they here?

Rubbing his forehead, the ache in his hand throbbing mightily, Blake informed Jane of the miniscule findings for Rudolf Chernobyl as well as the dwindling faith he had that anything of worth was to be found here, so close to the middle of nowhere, USA.

All she did was laugh.

He wondered if she'd gone off the deep end, food for sharks.

"You lead us to this bleak flatland hell and you expect anything else but laughter?"

He expected her ire. He expected derision of some sort, at least a mental slap via her slate-gray eyes. Perhaps she was simply delirious and about to kick him off the case and send him back to the smoggy confines of Los Angeles where he'd settle in and brood on life and perseverance and the cheerless answers he might find in a bottle of scotch. Then he'd get another call from another husband or wife in need of confirmation of infidelity, snap some unglamorous couplings, carry on as usual, and push the memory of Marlon and Jane Teagarden and this Russian freak, Rudolf Chernobyl, from his memory banks. He'd be happy to scrub them clean, fill them with a new kind of grime as he spent long nights staring at the ceiling while insomnia torqued his serotonin levels out of whack.

"There may still be a reason we're here, Jane." Though he felt any reasons were out to lunch, snacking on the bare bones of his patience and perhaps sanity.

"Of course there is. The lovely scenery. The blistering sun. The beaten down feeling that I've been taken for a ride when all I want is to find my brother. By the way, would you like me to get the tab for your dinner, too?" Blake watched her dig into her gray purse, pull out a black wallet, reach her hand into it as if reaching into an abyss, and wave a couple platinum charge cards in front of her smirking face. "Another hotel room, perhaps a penthouse suite" —she snorted, the thought of a penthouse suite in this dead end town preposterous—"or perhaps I should just give you a blow job and send you on your—"

"What the fuck is your problem? I've asked for nothing more than what you've proposed financially." Jane dropped the credit cards unceremoniously into her purse, though the smirk remained rigid on her face. "I'm trying to work through the ridiculous path that's been laid out, from a green limousine to a note dropped in an airport to fucking lizards scratching this town's name into dirt. I haven't a clue as to what's going on, yet I also know…I also know I am a part of this. Whatever this is."

Blake felt frustration dig his fingernails into his palms, both hands clenched into fists.

Leaning into him, her breath minty, trimmed in vodka sipped from a tiny bottle from the plane: "What good does that do us if—" She halted with an abruptness that surprised Blake, a crash-test dummy head-on and body jolting dance with a concrete wall, downshifting into deep thought, her pupils dilating, focused inward. Reading the message on the cranial wall.

"What?"

She put up her hand, swift to silence his verbal intrusion.

He waited, watching her as she closed her eyes, obviously trying to dredge up something from the gray matter disarray.

"The green limousine," she said. "I should have known before we stepped on that plane."

"What about the green limousine?"

"Peter Solon lives in 'the center of the world,' as he phrased it in the last interview he ever did, some twenty, twenty-five years ago. 'The center of the world'"—shaking her head, arranging the recollection—"no, no, 'The center of this world, America, land of those who erroneously think they are free, and home of the bored, bland, dead souls.' He mentioned his house. A blue ranch house—"

"A blue ranch house? A green limousine and now a blue ranch house?"

"A blue ranch house, the center of the world, as he knew it. A fucking blue ranch house."

Blake knew this had to be the reason they were here. He knew his instincts wouldn't set him totally off the trail or, more precisely...the lizards, the scaly messengers, wouldn't. They were meant to be here. He was meant to be here.

"Is that all I have to go on? A blue ranch house, somewhere in this vicinity, which might mean miles in any direction?"

"What do you mean? That was long ago, that interview, such a strange interview. The only one he'd ever given, actually. A diatribe against humanity, nothing more. Barely any mention of his two books, his literature. He was old then. Angry. Defeated. I can't imagine he's still alive. I can't imagine…"

"I need to find out if he is. There's a reason we are here. He may have answers pertinent to finding Marlon. At the very least, the blue ranch house might have answers."

"I'll get us a rental and—"

"No. I'll get a rental and I will go out and find the blue ranch house. Talk to Solon if he's still alive. But if not, there may be something for me to find there, anyway."

"You can't go alone."

"Can't? Look," he said, his hands on her shoulders, his determination holding her steady. "I am somehow a part of this. Trust my instincts. I know I need to do this alone. I will be back as soon as possible. There's a Hilton nearby. Stay in the lobby, the bar, and if I run late, get a room. Wait for me. I can't say how I know this is the only way to do this, but I know it is."

Blake continued to stare into her eyes, felt her body lighten, as if a weight had been lifted. Felt her give in. Her exhaustion was overwhelming. The life drained and he held her closer, lending her some of his strength to get on the shuttle and get to the hotel. He stroked her hair, ran his fingers through it. She did not stop him, not that it was a precursor to anything beyond compassion.

(*He remembered Claire's downy soft hair…*)

As he walked her to the shuttle, he said, "See you soon."

It was more for him than for her, as he wanted nothing to do with Peter Solon and whatever messed up mindset or devious secrets he might have, but knew it was the only path, now narrowing, he could take.

He spent the next ninety minutes baking in the car, the path unspooling outward from the airport. Jane and he had checked a ratty phone book hanging from a long dysfunctional pay phone along a wall in the airport for Solon's address, expecting to find nothing and meeting with their first success of this venture. Now, Blake pulled over to the side of a long strip of asphalt nudging dirt and yielding nothing but monotonous soft ocher fields as far as the eye and imagination could see. It felt as though it was scrubbing him bland.

The warm water tasted like metal and dirt, satisfying not in the least. He wiped his brow and rotated clockwise, taking it all in, looking for something beyond the fields and ground-hugging ranch houses. The houses all seemed as vacant as the fields littered with the occasional tractor and broken-down automobile turned to rust.

He peered into the deep blue, the sky so vast it swallowed all thought, adding to the monotony that surrounded him. Telephone poles stood crooked, cutting a path through the fields, their hides weathered by the elements. Cables strung out between them sagged and swayed sounding like the flapping wings of Pterodactyls as the hot breeze beat them unmercifully, before simmering down to a hum. The murmur of voices in transit, but never stopping out here. Down where he was, edge of a field that dulled senses and sight, the feral electricity of insects and phantoms and lost souls brought a chill to *his* soul; the one barely hanging on...

What was he doing here? Enough weird shit had already been shown to him, why continue? Avoiding anything more like the plague would seem the logical path. There would be no good end to this, but, then again, there was never going to be a good end to any of this. We were here, then we were gone, and for all but a few, those who trickled through clenched fists with purpose, what was the use?

Endurance? (Always endurance. The pin pulled from the hand grenade, waiting...)

As Blake got back into the car, a vulture landed in front of the vehicle, shrugged in a very human way, and lifted lazily back into the sky.

Time to tell Jane this was all a mistake, Solon or no Solon, being here in God's bleak country. Staring at the godforsaken land, wondering about life, death, and the conspiracy between both, their dreary conspiracy wasn't working anymore.

Blake turned the ignition and started on his way. He meandered a little ways more, knowing he would turn around and head back soon, but not wanting to hear any of it from Jane or any of it from his weary thoughts, drifting. No cars for miles. Silos again, still in the distance, but closer than before.

Perseverance? (Perseverance slipped a leg into the canvas sack of the three-legged race.)

To the right, color invaded his vision, leaking like a broken pen, staining fingers, paper, and intentions.

A blue house, long and lean.

A blue ranch house.

He slowly rolled up to a signpost at the intersection of an asphalt and a dirt road. "Broken" something.

Half the sign was torn off, or maybe the sign was simply a statement as to the present condition. The uninviting road, barely that, seemed rarely used. Stones settled in his path leading deep into the ocher ocean and to the blue ranch house, and perhaps answers.

Or possibly more questions. (Always more questions, it came with the private eye territory.)

He steered the car, rocking slowly as he did, toward the blue ranch house. Up close it looked more desolate than anything he'd seen so far. There was no way anybody lived here. Solon was old anyway. Blake wondered if anybody ever made it way out here and, if not, if he would discover the decaying body of Solon. A rare feast for the insects amid this banquet-starved desolation.

He turned the car around and parked a ways from the house, a necessary caution. Being out here any longer than he needed to be did not rate high on his "to do" list, even if, by dumb luck or wicked karma Solon was still alive.

The slats on the porch were termite-riddled and splintered. He had to do a minefield cha-cha just to make it to the door. Blue paint dusted everything, a shade of teal that might have been stronger once, but now, sun bleached it of its vibrancy. Even though it had obviously been a while since the last touch up, layers and layers of the same blue paint feebly clung to the wood. It was proof there never was potency, the blue here from the beginning lacked inspiration.

Before knocking, Blake leaned into the windows at each side of the door. The door might once have been sturdy, but it had been stripped of its strength by time, eroded by the elements, just like everything he saw out here. The thin curtains to each side, unmatched: the one on the left, off-white, with dandelions and sunflowers; the one to the right, faded orange decorated with thin insect figures with hats and baskets mocking the hustle-bustle of humanity—something he knew never happened out here—allowed him a view of the interior.

He twitched, noticing a quirky, scratchy sound, like electricity gone to rot—what a strange thought. Though strange thoughts and stranger revelations seemed the norm these days. He felt it as much as heard it, something that ate the ever-present humming, like the teeth of a saw attempting to cut into metal, but so low only dogs and the unlucky individuals with hyper-sensitive hearing could even perceive it. He opened his mouth, cracking his jaw with a loud pop.

To the left stood a wooden frame for a sofa, mismatched pillows piled in disarray upon it. A table that looked like the cousin to the sofa. Everything looked bone naked. Two doors, one opened and one closed. The open door led to darkness the measure of which Blake thought of as complete. As if light, natural or artificial, never had graced the room. That was it, sparse teetering on non-existent. To the right, a large bookshelf dominated the room, books stuffed every which way onto the shelves, tumbling to stacks on the floor. The lone bookshelf unworthy of the onslaught. To the right of the bookshelf, was a tiny desk on thin legs with an old typewriter on it, accompanied by an uncomfortable looking wooden chair. Another room, door open, showed the remnants of a kitchen, no curtains over the window above the sink. Even from outside, Blake could make out dishes piled on a table, a broken mug on the floor.

As he focused, he noticed roaches and moths crawl and flutter about. They drew his eye to the picture frames above the desk, to the right and left of the entrance to the kitchen. All of them empty. Though this could be anybody's house, something about the contents of this house made his instincts sing. This had to be Peter Solon's home.

No matter the strong possibility Peter Solon was no longer of this earth, Blake knocked.

The sounds in his ears, picking at his eardrums as an ant picks at a dead beetle, amplified, then ebbed.

He knew something had acknowledged his intrusion. Again, this was instinct cranked to Spinal Tap's ludicrous eleven. He knew somebody was here.

He knocked again, and then placed his hand on the door handle. Something brushed against his pinky. He pulled away swiftly, only to watch an insect that might have been a cockroach but might not have been, what with the discomfiting pale hue to its carapace; then again, carapace seemed negligible. It was more like skin, this strange insect's outer coating. Like a snipped finger with legs.

More insects slid up and down the door, the walls, and the cracked windows. Many of them were not like anything he ever had seen before. He wondered if the insects in the Midwest were so much different than those in the west.

He made sure it was all clear around the door handle and placed his hand on the knob and turned it. The door was unlocked. He pushed and it swung open, creaking as it did. The expected creak, the horror movie creak. Still, it made his hackles bunch and his free hand knot into an aching fist.

The sound in his ears, not from outside but directly touching his ears, amplified again. He put his fingers to his ears, knowing it was useless. Yet he could not help it.

As it ebbed, he said, "Hello." His voice seemed thin, hollow, and did not echo.

Another open doorway, dead center in the back of the room—strangely out of his vision from either window—led to a darkness that made the darkness to the right almost comforting.

His stopped breathing; the darkness swelled. He felt as though it would pour out of the rectangle and smite him on the spot. Drag him into that darkness where not even God was welcome.

One last time, then out of here: "Mr. Solon. Peter Solon." Parchment inscribed with invisible ink.

The house moaned and cracked, as if the wood were alive. A sound like nothing Blake had ever heard split through the rumble, like glass being chewed with feverish dedication by teeth made of gravel. Pops and whirrs; amplifier hum after a strummed power chord.

Then: "Who's asking?"

A voice shaped by these obtuse sounds. The voice of Peter Solon.

Blake stepped past the front door and into the house with a deep breath and a desire to be anywhere but here, in the presence of the man who had created the legend of the green limousine. Solon was the key. He would have to follow through. Even if his courage was on life support.

CHAPTER 18

TEAGARDEN

I know I must get to the end to appreciate the full experience, to shake hands with Burroughs and take the ride of a lifetime. But there's an increasing unease within each leg of my journey. I just want it done. What more does it require of me to get it done? How many more legs are left?

Drugs alter the essential machinations of the mind and body. That's part of the reason I do them: I have never been happy with either. You know this, dear sister. But the Centipede is altering me in confounding ways. I should have expected this, but you know how it is when one locks into a good drug ride? There's no looking back, just the desire for more. Yet this is not good, there's the promise of what it will lead to, but where I am now is bad; uneasy.

My ears are full of chattering sounds. Insects in deep conversations. Cicadas. Crickets. Others. Others with unpronounceable names and indescribable appearances. And incomprehensible voices.

Everywhere within my aural scope is like tinfoil being crinkled and stretched and crinkled again. My teeth ache as I listen. A rusty nail etching enamel, pain implants filling the rotting holes.

No, it's not listening. It is a cloak over everything, this chattering, this sound that makes my teeth ache and my neck twitch at bad angles and my stomach vibrate with a desire to join in.

Or not.

You see, where I am now is not a place that brings anything but uncertainty.

Where I am physically only magnifies this: a room, a large room. The building is a warehouse, gutted, left to die. The concrete walls are moist. The odor is musky, animal musky, yet tainted with decay and internal rot. It is the aromatic stench of architectural atrophy, of grease and dead skin, of dreams turned to scum and scraped off the rim of a glass of water swarming with primal life, to be swallowed without question. The presence of the odor is alluring in a textural way, yet poison to the system as cramping causes me to buckle over. It reminds me of withdrawal, something I never wanted to experience again. I immediately stick my finger down my throat, attempting to purge, but I fail as nothing comes up. I wonder if this is necessary? My nostrils, like twin mouths, insist I ingest these odors.

Each leg has altered me in such a way that my senses have been fine-tuned or, no, obviously, my senses are different. You remember my take on the dark frontier and everything I have learned here, right? A response to things being different.

But until now, I have not had an inkling of how different.

The Centipede manipulates everything.

The paradox highlights an essential truth about the life of the traveler of the dark frontier. Like an imbalanced scale, what we want and the results are always in conflict. We tear ourselves down in order to get what we need. Give our all in order to build ourselves back up.

I know I am not the same now as when I left, my dear sister. Time in the dark frontier has shown me so much, sowed the sickness of being, sewing it to the fabric of experience, ragged, yet well-worn.

My ears, or the sonic receptors deeper within my brain, read the wavelengths now. Unable to tune in, but able to decipher clips.

I hear so much amid the tinfoil chatter:

Marilyn Monroe says something I can't quite make out.

She's here, can you hear her? Let me hold the microphone up, where she's standing in the shadows.

There's Lena Olin, naked except for the hat she tips in my direction.

My steely erection, more proof of paradox. In this vile place, even the potential for bliss arouses. But that's never been my true path.

"You know you're fucking crazy, Marlon," Marilyn says. "I love you, I do. But the Centipede is a lie. You're wasting your time and not going to like where this is all leading—"

"Shut up! The Centipede is the ultimate experience. The Centipede..."

We are interrupted by a person who approaches from the shadows opposite from where Marilyn stands with her hands on her shapely hips, and Lena covers her genitals with the hat, an arm across her modest bosom. Rita Hayworth dips in and out of the darkness. Others too. Many others masked by the dodgy light. The person is humming. It is a murmuring grumble, throaty and masculine. It's almost musical, a dissonant symphony culled from a sentient vortex. Or a Wagnerian nightmare. But it's not that extravagant.

The figure lights a candle and I am witness to the man, if it is a man, of abhorrent girth, rolls upon rolls buried beneath a stained shirt of indistinct color that stretches the limits of the buttons.

I *hear* their struggle, the button's struggle...

Khaki shorts, the button at the waist missing, the zipper lolling down, unable to secure what bulges within.

No shoes, no socks, but he strolls gingerly through the debris. Some of it moves and I realize there are rats hitching along with his every ponderous step. Rats scrambling, rats climbing his plump calves. Rats everywhere.

How could I have missed them?

The figure unfolds a metal chair and sits in it. The metal strains in protest. The rats gnaw on the chair, chipping metal with ravenous teeth. Metal clicks and sparks in response to their assault. Blinking like stars, the sparks.

The man lights another candle, lets them both drip to the floor on each side of the chair—the first candle has already coated his ham hock fist, yet there is no reaction to this—and places each in the hot, hardening wax pool.

Light is set. The stage is set. I am ready for my performance. I need the next dose of the Centipede to send me on to the next leg away from here.

Far away from here.

Yes, I have lived among those you might think of as the scum of the earth and scum in general. Life means getting dirty, dear sister. Living dirty.

Cleanliness is next to godliness, they say. The eternally washed yet unfulfilled amongst you. Godliness has nothing to do with the goals of the dark frontier traveler. Freedom does. No rules, no regulations, all destinations slaughtered at the will of living at a heightened level of awareness. Every second is a potential revelation. But this place, this person…I am repulsed beyond any previous experience of filth. Yet I must consider my quest. I must consider the final result.

I must consider the broadest meanings of the word "different" and understand that is where this being resides.

"You know why you're here, boy?" the voice says. A heavy voice, the weight of wasted time swinging from the man's jowls. A closer inspection elicits a gasp. His features are those of a rodent, a human rodent, like the rats surrounding his chair and scurrying up and down his legs, his body.

Marilyn's voice burrows into my ears and only my ears as this man does not react to it. I think of him as Ratman; that is his hidden name, a secret only I know.

"You can't let him do this to you, just like all the other times."

I have to ignore her. The razor-sharp implication of what she is hinting at draws blood from memories.

"Of course. The Centipede"

"Fuck the Centipede. That's not why you're here."

Promise turns to ice, melts.

Marilyn, groans. Lena and Jacqueline and Rita and Sean and Naomi, sweet Naomi—I see them all, phantoms in the dark cowl surrounding him. Portraits of disgust, their faces etched with the deep lines of loathing that crawls over features and cripples their beauty as they stare at me. Judging me.

Your face, too, sister. I see you, too. Are you really here? Our eyes never meet to confirm my suspicions. You are not filled with disgust like the rest. Your look is one of curious detachment, as if you don't even see me. Feigning indifference at my predicament.

"I am on my way to Burroughs, to Ride the Centipede. There can be no other reason for me being here. That must be—"

He sniggers. Large paws scratch at his crotch, fondling...

"Touchy, aren't you?" Ratman pulls his hands from his crotch, reaches out toward me as if about to grab me, though the intent is meant more as cruel teasing. I want nothing to do with touching or allowing this grotesque creature to touch me. But just as swiftly, his hands divert to his crotch again, with more enthusiasm now. "Yeah, yeah, the Centipede is your sole purpose in this world of shit and fool's gold dreams. But that's not truly why you're here. You're meant to fulfill my request. That's the real point of it all, of this leg of your trip. Nothing more." He leers at me, pulls his shirt open. Buttons pop out toward me, BBs from a gun fired by blubber.

It is worse to see him unveil himself.

Though I cannot see him, somewhere to the far left and back, behind chunks of cinder and twisted metal, I hear Freddie Mercury—*Great King Rat was a dirty old man and a dirty old man was he*—and it's as if this man, Ratman, embodies that ugly creature.

I do not want to venture a guess about what Ratman's request might be. Whatever it is there's no avoiding it. I am here to get the next rig, to move forward. I just want to get it over with. His presence sickens me.

"Your revulsion arouses me," he says, that heavy voice like molasses pooling out of an excrement crusted asshole.

He starts to tug on his khaki shorts, and then stops.

"Pull these off," he says; demands. The voice is seared with depravity.

Yes, Marlon, take this in your mouth like a good son...

I scream and the contemptible person doesn't move in the least. Not even a jiggle.

Then, he rears his head back, cawing. A choking rain of laughter chopped out of the black night above. I realize there is no roof above us, but I don't see stars. The walls end in darkness. Dizziness joins the tilt of my head.

"What is your request," I say, knowing where this is headed. Sex, after all, being a currency here, nothing more. But with this monstrous person...

Tinfoil chatters ever more insistently, pricking my thoughts, draining more memories:

You need to stop with the drugs, Marlon. You've already got enough to deal with without enhancing your already unstable mind. This can only lead to bad places.

How can freeing one's mind be a bad place, Jane? My already freed mind wants more.

This is not freedom. You're trapping yourself in a cage you'll never be able to break out of if you insist on carrying on with your experiments.

You're just afraid.

It's just pot, man, Daryl says, putting his hand on your shoulder. You jerk sharply away.

He's not just doing pot. Ask Steve here. Ask Maddie. You're all walking a tightrope bound to snap at the weight of what you're doing.

Fuck you, bitch. I don't care if you are his big sister, Marlon knows what he wants, Maddie says, making a V with her fingers and flicking her tongue down the middle.

Fuck you, you say, but Steve grabs your arm before you can follow up and says, You should leave if you don't want to indulge, as I take out more of the huge allowance Father gave me, gives us, and hand most of it to Steve and Maddie, who take it and smile as one would imagine pythons might smile, and I swear their tongues flick out, crudely slit in half, dancing...

Still, I pause. My quest in question? No, I cannot pause. The Centipede calls to me. Burroughs waits for me.

Marilyn rages, "What the fuck is wrong with you? Gonna let this scumfuck do to you as has always been done before?"

She's right, I know. But I'm right, I know.

Paradox Complete.

"Are you back yet?" Ratman says, running his fat fingers in between the rolls of his belly and scooping out something white and moldy, looking like cottage cheese gone sour. He puts the fingers to his cracked lips and slurps loudly, not wanting to miss a bit of this snack, this appetizer before the meal, the act, whatever that specific act might be, with enthusiasm. Rats clamor for their taste of the diseased treat. A few of them bore into the folds with rabid singlemindedness. Focus is needle sharp and digging deep. I must get this deed done and on my way. Soon. Sooner.

"You're no boyfriend of mine if you let him treat you like all the others have treated you," Lena Olin says, wearing her hat again, pulling it down to shield her face, her view of my surrender.

As if I have a choice.

Tears stain my cheeks, burning.

"Enough delays. It's time for you to pleasure me. Pull these off, now. Or there will be no Centipede for you.

His power over me is complete. I will do whatever he needs. I must.

That's a good boy, son...

(I imagine a claw hammer tearing his skull open and supping on his brain. I imagine a chainsaw whirring into his bloated belly, dissecting him, a *living* autopsy.)

I pull off the khaki shorts, the effort extreme as they barely fit. I struggle as I work them over his elephantine thighs, revealing hideousness beyond compare. The rolls distend over his groin. His groin, hidden beneath more of that moldy, cottage cheese substance, white and sour smelling, epitomizing rancid to a degree uncharted by anyone but me. I would attempt to hurl again, but the futility of the act would fall well short of what I would rather experience: a purging of everything within.

"Get to it, boy. Start with your pretty mouth, before I take your asshole."

The thought of even touching Ratman annihilates my senses. I totter on my knees, woozy. Usually I would shut down and do it, just do it, close down self and do what is necessary to get what I *need*. But circumstances here leave me hesitant.

He leans forward, fleshy rolls threatening to plummet over me as a cellulite waterfall, and grips the back of my head with his hand.

"No Centipede until I fill you with my white, sticky disease," he says, that cawing laugh again. Knives being sharpened for the kill.

He pulls me closer to his crotch, roughly mashing my face in the horrendous human mold, smothering me. Within the mottled texture: movement. Lots of movement. As if a penis or three or more has awakened.

That's right, my boy. Take it all in.

He turns to somebody else in the room; many somebody else's, watching, breath heavy…

Daddy loves you so much. Take it all, wait for the surprise.

Somebody laughs; somebody groans. Somebody says, I want some, in a tiny voice that speaks volumes for the rest in the room. Mumbles of approval follow. A sick ritual has commenced, private and despairing.

Movement again, and a sudden splash of urine into my face, my mouth, the bitter tang bursting through the rotted cottage cheese.

Ratman guffaws as if in on a private joke.

"Ah, had to drain the lizard so's you can get to the meat, boy. Get to the meat," he demands, the slow flowing molasses intonations pricked by needles of desire punctured by desperation. His breath is a halitosis cloud, fog caressing heat-battered landfill.

Good boy. Good boy.

And the world turns white as father ejaculates in my mouth and we are alone again, not always, but he cherishes these times most, sells me otherwise and I wonder if he did the same to you, my dear sister?

"He's fuckin' loony, but he needs to stop this," Marilyn says.

"That cage your sister talked about is looking like a stint on death row if you continue along this path—"

This leg, I say, in my head, amid the turbulent clutter. The hurricane of anguish delegating me as its personal whipping boy.

"Boy."

Boy…

"You can kill him and take the rig and be on your way. No matter he gets anything more than he's gotten. This cannot go on.

Not like before. Not like before." My voice, in my head, joined by a defiant horde of pissed off girlfriends.

I pull my head from his fist, hair tearing. I don't care. This cannot go on. This cannot be the way.

"No," I wail, as rats start to chew through the walls. The echo bounces back, from the heavens where absent gods rarely ever tend to our world, yours or mine, dear sister, anymore.

Surprised, Ratman leans back, hands sinking into layered hips, and says, "Then no Centipede for you, you belligerent fuck." His hands slide down his oily rolls, settling on the white moldy crotch, and the three, perhaps four, five penises probing underneath for attention.

"No," I say again, firm.

"The dark frontier grapevine informed me of what you did to poor Nellie, fuck her and walk away. No shame in giving her less than what she wanted to know, what it means to be human. But that's not how it's going to pan out here, *boy*."

He pushes his girth up, swings and sways as I grab one of the candles and tilt the flame to his oily flesh.

Oily.

He howls and slumps back down.

"This is not the way this is supposed to play out. I want..."

"What I want," I say. "I want what I want."

"Why you little fucking twerp. I'll show you—"

I'll show you how much I love you, son. So much. So much...

"He's crazy, but is he right?" Marilyn says, to the shadows and the fading faces of all my ex-girlfriends.

"No," I say, a voice calmer, sadder. "Don't leave me."

"Then kill this fucker like you should have done to dear old daddy."

Ratman looks at me quizzically, as if enamored by a sideshow freak.

"Yes," I say, bringing the flame toward his face, his weighty arms unable to fend me off. My limbs bend in magnificent ways to avoid him and shove the candle flame down his throat. His eyes go wide and a scream gurgles amid the fire and wax, sealing him shut. *My hand* grips fire and hot wax, relenting not the least though pain should be scalding the nerves. I hold strong and fill his mouth, no matter the protests of his teeth or the jellyroll tremble of his body.

"Kill him. Put the ratfucker down," Marilyn says, her face crystal clear, a moon lighting this dark hub. Other satellites float around her, my ex-girlfriends all gleaming in approval of the task at hand.

I hold my fist steady, my limbs articulating impossible angles or, more so, improbable, but not for me.

Ratman quivers. His eyes bulge as red veins explode in the uncut cocaine whites of his eyes, his protest spreading. He knows his death is at hand, my leering satisfaction the last thing he will ever see.

I hear the rats whine and whisper, the language familiar. Not the language of insects or lizards, but of vermin. A language new to me, no matter the nights I've slept with them whispering close to my head.

But their whispers shift, translate as English, clear and cut to the marrow.

"Where's the rig, moron? Can you find it?"

I am flushed, distraught at their delight at my miscue. I've not seen it here. I've not seen it in this scoured, shithole Hell.

I've not seen it.

The moment stretches, my sanity a rubber band about to snap.

The laughter of rats is a hideous indictment for the deed I have done.

I pound Ratman's face. I pound his jiggling mass of blubber. I know where he must have hidden it.

He must have.

Desperation, the usual motivator, impelled me to start to dig between the folds, scooping out clumps of the white mold, some darkened by age. I sling the scum to the floor and the rats gather, anxious to dine on the morbid feast. I pull and toss and more gather, chowing down on the blubber-made buffet.

I turn to them, the rats, his rats.

"Tell me where the rig is and I will give you a feast worthy of a king."

"We'll have our feast whether you tell us or not, they say, in unison."

I think quickly, my brain hot-wired for the Centipede.

"I will take him out of here if you do not tell me. The feast will be left for other scavengers, but not you."

Universal disapproval echoes from the walls.

"Tell me, or he's gone."

The murmur of a hive-mind in action. They have a response within seconds. One of the rats climbs the rolls and settles beneath the large pink areola, the thumb thick nipple.

"In here," it says, signaling me as best it can to the roll beneath the nipple. I move the rat aside, dig into the roll, the moistness sticky, and relinquish my prize. The rig.

I back away and they take this as their cue. Ratman's body is instantly covered with rats.

I keep backing away until I reach a wall. The slickness appalls me. But I have no worries now. I have my syringe. The lone candle left in the room glimmers slyly at it. I see a clear liquid, with tiny divots like lizard scales floating in it.

I ready it for injection. My impatience as well as my abhorrence with this leg of the Centipede hastens my task. I need out of here now.

I am sickened at how my nostrils have almost become immune to the unrelenting assault they have withstood. I don't want to remember this place. It is the past. The past is dead.

I stick the needle into my neck, my jugular, press the plunger, and immediately, primordial dreams fill my head. My thoughts turn atavistic, primal. My thoughts turn inward, to my self, the human, the being I am becoming, and how it relates to the first spurt of life. How I am something new and special, not trash to be coddled by perverts in your world, or even my world, but special. Special… I am the one to receive the gift of Riding the Centipede. Me. Marlon Teagarden. Not you or anybody else. I am the chosen one.

Moments before the drug sends me on my way, there is a flash of blinding light and a figure. His words crumble, before the black velvet cloak of numbness takes me into its waiting arms. This is the first time during this whole journey it's felt like this. As if perhaps I am almost there. As if perhaps I'm on the downslope and will ease into the final stage.

CHAPTER 19

CHERNOBYL

Rudolf kicked down the already damaged door. Not only were the hinges shattered, the whole door flew across the barren landscape that was the decrepit warehouse in the middle of who the fuck cares. Rudolf was unaware of anything but need, his own need, and the need to round up Marlon Teagarden once and for all.

His need filled his head; his body was electric and alive and insatiable. He had only a taste, traveling along the dark in-between, waking in the real to revelations coated in hedonistic ecstasy, the control needed for his survival—containing the energy within—obliterated by another need, this one, to have just one fix, just one more fix. So his goal here, now—soon; *sooner*—was to get Marlon Teagarden in his grip and never let go until he found out where he could get more of—

What? The drug? What if it was only a heightened sensory overload while he traveled within Marlon's head? No, the drug had to be the engineer. Just one fix. Just one more fix…

So.

He burst through the door and there he was, on his haunches next to a fat man who flailed obscenely. This abundant, amorphous blob of a creature grunted and gasped as he tried to reach for Marlon—his Marlon; *his*—Marlon cranked his head in

Rudolf's direction and saw the light of Rudolf, the piercing light. His eyes squinted, blocking out the light. Blocking out Rudolf.

"Finally," Rudolf said, hurling his voice toward Marlon, but it was too late. Two steps into the battered shell, Rudolf watched as Marlon quivered like a heat ghost, misty and swirling and—

Gone.

"No. No!"

He watched the fat man finally tumble off a chair, that sighed in relief, onto his knees, pulling something out of his mouth. Clumps of something that looked like wax, half solid and crumbling.

Rudolf was swift to approach him, hands clenched then loosened, the joints never fully relaxed, he said, "Where did he go? Do you know his next destination?"

Gagging and spitting and still reaching into his massive maw, the man, who has the fidgety, illusive countenance one would associate with a rat, said, "The fucker got away. That little fucker got away without giving me what I wanted. That little—"

"Where did he go?" Rudolf said, gripping the man's damp shirt, pulling him close to his face.

Rats shuffled through the refuse and scattered to and fro.

The man pulled on Rudolf's hands, struggling for release.

"Look, buddy. I got no beef with you. The boy stole the drug, this leg of the Centipede. He's fucking gone. Gone."

Rudolf released the man, his fists raised in the air and let out a garbled vocalization of frustration that stretched into the starless sky, mating with the wind as it howled from the ridges of the decimated roof.

The man worked hard to gain purchase and pull himself into a standing position. His breath was heavy and smelled of sizzling fat and clotted meat and stomach acid trying to break it all down.

Rudolf brought his arms down and closed his eyes. He must regain some semblance of control. What was he doing? What has Marlon Teagarden—no! What has the Centipede done to him?

Asking the bloated pig anything would get him no information, he knew this already.

The man bent over with a grunt and a fart and attempted to pull up his khaki shorts. Rudolf noticed the man's filth-encrusted genitals. Visually trespassed over the man's sagging rolls and sweaty slime, sticky and stinking. Took in the whole of this human atrocity, a man who has let himself go in magnificent ways. What a horror, a travesty of life this man represented.

Rudolf dialed down, way down. Put his hand on the man's shoulder and squeezed.

"Ouch, hey…" the man said, slumping again to the garbage-laden, concrete floor. "Give it a break, buddy." He swiped at Rudolf's hand feebly.

The warehouse was silent except for a new sound, a crackling sound, like metal being chewed that lived in Rudolf's head. He did not like it. It was a constant reminder of what he needed. It was the sound of his world being siphoned into the void of self-annihilation, which only made him squeeze the man's shoulder even harder.

The man screamed in protest. His clavicle, even beneath the layers of fat, snapped. Tears poured out of slit sockets. The man looked up at Rudolf, pleading as he struggled to disengage Rudolf's clamp-screwed-tight grip.

Rudolf let go, his breath even and his control as close to balanced as he'd felt in however long it'd been since he passed through the in-between.

He'd lost track of time.

Time did not matter anymore. What mattered was the drug. That's all that mattered.

No, control. *Control* mattered…

He steadied himself. He needed something to remind him he was the one in charge of his body. He reached deep within, to the core of who he was, of what he was, and gathered that something, ready to make a stand for himself.

He squatted down on his haunches and put his hand on the fat man's damaged shoulder.

The big man flinched, not wanting anything more to do with Rudolf Chernobyl. He scooted away from Rudolf, rats nipping at his ankles. He swiped at the rats with equal success. They clung to the flab; he swatted again.

Rudolf took it all in, called up his core being—that one truth that superseded the rest—and proceeded accordingly.

"Have you ever read a book called *1984*, written by George Orwell?" he said, eyebrow arched, hands on his thighs. Fingers flexed.

The big man leaned back and up, though still on his knees as if silently praying for Rudolf to leave him be.

"What's that got to do with anything?"

"Just answer the question…sir." Rudolf's words hissed like the birth of fire, vehemence coiled in every syllable. His eyes brightened and he immediately toned it down. From the inside.

But the man's eyes grew wide as he noticed Rudolf's eyes a wonder of strangeness he had never witnessed before.

Taking the better path, the one not marked on the map that led him to this point in his life, the big man said, "No. Never read the book. Don't much have any use for books."

Rudolf extended his arm toward the man's knee, where a rat circled as if blind, yet driven by the nauseating stench and promise of meat to feast and said, "Allow me." He snatched up the gray rat. Another rat scampered away, while two more, brave and ravenous, replaced the first in the queue of sick need.

Rudolf grabbed both in swift motion, clutching all three tightly in his large hand, their squeaking the glum chorus to events that transpire in such gloomy places.

"Too bad," he said, about the man's lack of having read the book. Knowledge might heighten what was going to happen next, but Rudolf really did not care. Care, compassion—never one of his negotiating tools. Sadism and the bliss inspired by immense cruelty, humiliation—these were the things that Rudolf was made of.

"There's a scene in which our protagonist, Winston Smith, is made to wear a cage over his head."

The big man scooted back again, his swishing motion distributing garbage and wayward rats out of his path. His forlorn expression indicated he wanted nothing to do with Rudolf's intentions, whatever they were.

"No, no." Rudolf shook a finger at him.

"Please..."

"No, you repellent excuse for a human being, who is even more repellent than most human beings who repulse me with their mere existence. At least those who waste their lives crawling through the slime as if it's a road to heaven."

"C'mon, buddy—"

"No, no. Never. We could never have been buddies. Look at you, draped in deplorable attire and having let yourself go. No, we have nothing in common," he said, though a thin sliver of their relation twitched in Rudolf's boiling brain pan, where addiction resided in the petri dish, waiting to express itself. He bared his teeth, the rabid dog, the furious orangutan.

Closing his eyes, he said, "There is a scene where our protagonist, Winston Smith, is made to wear a cage over his head. At the opposite end of the cage, there are rats. The first of two doors is raised, moving a rat closer to Mr. Smith's face."

"What the fuck does that have to do with anything here?" the big man said, but he wasn't that stupid, was he? Rudolf waved the fistful of rats in the man's face.

"I don't have a cage. I don't need a cage. I don't know where Marlon Teagarden is off to, but I will find him. I will," he said, nodding with certainty. "I know exactly where you're going, though, fat man."

"No, whatever you got in mind...no..." He raised his flabby arms, inconsequential shields to the ministrations of Rudolf's mayhem.

"Oh, yes, yes. You're going to be food for these rats," he said, as he pounced on the man, sickened by his presence, while he stuffed one, then another, then the third rat, into the man's gaping mouth, both hands pushing with all his force. "They will start from the inside."

The man's jaw opened wide and cracked loud.

Rudolf seethed as he stuffed the three rats deeper inside, grabbed another rat nibbling on the fat man's revolting loins, and stuffed it in as well.

They filled the mouth, the throat and blood from their chomping teeth coated their gray and brown bodies, the big man's lips and cheeks. As they tore through his toad-like throat, the big man's eyes rolled back in his head.

Easy prey.

Rudolf dropped the still jerking man to the floor. A flash flood of claws and hairy bodies and rodent glee covered the man, sliding into the folds, slurping and gnawing and tearing and eating him alive. Alive, but not for long.

Rudolf stood tall, pleased with his presentation, his exhibition. Another standout piece of art created by his hands. But that wasn't why he was here. He wiped his brow on the sleeve of his shirt. What he needed was the drug, the Centipede. He needed to find Marlon Teagarden before he slipped through his fingers forever.

Rudolf centered himself. There would be nothing to latch on to. Marlon was in that place in between. He could not go there unless he was already homing in. Which meant he would have to wait until Marlon's signal surfaced again, like a buoy bobbing up to say, hello, here I am.

He reared back and wailed into that ebony wasteland above and stomped out of this piecemeal shithole with more determination than ever before.

CHAPTER 20

BLAKE

"My name is Terrance Blake." He removed his black hat. "I am a private investigator." Blake found himself flexing his fingers along the rim. His jawbone slid sideways with the clunky insistence of tectonic plates shifting and settling. When it clicked into place, the sound was akin to the hammer being set on a pistol.

"Do I know you, Terrance Blake?"

As before, the voice seemed to take the odd conglomeration of sounds floating through the empty space and spin, fold, and manipulate them into a semblance of speech.

"No, sir. I've just a few questions and can be on my way."

"Questions?" A sound as if Solon was moving about in the darkness. There was a sense of space being rearranged.

Blake realized his toes were also joining in the anatomical discomfort, scrunching and stretching and scrunching again.

"Have I done something worthy of questions?" The sound that followed tickled deep in Blake's belly. He thought it laughter, as if Solon was laughing at him, but the tickle passed the point of delight and dived head first into pinpricking torture.

"No. Not exactly, sir."

"Call me Master, Terrance Blake." The tickling again, branching out to his thighs. Burning.

"Excuse me."

"Am I not clear, Terrance Blake? Call me Master. All my acolytes as well as lesser beings address me in this manner."

He was mad, this much was certain. Blake exhaled slow and long, attempting to set free the weird sensations he felt within his system, to no avail.

"Blake. Call me Blake. Just Blake...Master."

"So, what shall Master and Blake discuss?" The tones were surrounded by discordant clatter, not big sounds, but small ones, circling as vultures around Solon's vocalization.

Comrades to the lone vulture Blake had seen outside, for sure.

"Sir—"

"Master." A buzzing joined the clatter, the busy ambience, and stretched out after Solon's words died. Bees. Perhaps wasps. Blake glanced around the sweltering confines, noting insects and lizards and more of those that defied description, but no bees or wasps—or related, unknown flying insects—anywhere. He contemplated leaving, just leaving, but there was no reward in cowardice. He had only one option.

"Master."

A sigh of satisfaction emitted from the dark room, the bristling void. The buzzing had eclipsed all other sounds at this point, besides their voices and Blake's noticeably audible breathing.

"I've a question about the green limousine."

A murmur Blake could only think of as an extension of curiosity like the twitch of invisible antenna. Antenna branching out from within the consciousness of Solon.

"A fan? You are a fan, Blake?" Solon's voice clapped hard in speaking Blake's name. Blake thought the sound similar to a singular applause in recognition of his stalwart determination to even have found the recluse.

"No, sir."

A grumble from the void, more movement. Space expanding, as the wings of a large bird.

"Master. It's just the only thing I have to go on in a case I'm working on."

"How do you mean?

"I saw a green limousine in San Francisco as I was searching for a runaway, the focus of my case."

The void dilated. Blake sensed this and had to rub his eyes, an excuse to shut them, block out the impossible shifting of geometry. The buzzing rattled around in his head. He shook it, as if it was real and this action would set it free, as if something would fly out of his ears and leave him be. Perhaps winged monkeys...

"You saw a green limousine. Rare as they may be, I'm sure there are many green limousines, Blake. Why do you think this has anything to do with me?"

"The person, the runaway, I suspect..." What did he suspect, really? The evidence was flimsy at best. Still... "I suspect the person I am searching for had entered the green limousine and—"

An immense crash and earthshaking rumble blotted all conversation and thought out for the extent of the fit. An abhorrent stench seeped out of the darkness. Blake thought, if rage had a smell, this would be it. It clogged all pores. It singed nostril hairs. It burned the back of his throat, curling up into his brain. It was acidic as much as odorous. The buzzing amplified as if it was embroidered into the house, the wood, the foundation; the air and sunlight beyond the front door; the heat. All of the reality out here, as inconceivable as that might be.

The first "word" was indecipherable, yet furiously vehement. The second word was "Burroughs."

With all he knew about this case, and the literary connections, he knew the Burroughs noted here had to be William S.

Burroughs. Dead for almost twenty years now, but a center of fury for Solon.

"William S. Burroughs?"

"Of course, William S. Burroughs," Solon said, followed by more of the vocalizations that had nothing to do with human language.

"What's he got to do with the green limousine?"

"Nothing. And everything, the conniving thief."

"What do you mean?"

"He stole that from me. The green limousine was my invention, and he's degraded it with his manipulative sense of ego. He knew it would rub me frantic, but he does not care."

Blake covered his face, the smells making him woozy.

"Decided to utilize it as a doorway for his ever dreamed of yet never successfully attained promise to the traveler of the dark frontier bequeathed with the gift of Riding the Centipede."

Madness reigned, but Blake knew he had to push on, now that the green limousine had triggered something of possible substance amid the locomotive impetus of this ride on the crazy train.

"What are you talking about? What is Riding the Centipede?"

Deep inhalations within the void pulled on Blake's cheeks, his ears; made the door frame fluctuate, as well as all of the empty frames on the wall. Blake thought he could perceive a shape beyond the dark doorway, yet what he perceived was not human.

"Don't look too hard, Blake." His name again, a whip snapping against an already welt-riddled back.

"Answer my question." He spat without tact.

This seemed to amuse Solon as the ambience within the room piped down. Even the buzzing, though now Blake noticed a lone bee exit the void; and another, plump as a plum.

Calmer: "Answer my question, Master." Blake felt himself bend without breaking, but it was getting close.

Now that Blake was reconciled to subservient status, the pleasure in Solon's quirky vocalization was evident as he relayed the information.

"Riding the Centipede is Burroughs' gift to the dark frontier traveler in search of the so-called ultimate experience. The ultimate experience being drug related, of course. Each leg of the journey to Burroughs, another drug is ingested, preparing the traveler for this ultimate experience. Experience leaves scars. On the flesh or deeper."

A curious aside, then back to the mainline.

"What the traveler does not know is there's been none who have made it to Burroughs so far. It is rumor. Perhaps a lie played out for his amusement, testing the mettle of the chosen one's. I only know there's a sense of validity to it because that bastard used the green limousine as a snide comment on my writing."

Blake swore the empty picture frames swelled slightly, as if breathing.

"A mocking smack to the truth of what I know. About him, myself, this world; all worlds, interconnected. All of it. He degraded my creation by demoting it to simply being a doorway in his little game."

This made zero sense to Blake, yet he listened on.

"He's always thought his work superior to mine. Even if he stole from it for elements found in much of his work. The use of the language of insects in the unabridged version of *Naked Lunch* being his most blatant—"

Solon screamed, or at least let loose with a sound related to a scream. It was a tone that scissored through the air, slicing into Blake's mind, body, the house itself. Insects froze and tumbled from walls; lizards hung on a few seconds longer before joining them. Blake buckled to his knees.

"—his most obvious example. Yet, he never had the heart to release that version on the world you live in, only down here. Where it sits amid the midlist titles and well below my masterpieces. You see"—pausing again, a sense of bringing composure to the shadows, as if one was brushing lint off a suit, plucking the finer pieces—"Burroughs is a man who dreamed of being an insect, but did not understand the true sacrifice inherent for success: letting go of one's humanity. Completely. A harder task than mine."

"Which would be…?"

"I am an insect who dreamed of being a man, if only to coordinate the uprising of insects to our rightful place in the world. It was easy; humans are easy to assimilate. But it was not worth the effort, as humans do not have the capacity to understand the magnitude of my stories, to embrace the essence of their inherent insect logic. We need the gates of distant, primal cognizance to swing open, in order to take command. At this time, human knowledge is not the equal to the task. So we wait. I wait."

Dear God. Blake had never heard such madness. Perhaps that's why Solon lived in isolation, probably writing more of his unsuccessful tales, jealous of a dead man, angry at the world.

"You don't believe me, either, do you?"

Blake did not answer. Instead, he had one more question and then to leave, to drive with haste away from this sanity-blasted wasteland.

"Why did I see the green limousine? What do I have to do with this…Master?"

Blake could swear the darkness bulged out from the door frame.

"You are a part of Burroughs' frivolity."

"What is that supposed to mean, his frivolity?"

"Oh, it's all quite comical if you ask me. You're chasing an idiot chasing a rumor chasing its tail." The tickling rippled through Blake's whole body. Back to standing, he almost buckled again, but held on.

"Give me something real. You created it. You must know its use."

"Of course I know its use. Burroughs, that shit, just subverted it for his own means. Meaning…"

The tickling stopped, though no words followed. Sweat beaded and raced down Blake's forehead.

A few insects and lizards, perhaps those relieved of their incapacitation, started up the walls again.

Blake noticed many of the frames had burst, the splintered remains still attached to the walls. When did that happen?

Back to the here and now, but not for long. He needed the too hot sun and miles and miles of asphalt behind him, with his foot jammed on the pedal, pressing down with all his might.

"Meaning?"

"Well, why don't you ask Burroughs what it all means?"

"He's dead. He's been dead for years. What the hell kind of madness is…any of this?"

Turning to walk away, frustrated and angry for listening to any of this madman's verbal shenanigans. Beat down, he'd had enough.

"He's only dead in your world, Blake. He's only dead *in your world*."

More of the fat bees, which did not exactly look like bees — everything about this ragged outpost of land seemed wrong, alien; different — clamored for light, eager to drink it in. Growing fatter with the slaking.

Worse yet, the darkness shifted, stirring his cranial cauldron with the bleakest imaginings. Blake flinched, froze, and flinched again, taking in the movement that coiled into his very being.

The darkness separated, as the Red Sea had for Moses. But this was not Moses. This was Solon, about to step out of the concentrated abyss and into Blake's world.

CHAPTER 21

TEAGARDEN

Thin metallic laughter filters into my head.

I rub my ears with arachnid fingers. I jerk my hands from my ears, take in the slow twitching fingers crawling through the air. Spider legs massaging the ether, spinning invisible webs.

Are you there, dear sister?

The difference is palpable.

Ch-ch-ch-ch-changes...

My vision blossoms into sight, a different sight, yet how, I am not sure. You know how sometimes you know something is not the same, but figuring it out is impossible? Like when a person puts on contacts and their eye color is different, yet it is such an unexpected thing it's hard to put a finger on what is different. It's like that. Though in the difference, I do notice motes of dust drifting in the darkness. Something I would rarely notice before, without a ray of light, a beaming bulb. Odd, but not unwelcome.

That's when I notice it's not motes of dust. It's some kind of flying insects, as they swarm as starlings and disappear into the distance. The dark distance. The dark. Why do I think distance? Just dark. They disappear into the dark.

But there is a distance as a light bobs from within it. A train at the end of a tunnel? More like a wick lit at the end of a stick of dynamite.

I am so morose. Morbid.

Are you morbid?

The metallic scritch-scritch continues. A conference of sinister, sentient shards of shaved metal. Or insects. It reminds me of what I have heard of the language of insects. Sort of.

The light approaches, a torch. A figure in a robe, hood pulled up over his, her…or its head.

"Well, well. You're the first ever to make it this far." The voice is akin to boiling water bubbling over the edge of a pot. Recollection sets it within the realm of the language of lizards; perhaps.

I squint and yet, with the torch held to its left, the figure's face is nothing but eternal night. Something shimmers in the torchlight there: stars, constellations, messages…

The illumination from the wavering flame flickers off the walls, the shadows alive, or perhaps the light between the cracks is alive. Brick into stone. Color indistinguishable. Brick and stone and strange creatures rushing about. I flinch as something brushes by my hand. I let out a tiny yelp of surprise.

"Stand up, let's get you on your way." Bubbling, seething. The seething accentuates the lizard-like quality, almost a hiss.

I'm only too happy to be off the hard, cold floor. The place feels like a prison cell. Isolation. A mausoleum.

I emit a skittish sound, laughter in a way; serious changes, more evident. But when I speak, it is my regular voice that cuts through the rising rumble of scritch-scritch-scritching. At least in my ears, my head.

"The Centipede."

"Yes, yes. You are the first to make it this far. But there's much more to your journey. This leg."

As the words take shape, I sense this language is not a common mode of communication for this figure, or perhaps it is antsy to get on as well. I am reminded of Daryl. There's something of urgency in its unseen stride. It seems to hover, the robe draping over whatever legs it may possess, human or covered in scales reptilian, or many other possibilities.

His face is a wasteland, damned to eternal vagaries… though I expect here, wherever here is, it does not matter. I am only too glad he turns away as we start on our trek.

I am bristling with eagerness, though. Cannot help myself. Especially if I am the first to make it this far. Get me to the end, man! I start to ask the only pertinent question circumstances allows, when something flutters in my vision, distracting me.

It is a huge fly wearing a mask, an almost human face. I am reminded of the fly with a human face caught in the web at the end of the original version of the movie, *The Fly*. I wonder if I am caught in a web. (*Help me.*) Its wings are pale and decorated with letters which are impossible to read while it's in flight. I think this and it stops, glides, and I read: *A fly when it exists, has as much being as a God.* My internal files pull up Soren Kierkegaard as the originator of this line…or was it Brundlefly, Jeff Goldblum from David Cronenberg's reimagining of *The Fly*. Seems a succinct assumption under my present condition, the metamorphosis I am locked into.

Gregor Samsa would be proud. Kafka as well. Though in taking a quick glance at myself, I am me. Human. Paltry. Inconsequential.

Pity.

The mask evaporates, yet through the fly's mouth aperture it says, in a voice rippling as a river of gravel, combining English with the language of insects, "Imagination is the voice of daring. If there is anything Godlike about God it is that. He dared to imagine everything. Of course, that might also depend on whose imagination one bows to. Who is your God, Marlon?"

The first part is familiar, Henry Miller, though the fly has taken liberties to add its two cents or nonsensical aside, tilting the notion into the realm of the curious.

I am about to respond when the hooded figure turns to me, that face, bleak and hollow, and says, "Don't listen to it. To them," signaling to the abundant insects and lizards and compelling abstractions of both skittering on the walls. All eyes on me. Dozens and dozens of eyes on me."

"They are minor players in your quest for the Centipede. Don't allow them purchase in your mind, now that it's being shaped to accept everything you are to experience."

The sounds in my ears, in my head, escalate. As if all of these creatures have slithered into my ears and have decided to feast on my brain, my thoughts. I open my mouth wide, trying to force a yawn, something—an escape route?

"Don't tempt them, fool. They would be more than happy to fill you, take you from within. End your quest at the door of completion."

Which makes me think of the obvious question events had distracted me from asking.

"What do you want? Need? In exchange, y'know?"

The bubbling pours out of him. There is no indication of this in that void of a face, though astonishingly, a three-headed lizard weaves a herky-jerky trail across the dark façade, raising not the ire or inclination of the figure to stop with the abrasive bubbling: laughter.

"It's not what I want. It's not my place. It's her place. She's never expected anyone to make it this far. She's...preparing herself."

There's an ominous quality to this phrase. I sense it in my bones, my gut.

"Preparing herself?" I ask, following up with the more pertinent question, "Who is she?"

The figure ignores me and mumbles, "Pretty herself up for you, in a way."

In a way, he says. This figure dressed in shadows and secrets.

"When?"

"When what?"

"When do I meet her, this mysterious she?"

"Don't be so anxious," he says. Another lizard-like creature — the legs are like...the motivation is like a tank, the rolling of wheels in a rigid track — caresses the void within the hood, before sinking into it without a struggle.

"You'll get to her soon enough. She's the last leg before you meet up with Burroughs."

This news fills me with elation. Finally, almost there. No matter what she wants, I will fulfill it and be with Burroughs sooner than later. Soon, soon...

"Why are you smiling?" the figure asks, before turning to face the darkness ahead and continuing on our way.

"The ultimate experience is soon mine. That's why I am here. That's the whole purpose of what I have gone through just to get here. Wouldn't you be happy?"

"Happiness is a conscious choice, not a goal one can set and achieve through some rigorous task. And getting here does not mean there's a there from here."

The bubbling simmers, oily. Spattering.

Not a there from here? Why would I be here if there wasn't?

I step on something that steps back, a foot on the ground, but no, a large toad with the imprint of my worn Converse sneakers on its back.

It croaks and within the throaty timbre of the croak, emits a sound that resembles the word *asshole*.

Sidestepping, I continue with my conversation with the one I think of as my guide, leading me to a promised land like no other.

"Just get me there and let me deal with it." Obstinate, a bit harsh, but I don't care. I sense how close I am. My veins sing a chattering chorus. Of course!

The bubbling which had turned oily and spattered sporadically gains strength, spitting vitriol as my guide speaks. "Don't think it's going to be anything you want to do." The cowl shakes side to side, but the messenger does not turn to face me. "Don't think you have a clue what's coming up."

"It doesn't matter what you..." But the words stall, hesitate, not in the actual speaking, but in hitting the air, my eardrums, perhaps the messenger's eardrums, means of hearing—whatever the fuck ever. Then the words rush past me, bunched together.

"What the...?"

Again, delayed, then slingshotting ahead. My tread slows, and I notice even that seems out of sync: the echo of footsteps hits me before my foot stamps the ground, though that might simply be the audio reflection of the previous step. It disorients. I do not like it at all. My stomach lurches.

"We're almost there," my guide says, not turning to tell me this. Its voice sneaks up from behind. I don't turn to check if another has hitched along with us. I know it is the figure in front of me.

The brick and stone walls are negligible as we approach a door, buried beneath a wallpaper of kinetic wonder as creatures of all manner roil in orgiastic glee all over them. It is magnificent and it is shocking. More surprising is the door glittering in prismatic radiance, as if carved from crystals, though I cannot see through it in any way. The slanted slash and angles of the appearance is wholly impenetrable. The torch inspires variations on colors within the flame to sashay along the cubist abstraction that is the door.

No insects, lizards, or indescribable things trespass upon this magnificent door.

I am in awe, mouth slack and something climbs in and I try to spit, to close my mouth afterwards, but neither action is met with success.

My guide turns to me, perhaps hearing my struggle, and reaches out with a black-gloved hand—or possibly a hand as velvety rich and dark as its face—and plucks the offending thing from between my lips. The thing dangles from the dark fingers before my guide flings it to the wall. It is immediately immersed in the thriving tide.

"I told you to keep your mouth shut unless you want to be fodder for us."

Us? So he is one of these creatures? Just because he wears a robe does not mean it has any allegiance to humanity.

I spit out of habit, clearing my tongue of the creature and this other creature as my guide says, "You will do exactly as she requests. Understood?"

"Of course. I need this, to get to the Centipede."

"Of course, you say. Without knowing what she wants."

"It does not matter. I will fulfill it without delay."

The bubbling ceases. The water within his throat frozen. The words come out crisp and clear.

"Of course you will." A mocking retort. "All you need to know is that if you do not fully give of yourself to her request, well—"

"Haven't you been listening? My quest is at hand. She is the final stop, the final leg, before Burroughs. There's no turning back now. I am firm with my statement. There is no doubt in my cold heart."

"Listen up, confidence boy. Once I ring her up and this door is opened, you're hers. Completely. We out here do not want you to fail, you know? You better be everything she wants and more. Because you don't want to piss off the Reptile Queen. We don't want you to piss her off. Especially when she's hungry…"

With this, my heart sinks. My heart drowns. Perhaps I saw this coming, my instinct felt this coming. The Reptile Queen.

I have heard about the Reptile Queen and her ways. But meeting her is something I never expected. She doesn't take guests. She takes. On what level, has never been explained to me. Rumors left to rumors design and the imagination of the receptor.

"What are you trembling for?" my guide says. "Shall I refrain from pressing the doorbell and alerting her to your presence?"

"Go…go ahead."

My guide hesitates.

I nod, thinking, what the hell is *Especially when she's hungry* supposed to mean?

Hungry for what?

Hungry?

Shit.

But I must. Nothing can get in my way of obtaining the Centipede. Nothing. Not even the Reptile Queen.

My guide presses a finger—gloved or not, it does not matter—to a round white space, a button. I hear a polite ding-dong, almost comical.

The door opens. The lights and colors simmer to pale.

My guide backs away, bumps into me. I feel his sponginess. The creatures upon the walls thrust backwards, growing thick where bodies trample bodies for escape.

The scritch-scritch sounds eating all thoughts are eclipsed by the swell of dread. Silence, deep and inconsolable. The moment the nightmare becomes real.

My guide nudges me forward.

"You don't want to piss her off. Go. Go now."

I enter…

CHAPTER 22

CHERNOBYL

The room was humid, the heat blooming inside him, an organic generator he needed to switch off.

He closed his eyes, concentration aligned for the first of two tasks on his agenda, having noticed a light sheen on the painted skin of a Caravaggio. The paint was coming alive, something he could not allow to happen.

So his breath slowed down, life internalized to sharpen his control, and he remembered what it meant to be human, simply human. A paradox of ideals as it's the part of him he feels most in conflict with. Nonetheless, he sensed it was the only way to stop what fumed inside him.

Cooling. Cooling…

Sitting on the floor, the ashen reminder of the chair and his clothing swept to the baseboards, but not away. He needed the constant reminder here, where he found salvation, away from the turbulence of duties and the people who inspired him to carry on with said duties, to better acquaint himself with the depth of the power the drug—the Centipede—wielded. He needed to know there was something more potent in the world than Rudolf Chernobyl.

Need like this was a new religion, one he could put his hands together and pray to—hallelujah!—or put his hands around a throat in order to get to know his new god better.

Legs crossed, he was locked into the lotus position. Naked. No wasting clothes this time.

The buoy had bobbed up after hours of waiting patiently to reconnect with Marlon. Rudolf was hooked into Marlon Teagarden, taking in the imagery, though this time, darkness, roiling and magnificent, was the most prominent detail he obtained. A darkness that seemed alive.

At first he was angry. Usually, the images were lucid. Well-lighted or, at least, lighted in some way. He realized as his anger simmered, the only light in this imagery sputtered inconsistently, undecided as to whether it wanted to participate or not. With this thought, he realized it was true light, true to where Marlon Teagarden was. Anger was the wrong response. Just pay attention and trust his eyes, his gifts.

Where was Marlon?

In this stage, before he injected the drug and abruptly cut off the internal homing device, it was easy to decipher his location. The map brought up by his internal radar indicated Marlon Teagarden was in Louisiana, somewhere around Lafayette. On the outskirts, not quite digging in.

This did not matter—

—*curled into the fetal position, a reminder of beginnings, his feeble mother, his true father, but fading as a humming, singing tone framed in harsher sounds—as if fingernails were scratching at his pleasure centers, the endorphins anxious and spreading wide to take the assaults, wanting more*—

—as he was not going to make the mistake of losing track this time, running to a destination found, yet lost upon attainment. Not after the last time.

Sitting again, focused. Determined. Hungry...

He watched more, the images like cracked glass, chiaroscuro impressions pulsing on the periphery, yet all he could do was watch. Watch and wait. At some point, Marlon Teagarden would take the drug again, the Centipede—

—moaning, sweating; screaming rode the moans to a pitch that threatened to shatter focus, sheared off anything but intent, need. Need. So hungry, his veins. His mind. His body. Him—

—Leaning forward, a puddle of drool on the floor.

Upright again, eyes sealed shut, internally watching.

Patience was a bitch in heat without a cock to fulfill the need. The need.

He had a moment within his own thoughts, mesmerized by the cracked glass imagery and a sense of ponderous dread that wrapped around him as an army of octopus tentacles would, dragging him down to its murky depths. A neon declaration of a moment, bright as the addiction to which he had succumbed. Not even knowing what it was, only the how, and this path. The moment itself was unclear, yet the stained quality was what muddied his being in a way he could not comprehend, yet he needed some *thing*, this drug, as he'd never needed anything before.

The singing in his head was not voices, but vibrations. Tones tinted black and made to suffer if not for the promise whittled within the process. It remained constant, unwavering as he followed Marlon Teagarden as the journey continued, past the cracked glass and into something that made even Rudolf blanch.

Holding on. Holding on. Because he had to. Because he must.

—sprawled on the floor, contorted, distorted, all willpower aborted for the new god, the only one that mattered. The Centipede...

But first, this—

CHAPTER 23

BLAKE

Blake had no patience for any more of this, no gumption, no courage. He rushed for the door, slamming through the fragile exit. Wood disintegrated as his body crashed through. His foot sank into the aged, termite-riddled wood of the porch; termite-riddled, or some kind of freak insect he could not comprehend. They flourished here, quite obviously. He yelped in agony, a shocking sound coming from a man of his stature, yet circumstances demanded a yelp, so a yelp was to be had. Nonetheless, it did not stop his forward momentum as he lifted himself from the deluge, swiping an array of strange creatures from his pant leg.

Glancing back, the buzzing amplified, his eardrums quaking at the intrusion, the outlandish aural assault. Dozens of fat bees passed through the doorway, a mish-mash of bumper car colliding bodies swarming toward him.

"Wouldn't you like to stay for tea, Blake?" His name: the clap of gunshot in a distant field; again. "Wouldn't you like to stay for tea and destiny?" Solon said, the vocalization more akin to white water rapids than anything remotely human.

Blake was up and running, listening to the din behind him, but not turning to look for fear of seeing his pursuers...or Solon. At his car, he fumbled for the keys, suddenly realizing his right hand was throbbing with pain, something the tumble outside the front door had magnified from the usual dull reminder that lived in the crooked fingers, the knobby, nuts-and-bolts knuckles.

To open the door, he switched the keys to his left hand, rendering the act slightly off, unnatural, not by rote but by jittery function. Concentration was necessary, willing the fingers to just slide the damn key into the hole and turn.

Time held its breath. The buzzing intensified. Solon's laughter had nothing to do with laughter; it was a malicious thing. It was taking roost in the flayed carcass of Blake's withered sanity.

Blake stumbled into the driver's seat, cranking the ignition, again with the clumsy left hand, reaching around the steering wheel just to get the key inserted. It started up immediately. His foot slammed the pedal to the floor and the rental exploded into motion, kicking up clouds of dirt, gravel.

The bees thumped at the roof, the windows to the right side of the car. The windows cracked at such blunt insistence, but the bees did not splat to death as might be expected. They bounced off like rubber balls.

The dirt road ended and he yanked the car onto asphalt. The rubber gripped hard and fast and Blake punched a hundred before his breath caught up with him. The rearview told no lies. The fat bees and Solon were somewhere beyond view, perhaps in a realm where nightmares held the reins, but not here, not with him as he sped back to Jane, to relay this mad news, yet not to deny it.

Solon implied Burroughs was still alive. Blake knew Burroughs was dead. Yet, with what he'd just experienced, he was more inclined to believe the former.

He prayed to a God he barely acknowledged, said out loud, "Dear God," but the prayer turned to mist as they always did, nothing more than a moment of weakness inspired by Solon.

Within less than a half hour, the airport cut across the horizon, a control tower dead center, a small plane landing to the right, a larger one lifting into the deep blue. The Hilton and a lobby and a bar, sweet Jesus, a bar...

"What did you find out, Blake?" Anxious to know now, not five minutes from now, but this moment. Jane's impatience sharpened the fresh lines across her forehead.

Blake finally felt he could breathe again, so he held up his hand and wandered into the bar.

"Tell me something."

He ordered whiskey, straight up, no frills. The burn as he swallowed it was as close to heaven one gets on this earth, he thought, tapping the counter, refilling, and slugging it down without delay.

Jane sat next to him, her eyes pensive.

Blake saw this and ordered two more shots.

She said, "No."

"You're going to need this."

She took his word and they both tilted their heads back, taking it all in, burning as one, and the world seemed to simmer to bearable.

"Did you..." Jane stopped.

Blake's actions answered her question. Get to the point.

"What did Solon have to say?"

There was no dancing around the lunacy of the tale. Get to the point, indeed.

"Solon said, more or less, but more, much more, William S. Burroughs is alive and to ask him what it's all about." Blake smiled. It was a chipped mask.

"Burroughs...what? He's been dead for almost twenty years. He's dead—"

"Well, my inclination is to believe the hard evidence, yes. But after going to that house, with all its rare accoutrements and squirming inhabitants, I'm banking Burroughs is still in the game. How, why and where, well, these questions are outside of my scope of knowledge. Outside of my former understanding of the world I live in."

"But he's dead," Jane said, her voice trailing off: shadows leading the day into darkness.

This day was winding down. They had no game plan.

The silence was external. Inside his befuddled mind, the machinations of thought ground gears into dust, and logic into folly.

"Burroughs died in Kansas City," Jane said, the look in her eyes searching, pulling up information through the clutter.

"Your point?"

"If he's still alive..."

"Was he buried there?" Blake rearranged himself to face her, swiveling on the barstool.

Jane closed her eyes, movement underneath the lids. "No. St. Louis." Still digging, the spade of thought sinking deeper. "Bellefontaine Cemetery. St. Louis, Missouri."

Blake chewed on the information, not liking the taste, though he did not feel strongly about it, he said, "I guess we're off to St. Louis, then." Conviction lacking, yet what other options did they have?

"Wait!" Sitting taller, she scooted the barstool closer to him and started to laugh, a delirious undercurrent to whatever was next.

"Wait what? Tell me."

"A green limousine. A blue ranch house." She started to slap the palm of her hand to the counter.

"Another?" the barkeeper said, toweling a tall, thin beer stein dry. Jane shook her head, no, no.

Blake leaned into her, questioning: "What's going on?"

Her eyes were lit with a lunatic sparkle.

"A green limousine. A blue ranch house. Do you know what Burroughs' home was in Lawrence, Kansas?"

Blake awaited the revelation, eager but silent.

"A red cottage. A red cottage!" She leaned back, her left foot seeking the floor. Ready to run.

Their eyes met and the mutual laughter of the borderline insane erupted between them. The bartender, short black hair combed into a gel stiffening helmet, gave them a wary look.

"Barkeep," Blake said, exaggerated gesticulations adorning his words. "One more for each of us." Looking at Jane, knowing all common sense had left the building with Elvis, and perhaps with a devious locksmith intent on keeping common sense out forever, and said, softer, "One for the road."

With glasses filled, they clinked them together, an unspoken toast to a path most daft, shook their heads, and welcomed the burn one more time.

The end was nigh. The end of this journey. With the evidence at hand, perhaps it was the end to reality as they knew it. So be it, thought Blake, never one to coddle this reality with much enthusiasm anyway, no matter what waited for them at a red cottage in Lawrence, Kansas.

CHAPTER 24

TEAGARDEN

The door shut behind me without my assistance. A soft snick and silence. The shimmering crystalline skin fades to shadow here. The walls of the chamber are chiseled much like the door. Though the geometry is all edges, there's roundness to the color, if that makes sense. Ebony dominates, yet there's lights flowing within the walls. A swimming luminescence that reminds me of video clips I had watched of creatures found at the deepest depths of the ocean. I take it in, fascinated by the architecture, yet the circumstances stain the fascination with a layer of fear I've never experienced in this life.

This is the realm of the Reptile Queen. If the rumors are true—and we know about rumors, don't we, dear sister?—her intentions, her passions, her existence, is not one my presence wants to discourage.

Give her what she wants and move on. Give her what she wants without hesitation and move on.

But we know how humans are in situations steeped in dread, don't we?

I remind myself of the Centipede, and why I am here.

I bear down, take in the area, the chthonic wonder…and, at the far end of the cavern, I see her in all her monstrous splendor.

My gorge rises, not as a reaction to her grotesque magnificence, more so because the fear is solid now, a weight floating within me. It binds my feet. My steps are clumsy, hesitant, as I told myself not to be. My thoughts whir as an unhinged saw blade, dulled teeth unable to bite through the terror stifling my blood flow, my purpose. Frozen, I feel as if I am in an iceberg. I'm trapped, yet my slow progress melts the iceberg, leaving a puddle of water and perhaps urine, my solid dread made liquid.

She sits, squirming, constantly moving. Ripples dance across her body, at least as far as I can see. Clarity confuses the issue as I approach her. Kinetic is the word: her body is kinetic as the walls outside of her domain. Alive. Everywhere. Scales reflect the lights that abound in the chamber walls. Flat, shaped as arrows, rippling as she breathes.

But what part of her breathes?

There is a head adorned with a crown of snakes to rival Medusa's heinous headdress. One large eye with two pupils, rubies red as blood, yet rimmed in emerald shadows. In seeing this, there's almost a faux 3D effect, the orbs pulsing outwards, toward me. I do not see a nose or ears, but, of course, being related to reptiles—though something more, quite obviously something more—these might be buried amid the nest of agitated snakes coiled around her head. Snakes, awakened by my presence, snap at me, tongues split, tongues pierced—so odd, this addition—and fangs, two or three layers, the mouths long and lean, dripping venom. It sizzles on her scaly flesh, yet does not seem to annoy her.

The mouth, though... *her* mouth. Her mouth splits wide as the head is tall, including the pompadour of snakes. No lips, but a smooth, leathery, cauterization-of-the-wound look to the smile. And she is smiling, leering. Her mouth, curled at the edges, her glee is obvious. No fangs, just a row of jagged teeth, like crags across a mountaintop. Uneven. Prominent. Vicious. What will she want in order to get me what I need?

What I need.

What I *demand*.

But there's more to her that meets the eye, and blinds it with such perversion. Her limbs, many of them, with pincer-like appearance and spikes at the tips, are sealed with an armor of scales. Her breasts, many of them as well, with... uncertain nipples, large areola with thick protuberances jutting from them, have a sense of fluidity that lends them a quality of malleability.

She seems a shape-shifter, waiting to shift. I've only two shape-shifters in my travels. Her inconsistent, fluid qualities reminds me of them.

Finally, at the center of her, a large vagina trimmed in teeth like a shark's. Drooling in anticipation. The lips of her crimson labia pucker and blow me kisses. They join the mouth on her head in leering, her undefined desires worn on her sleeve... if she had one.

Below the vagina dentata, the dark nub of her anus, equally as preposterous—yet wondrous as well; different, remember...different—the spoke-like creases puckering as the lips would, no teeth here, but a tongue of shit protrudes, slick and shiny. An oily tongue from within the vagina snaps out and wraps around it, this soul kiss of the blackest designs one to mesmerize as these tongues battle to no end, yet beads of moisture rise along the genital tapestry.

I turn away, and her voice invades my head.

"Too much for your puny human mind to comprehend, aren't I?" The words are clear, the voice almost beautiful, feathery, ethereal. The contrast is staggering.

I can show no weakness.

"I've been a traveler of the dark frontier for years. My mind has acclimated to the eccentricities of this world, and welcomes them."

"A traveler of the dark frontier?" she says, her voice soothing as butterfly kisses. "A bridge, only. You've no idea what you've got yourself into."

The large mouth curls upward in amusement, with knowledge I've yet to attain. The snakes haloing her head laugh, their "voices" as hers, almost soothing. I feel light-headed, adrift in the ether, the wispy tones affecting me somehow, some way…

I shake my head from the distraction, the mind in flux.

"I know what I've gotten myself into. I want to Ride the Centipede. There is no other goal—"

"Of course. The Centipede. Such a meager aspiration, but you humans and your puny minds cannot envision more than that, without sinking into madness. Unless you're already there, eh, Marlon?"

"How can a desire to partake in the ultimate experience be construed as being mad?" I say, defiant in my quest.

"It's all semantics, I guess," she says, the body in motion, adopting an eel-like shrug. Almost human in a way, yet so alien amid her incongruent anatomical construction. "No need for me to question the inadequate designs of humans. I like William." She nods, as do the snakes, all in appreciation of Burroughs. "I do this for him as much as for myself. He tells amusing stories and I like to hear them. But they are human stories. That is my interest. Sociological, I suppose." She laughs, the feathery tones joining as one, a wing, sweeping away my contentions, yet I do not care. I am close to my goal. No time to linger here longer than necessary.

"What do you want from me, to get me through the final leg of my journey, to Burroughs and the Centipede?

"So eager, Marlon. I don't think you've got what it takes to go all the way, though you are the first to make it this far. I never contemplated one making it to me. And what I want.

"No games. No more delays. I need—"

"What I need," she says, completing my sentence but the statement is one for both of us.

She squirms on her throne, something manufactured from indecipherable bones clumped together into the chair-like shape, decorated with a lattice of interconnected exoskeletons, polished black and brown, gunmetal gray and never-seen summer sky blue. She lifts her massive body from the cramped confines. I lean back as she stretches, twelve, fourteen feet tall. Her snaky heads reach for the ceiling, flicking tongues at it, licking the walls, before settling their attention back on me. Their attention? It is all her, this monstrous beauty, flexing and flaunting her power as veins ride the cartography of muscle beneath the scales, yet still quite visible. But with the movement, the sensual flow, I am reminded of the rumors and her insatiable appetite for the perverse. I cannot imagine what she wants. Can it be any worse than what Ratman wanted? Look how that ended up... I know, no matter what, I will have to shut my brain off and get to whatever it is she wants once she makes her request. Will it be something of a sexual nature? A quest for humanity, to further her sociology studies? Something of myself as yet undetermined? That is the way in some situations. Shut down to move forward. It is the way of those who live in the trenches and travel the dark frontier.

Her nipples drip and I first think—milk?—but it is not milk. It is saliva or some related liquid, and her nipples split into many mouths as well. More mouths—for what purpose?

"What I need is for you to let go, Marlon."

"Let go of what?"

I know I have taken another step back as she looms over me, then forward. It's a dance of fear, a waltz inspired by trepidation.

"I need you to let go of...everything." The last word somehow lengthened, additional syllables added, embellishing it with a gruesome quality.

"What is that supposed to mean? How can I fulfill anything by doing nothing?"

"You're not paying attention," she says. Her desire coats the floor, a viscous puddle. She slithers in it, undulates with blatant appreciation, obviously enjoying the sensation. Sighs of pleasure brush my eardrums, though needles tip their reception. My foot slides as the puddle spreads out to me, but I keep my balance. In this dance, she is in the lead.

"I need you to let go of everything you have ever believed in. Everything that makes you human. Everything that matters, except your need for the Centipede."

Of course, I think. There is nothing else that matters. I can give it all up because nothing else matters as much as the Centipede. Just this one thing…then it is mine!

"Fine. How do I go about letting go of everything to your satisfaction?"

Her smile is something to behold. Then, the words: "I'm hungry."

"Hungry?" I say, though there is a frisson that the situation inspires, rubbing at my cerebral cortex with the gentle insistence of pumice.

Hungry, she said. Hungry, my cloaked guide had said. Hungry for…

"Through me is the final leg of the Centipede, Marlon. *Through me*."

"You mean…"

And she is on me, spikes digging into my flesh as she pounced. Snakes nip at me, tearing off my clothes. Fangs slice into flesh with buttery ease. Her weight suffocates, but that isn't even the worst. The mouths of her nipples join in, the scalpel incisions of the fangs there injecting me with venom that paralyzes. I am made stone for this derangement of Medusa.

Then she dines.

She sets her grinding vagina on my freed cock, the lips inspiring an erection, an impossible erection, yet the meaty fullness is only necessitated to better dig the barbed teeth jutting from within her into the flesh. Pulling and tearing, the pain incomprehensible—arms torn off a rag doll, defenseless— stuffing the meat into the maw as the tongue from the anus scoops my testicles from the ruptured scrotum and slurps them into the stinking orifice there.

The pain is excruciating, bending all meaning of what I thought were the limits of physical pain, creating new icons to bow down to in the process. Such knowledge, such wisdom, but to what purpose? What if she is only defiling me, slaughtering me, to feast on the remains, for her own means, and all this journey has been for naught? I am a victim of battle before battle has been waged. I am nothing but pain and putty in her hands, mouths. I am frozen; again, I am stone.

She leans in with that large mouth and that one split-pupil eye and says, "Through me is the final leg. My acidic juices, my internal digestive tract, are the penultimate extension of the Centipede. Through me is the path. Through me is the way. I am the light. I am the needle."

She sounds like a demented god.

"Stop thinking beyond sensation. Pain of this magnitude demands participation. Nothing more matters. Oh, it will all lead to the Centipede, but right now, all I need to do is eat you alive. Devour all of you, your wayward thoughts and delicious flesh, creamy organs, breaking bones — all of it. Grind you to gruel. To shit."

I want to scream, but this experience, no matter the enormity of suffering, has to be endured without possibility of release. Screaming is not an option, anyway, what with the paralysis. I am bestowed with the experience. *Are you experienced?* This experience, all that I am. The many mouths with the many teeth nip off chunks of me, slowly gnaw me to…death?

How could death lead me to…?

Death is only the beginning…

But it won't be exactly slow as I watch the Reptile Queen's mouth grow wide, jaw unhinged, slack, her throat as my cloaked guide's face, a wasteland, a void. The alpha and omega of *my* personal infinity.

She covers my head, clamping tight, asphyxiating me as she tears through the throat, tears my head and my reeling brain from my body. As she decapitates me. I thought she might ingest me whole, as a snake would, but she's simply joining in, taking some for *this* mouth. Though the reality of the situation is obvious: I am the feast to be savored by her *many* mouths.

And my consciousness does not waver. I am awake and mentally taking it all in. It only magnifies the travesty at hand, as I sense the mastication of my head, the skull pulverized, the brain turned to slush. The meat of me, ground down to digestible pieces. Human hamburger.

She takes all of me.

Time truly has no meaning. It is interminable, and sadistic as fuck.

The acids scour me, even the consciousness, somehow, the consciousness. I travel for what seems lifetimes in her belly, her being. I register fleeting thoughts that only heighten the pain.

Pain is my god.

Pain is my being.

I am God. The God of Pain.

Time is elastic.

It is

Now.

Now is forever.

All within the span of a millisecond.

Finally. A moment where the pain recedes—a black tide, perhaps rearing back, with a tsunami to follow.

How much more?

How much more?

And I sense it: expulsion. After time immemorial, but perhaps only hours, a day or two, three, I sense all of me somehow released.

I sense the plop of me as I hit a surface so cold it stings. Compared to the preceding experience, I welcome it. A reminder of real pain, something *less* than. Something bearable. This experience, perhaps ceasing. This experience, one to cherish? I venture not, if the end result is not as I need.

I feel rough spears poke me. I feel soft shards of me being licked off the anus—it must be, having been expulsed, having been shat out of that monstrous beauty, the Reptile Queen—and spitting me out. That abhorrent mouth worthy of a deep kiss if I am where I need to be.

Where I need to be.

The process continues.

I feel a limb, a leg, whole again.

I feel kidneys swell and vertebra sing.

I feel thoughts intensify and heart throb, quiver and forcefully re-ignite.

The shit of me. The shit I am.

I feel another limb, distinguished as an arm. A leg, joining the other. My torso, the foundation for the organs.

My tongue tastes my slimy lips and I almost regurgitate my self, turn myself outside, inside. I have no firm idea beyond the manipulating of me.

Smells cluster as one in my nostrils, repugnant, yet so intoxicating.

My ears whisper to life; they hear a voice—not a voice: humming. Feathery and focused. A sing-songy soundtrack for the outlandish task at hand.

Once I am rolled and licked clean by the tongue it teases the labia lips open. My first sight now is the teeth-lined vagina, smiling in a way. I see the Reptile Queen toil as I never imagined she would, this task hers to complete, for her friend Burroughs.

Please.

"There," she says. "All done and as ugly as ever."

I prop myself up on my elbows, take a long gander. Even my clothing is part of the deal, amazingly stitched back together—as

I have been—with no signs of having been damaged in the first place.

"You know what to do, right?"

Breathing, taking in the stale, diseased air, realizing wherever I am is not a place where cleanliness has ever trespassed. No, wherever I am is the pit of all filth. It is a shrine to all the garbage that fills our heads, our bodies, our existence, without the trespass of any gods. But this observation subsides; the smell is only stale. My awakening nostrils are adjusting to regular function and not the onslaught of filth. The onslaught of filth is within me...

The thought is eclipsed by the hiss of a cat; and another. The Reptile Queen pulls me from my swivel-headed surveillance, to face her one large eye, both pupils burning as suns about to supernova, the core gone white and blinding.

"You know what to do?" she says, nodding her head to the left.

"Oh, fuck," I finally say, feeble words to express the completion of this leg of my journey.

She shoves me toward the left, where she directs me with her head nod, and I see it. An empty syringe sitting on a velvet cloth on a block of marble, like a table, or a tomb.

"If you think that was fun, wait until William gets into your blood," she says, before peering over my head. "I must go. I've got...things to tend to. And I'm hungry again." She laughs, a pillow gutted and feathers filling my ears, and steps back, once, twice, before turning to steam and disappearing.

I walk toward the syringe. Reach out. Hesitate.

My hands are moist and I cannot remember if this is simply a result of what I have gone through, or if what I have gone through is fuel on the fire that is my anticipation. It does not matter. Everything within aligns as it always does. My heartbeat races. The track of my arteries and veins greets unlimited velocity as corpuscles attain optimum speed. There are no winners here. The rampant blood only magnifies the need.

Blood is a dissonant symphony in my ears. The rapid transit a locomotive I can hear now.

My hesitation is only a sign of relief.

I step closer and a handful of cats circle my legs, before scattering into the darkness.

I've known anticipation. I *live* in a state of anticipation. Right now, with the promise of Riding the Centipede so close, anticipation is all I am.

I calm down and force myself through the steps. I pick up the syringe, feel the weight of emptiness, yet also the promise.

I turn to look behind me, where the Reptile Queen had gazed, as if I might receive a transmission.

What I see annihilates all expectations.

CHAPTER 25

CHERNOBYL

A throaty drone signifying protest pulsed from within, bypassing the throat and centering on the amygdala. Rudolf Chernobyl, never one to empathize with another person's emotions, found himself hooked into Marlon's innermost sensations: dread; fear. But beyond fear, obstinate ideals crept around the periphery. Perhaps the scent of defiance. But the truth was what flooded over Rudolf, bulldozing its way into him: dread; fear.

Abstractions mounted and then crumbled. A menagerie of roiling life abounded: reptiles, snakes, insects, humans, yet all grafted together, a conglomeration of the anatomically obscene, mutated, distorted—monstrous. All of this fluctuated, folded inside-out, outside-in, stretched, bending in ways that seemed crippling. He saw this behind his clamped shut lids. Clamped shut, yet quivering—*wanting release: please, open now, free me, free me. Not wanting more of this. But the need eclipsed everything...*

Mouth hung slack, hyperventilating. Breath coming fast and harsh, a sandstorm in his throat. The drone clipped, hung out to dry, arid, burning.

The sensations he received empathically struggled for dominance. Dread and fear versus obstinance, defiance...and something more.

The need...

Rudolf's own insatiable need—hooked into Marlon's insatiable need. It sung in his veins, his body, and his brain—

—*sprawled across the floor. Sweat bubbling out of pores. The generator grinding unmercifully. The heat nurturing the pinpoint tumor of atomic energy—the closest acknowledgement of soul within his soulless being—inspiring it to branch out, weeds taking root and growing, pushing through the hard earth with determination. Pushing up through layers of skin, digging from within with a spade made of the lumpy, misshapen tumor/soul: obstinate; defiant—*

Sitting again, shaking. Whatever was in motion was different than any other experience he's had when using his internal homing skills. This time it was more full-bodied. Lethal. Experienced; to be experienced. (*Are you experienced?*) Holding his own in a necessary fight he does not feel confident in engaging in.

His veins let him know this much. They chattered in the language of addiction, their anticipation the crux of his existence.

(Feed me! *Feed me!*)

He was nothing without the anticipation: a vacancy in the vast art room. A discrepancy in the molecular structure of air, space. The drug was his God. All else deemed inconsequential.

—*flesh in revolt, different from the malignant tumor/soul nudging for the freedom to roam across his body, on the outside. Something Marlon is experiencing, channeled through him, the dials searching for static nightmares—and finding them—or possibly avaricious secrets within Rudolf's reeling mind. That which connected him to Marlon rose up from within and seared his flesh, flooding up and out of pores, insistent. The horror that was his true self clamoring for freedom—*

He pulled hard on the reins, no matter the need, the unquenchable need, he needed balance, to fulfill both yearnings, both extremes. His life depended on it. The tumor/ soul throbbed in protest, but somehow, Rudolf kept it at bay.

Mostly at bay.

(*Liar!*)

Marlon's world went black. The homing device stayed precariously connected, but the drug was not just inside Marlon's veins and mind, it surrounded him in a way incomparable to anything Rudolf had imagined a drug could do. It's as if he was bathing in it, swimming in it; hanging ten with narcotic sharks.

An obliteration of sorts in motion. He sensed (*completely*) the annihilation of Marlon, yet Marlon's destruction did not lead to death.

Transformation. Transformation takes hold.

For one of the rare moments in his life, Rudolf sensed pain. It was peripheral here, not all-encompassing, but it almost crippled his pursuit. He gasped, suffocating with the effort of trying to breathe. He emitted a squished squelch of a cry, a windpipe being squeezed tight, and knew this could not continue. It would shred him to pieces, shards of self and narcotic sharks, indistinguishable. Pain was something he knew only from afar. He distributed it, curious at the responses, but only with his birth and now, this moment, it stifled his breath, threatened to grind bones into powder. Promised to know him as it has never known any living creature. Not even Marlon, now.

Rudolf's intentions stumbled to the forefront. The knowledge within told him that this process would not be swift. For him to endure the whole thing would extinguish his being, something he *might* not be able to sustain. A strange thought, as annihilation should be total, yet this molecular breakdown seemed a birthing of sorts.

(Reborn: *Hallelujah!*)

Understanding passed through Rudolf's thoughts. This part of the process was readying Marlon for the final stages. It was readying Marlon so he could Ride the Centipede.

Rudolf could not let Marlon succeed. Go through the process, this hellish stage, but he must get the drug for his employers.

(He thought this but the chattering of his veins reminded him otherwise.)

(He swiped the thought away, the chattering veins laughing at his attempts to silence them. He would bring his employer to the end game. Rudolf Chernobyl was a man of his word. Decisions afterward, well, he'd make them when all the pieces of the puzzle had been connected.)

So.

Rudolf sensed momentum. A path. From here to there.

—pain, sweet self-annihilating pain. It kissed him and the tumor/soul throbbed, ecstatic—

He sensed direction. The path. Striding forward, somehow moving beyond Marlon and into the swampy terrain of the undefined. Surging, moving within the black currents. The dark clings to him, becomes one with him. A muscular force; a liquid disintegration. An ululating progression.

(Revelations at every turn.)

The darkness here was alive.

Inertia, without struggle.

He wondered what he could do to move the process forward swifter—

—swimming, legs and arms in motion, the sweat coating the tiled floor, the quest of the tumor/soul curiously abated; for now. Fingernails pry up and loosen tiles from the floor, the western motif designs crushed to shards in his strong hands, much as the threat or impending truth his bones were to meet mere minutes, seconds, ago. Drawing blood he does not feel. He is not here, in essence. He is—

—there, driven by the destructive seduction of the drug, the Centipede, as time becomes trivial, as it should be. It should not rule lives, yet right now, patience is an ebbing tide of promises wrapped in Euphoria's alluring arms.

It goes on…and on and on, when his breath ceases, strangled, gone.

Moments drowning in air.

Moments that linger as centuries, decaying—no—*decayed*. Dead. Yet not. Life compresses to will. To something less than being. Yet still present. A shadow of promise.

Are all promises lies?

Rudolf remembered again his birth, the wonder of existence, of life. Cherished gift. Cursed blight.

Confusion compelled him to branch out, within. The tumor/soul still there, observant, but allowing him whichever means he needed to be. To be Rudolf Chernobyl. Force of will. Driven by need.

Need.

The diseased elixir.

Rudolf used the need to pull himself from the clutches of the drug—the Centipede—a preposterous conflict of ideals, yet necessary to achieve such a daring objective.

His lids opened within the dark realm that Marlon Teagarden has yet to know. A destination, clouded, but his to define. The homing device illuminated as a white shadow of itself within; the negative positive. The white glow was a reflection of upcoming events for Marlon but not for Rudolf. He was already here. There.

Marlon was still traveling. Rudolf knew this. But Rudolf has made it to the end game destination. He glanced around, taking it all in, reading the map, knowing *his* next destination.

In the large room, oils liquefied, dripping off sagging canvases that coated the floor and his body with the evidence of his journey. He growled in anger, sighed afterward in joy. Growled again as he stood. His penis was rigid, but he held orgasm in tow. Not now. He had places to be. He could not hesitate. Though it seemed to have taken long, this maligned journey that had corrupted the room—along with the scarred, melted paintings, divots have been ripped from the floor, piles of crushed tiles like ant hills devoid of insect trespass—time may be immeasurable within the realm of where Marlon was.

Yet, there is no sign of Marlon. No, he has not made it to the end of his journey. His destiny.

So, time was of the essence.

Rudolf strode toward the door, the knob hot in his grip. He swung it open and his body tingled at the rush of cool air.

He turned to his right and walked to the bedroom. Making a phone call and setting a meeting place. He pulled a white suit from the closet full of them. When passing the mirror, he was struck by his transformation. His fists knotted into heavy hammers, but he regained control. He had no time to waste on vanity.

He drew a white leather trench coat from its roost in the closet, along with a hooded, cream-colored fleece jacket, the better to fly under the radar. His less than attractive appearance demanded such precautions.

His tumor/soul was leaking out. Perhaps, yes, perhaps that was the truth. His fists clenched tight again. There was no soul here. Only existence. He'd deal with this…imposition, and get back to his former appearance after he had attained the drug.

That was all that mattered now. That and keeping his word. His employer has been informed and all parties would meet up, but the scenario would not play out as planned.

He pulled the trench coat over the hoodie, the white cowl a halo above the impurities seeking freedom.

This would have to do. He was dressed in the appropriate manner to meet his destiny. One he's sure would bring him the ultimate experience.

CHAPTER 26

TEAGARDEN

If this figure is Burroughs, it is not a Burroughs I have ever imagined. I've seen photos, watched videos. The only thing this figure has in common with Burroughs, as far as the shadows allow me to see, is a lanky exterior.

I wonder if I've been duped and this is just another leg of my journey, with many more, an eternity more, to follow. Or if Riding the Centipede even has foundation in my reality, dear sister. Is it all a sham? The anticipation renders all thought inconsequential. Yet holding the syringe in my ready fingers—the empty syringe—I know, somehow, this figure is him. It *has* to be.

Perhaps approaching will clear out the shadows, sunlight over rolling hills, and the man I expect to see will appear.

Perhaps the transformation I sense is woven into my physicality has altered how I see things.

(Perhaps this whole journey has been the result of a mighty powerful hallucinogen…)

—*buy the ticket, take the ride…there's no turning back from the other side*—

("Do it," Marilyn whispers, from the brackish pool of my subconsciousness, somewhere way back there, where whippoorwills screech and wail.)

There is one way. Only one way.

Still standing at a distance, I raise the syringe to eye level. I pull back the plunger, and then compress it, clearing out all the air. A soft hiss passes through the eye of the needle.

A cat sprints across the cold floor; two more follow. I hear soft purring and sounds that relate to soft purring, yet none of this brings me comfort.

It was common knowledge that Burroughs liked cats, though...

I stretch my arm out and it literally stretches, rubbery and laced with ribbons that rise up, ready for action. Ready for the needle.

The veins protrude like mountains on a relief map, but I have no expectation of relief, only more. More.

(Something more...)

My right hand hovers over the mountains, the needle held steady, my fingers concrete and precise. I don't even need to tie off. My veins are so eager they demand participation, now.

(Chattering, chattering...)

I no longer feel the pinch of penetration as the needle punctures flesh, though sweat trickles down the sides of my face, my hairline damp—a muddy riverbed.

I inhale with slow, concentrated purpose and depress the plunger, pulling back, the syringe filling with blood, crimson flowing swiftly. Tiny creatures accompany the surging fluid. I see tiny limbs flutter as if these unknown creatures are swimming. I think I see a few doing the backstroke. Faint light illuminates what lives within the syringe, my blood; my body.

Even in the act of taking and not receiving, the deed carries weight. I exhale as the syringe fills, pull the needle from the yellow flesh, press the crease to my side into the tattered The Doors T-shirt, staunching the flow. My awkward pose does not matter. I make way across the dark room and nothing changes. The figure seems...inhuman.

Distinguishing human from nightmare—no—from that which should only be perceived as different, seems a dicey task. I want an arm, a vein to fill, to initiate the final stage, the final leg. I must feel around the seemingly slumbering creature. Burroughs, sure, but a *transformed* Burroughs, as I feel I've been transformed. I reach into the shadows and my fingers wander within the darkness. Touch interprets the sensation of fabric, cross-hatched threading. The blanket of shadows is quite literally a *blanket* of shadows...

A seed of unease takes root, but I bat it away. Why allow fear a foothold when I am so close? Burroughs may be different than expected, but what does that matter? After all I've been through, especially the previous leg, why even consider hesitating?

My hands continue to trace over the figure, lightly seeking an arm, a vein.

A low rumble vibrates under my palm.

I don't allow my surprise to hinder my search. The vibration seems indicative of the torso, the lungs inhaling then exhaling stale air, aware of my intrusion. The rumble voices displeasure, yet I sense it is directing me. I move my eager fingers toward where the arm should be.

Peeling the thin fabric as one might the skin of a plum, the darkness slides aside. The dim light from around me, the source of which I'm uncertain, reveals a thin, long arm, barely more than bone covered in a dull, greasy, grey flesh. Odd blades like curved spikes along a lizard's spine, or perhaps the prickly, thick hairs that dress a tarantula's body, are evident here. Yet they are scattered along the length and do not dominate.

There are blue lines beneath the sickly flesh. A simpler road map than I am accustomed to when injecting myself, yet one that I hope is sufficient enough to accomplish my task.

I aim the needle at a blue vein, to the indecipherable ink pen scribbling, the cursive scribble of life. The chorus in my head lifts to heavenly heights, yet the chorus itself is laced with aural debris. Slivers of distortion knot and tighten; tighter.

As the needle approaches the arm, the blue line squiggles. Alive. A worm seeking the surface.

My mouth hangs slack.

Blood has coagulated from my recent puncture. It's sticky as I open the crease to use my hand to hold down his arm. I steady myself and apply the needle to the blue line.

Pushing it in.

Pushing the plunger.

Crimson vacates the syringe. Blood, sweet elixir of life… and life again?

Wakes the legend.

As the plunger pushes to the hilt, Burroughs' body sucks in a deep inhalation of air. The sleeping giant awakens. The dim light brightens.

I see him now, this thing as much insect as man, yet morphing as the blood surges into his body.

I pull the needle from his arm and back away. His transformation is instantaneous as opposed to my slow metamorphosis. He bloats, a balloon being filled with air, though the crackling and crinkling seems of a wooden derivation.

A growl, yet not from deep within, more like skimming past the lips, as if the lips were made of aluminum, smooth, yet metallic, rises as smoke from an industrial complex. *It is visible, dirty, a stained white cloud, blooming.*

Something else rises up, a cobra from the basket of his loins. No, of course not (of course not?). It's his penis filling with blood, with life and length…and insects flood out of the swollen glans, pouring out, twitching along the pulsing veins. Underneath the skin of the shaft and all over the stretched taut flesh. The sound of his orgasm, from his mouth as well as emanating from the insect traffic gushing out of his penis, is of a tonal quality I've never heard before, never perceived. A sound so foreign it eludes classification.

The sound draws a response from the cats lurking in the shadows. A chorus of screeches and purring that hums harshly, burrowing into my eardrums.

It goes on and on: the vocalizations of unknown pleasure as well as the insect ejaculation. The body fills out as well. Not a lot, Burroughs was a lean man, but enough to mask the insect within, the insect-like creature he was while sleeping. (Sleeping?)

"God *damn* the torpedoes, been a long time since I've shot a load of such sphincter squeezing articulation, my boy. Even the hemorrhoids will be whistling dixie in appreciation of their parole from just hanging out and feeling ignored. Been waiting a long time for somebody to get this far."

The voice, the inflection, is unquestionably Burroughs', though it is different as well. The droning quality is spiked with battery acid, charged and clearing out perhaps years of silence. A few insects, also of an unspecified species, scurry past his lips as the white smoke turns to silver.

He sits up, pulls the shadow fabric over himself. The shadow fabric now a motley jacket, the moldy smell and abrupt movement releases moths from the sleeping folds, indicative of the many years it has hung over his prone body. Steaming fluids that plume from pores, jetting in little bursts all over his still gray flesh like geysers, pass through the shadow fabric. Their interference trims it all in a moldy green hue, before shimmering and fading swiftly away.

"Did I send for you?" he asks, staring at me with eyes the pastel orange color of a Monarch butterfly's wings.

"Yes," I say, not one to contemplate beyond need. "I am Marlon Teagarden."

"Marlon who?" His cheeks are hollow, excavated as empty graves.

There is a moment like glass being blown, frozen, shattered. A slow-motion sprinkle spattering like blood from an open jugular across my thoughts. I open my mouth to speak, but he beats me to it.

"Worried you, didn't I?" He laughs, a sound akin to the caw of a crow; many crows, actually; a murder of crows. A murder...

He plucks insects off his still erect penis, their bodies turn liquid then crusty. He crunches them between his blackened teeth.

"Nobody's ever gotten by my scaly mistress before. Nobody's ever made it this far. Lost souls but not lost enough. Not true explorers of what you call the dark frontier, but my associates who travel the same margins call by many names."

I am struck by the awe of being in his presence, of making it to the end, but need to know specifics, to calm my jangling nerves.

"How long will it take?"

"Anxious, are we?" His smile is feral. His smile is lethal.

I nod my head.

"You know what you've gotten yourself into, eh, kiddo?"

"Yes," I say. "Just tell me something, anything..."

"Time does not matter to the dark frontier patron, as you know. But for the sake of putting your nerves to rest, it should be about two hours for your blood to acquire what's necessary for you to experience as I do—"

"The ultimate experience, yes."

"As close as you can get to experiencing the multitude of everything unimagined without being me. Though if you think you have a clue as to what to expect, kiddo, you haven't the foggiest."

"Unimagined?"

"You have no idea."

Again, his face tightens, the savage knowledge of what I am to experience, of what is next, sculpting it with a patina of mystery. It is not a comforting transformation.

He has been stroking a cat the whole time he's been speaking. More than one, I can see. A bustling furball of life has nudged his erection to one side, staking claim to his lap.

"I made it past the Reptile Queen, I'm sure I can face anything now."

The cawing is a crowd, much more than a murder; a war. After a long spell, it subsides, and he says, "What you experienced with my scaly mistress was but the tip of the needle of what is to follow. The puncture, without depressing the plunger and filling you with the narcotic elixir that is me, my mind, unhinged and freefalling."

"The Centipede."

He curls his lips, a brow, his eyes full of sadistic glee.

"The Centipede, of course. A catchphrase name, like Horse, Angel Dust, Dirt Goblin; like your modern methods of enlightenment via destruction. Krokodil. Penny Pincher. Triple Crown. A name built on paradox as I detest centipedes. Venusian slime. Truth is, as surrealist painter Sal Dali once said, 'I am drugs.' It was a statement of intent. A challenge to the Bourgeois, the snobs and capitalists. The elite, at least within their own minds. 'Take me, and see.' It was not as one might suggest, ego-inspired"—his smile again, so full of ambiguity—"but an invitation: take me, and be'."

"Many of the surrealists, much like paranoids, know a thing or two about what's really going down in the world up there." He raises a skeletal phalange, the thumb, indicating up there. Above us. "They know without the perverted psychological baggage, even if the perverse might be part of their makeup. Many of my fellow literary cohorts also get it, this thing called life, forever expanding after the physical body as you understand it, dies. Yet not in a sense those who experience afterward can describe. The point being…" —he pauses, for dramatic effect or an exercise in cruelty, something I did not expect, yet deep down, I think he's just having some kind of mischievous fun at my expense—"I am drugs. I am *the* drug. Call it what you will, any worthwhile human with the buckaroo hullabaloo to get on in this thing called life, existence, would be clamoring at my feet to experience something beyond the generic. The bland. I supply this. I am the drug. The narcotic personification of the black meat, the thirsty devil. The puckered asshole of fate."

My head spins with the information, a lit match to a forest. Burroughs in a chatty mood. No matter the tinge of nonsense inherent in it all. Perhaps nonsense is the true god that deserves our faith. Perhaps nonsense reigns supreme to those who "get it."

"You'll meet them all," he said, the look on his face not lethal nor sadistic. Filled with awe, because he knows what I have coming.

"Meet…meet who?"

"Pay attention, kiddo. Haven't you been paying attention?"

"Well, yes, but…"

"No buts, unless you're talking about sharing something more than your blood." He leers, though the leer is a flash, and not laced with perverse or malevolent intent. "I will sodomize your mind, not your flesh. Here, that's where the fullest experiences dwell." He taps the side of his head, the spindly nail digging into the new flesh; a bead of blood—my goal leaking out? "Here, where you will join in the chaos of release from your humanly ways and the skincage husk. Here where freedom abounds, simply waiting for you to let it frolic.

I think about it all, want it all, please, go ahead, sodomize my mind, split the hemispheres and fuck my cerebral cortex. Time cannot move fast enough.

"I will meet others as well? Dali?"

He nods his head.

"Ginsberg? Rimbaud? Kerouac?"

All met with hearty head nods and my anticipation is plastered across my face.

"There's always more. So many more. Unlimited."

I reel off more names, then an obvious choice, though I am not sure if he's dead or alive or...

"Solon?"

Burroughs stops on a dime, all momentum sucked dry.

"I mean, I'm not sure if he's dead or not, but..."

"He's been dead for many years. Actually, he's never been truly alive in the world up there, the sappy bastard. Sad sack and quite antisocial. You could probably meet up with him, but not in this way."

"Why not? He's a master craftsman of the bizarre."

"He's a pulp hack with haughty aspirations never fully realized. A smudge given time in your world, my former world."

"What's that supposed to mean?"

"He is an insect that dreamed of being a man...for all the wrong reasons. Fame. Fortune. I am a man who dreamed of being an insect. In essence, expanding beyond the range of normalcy that runs the world I lived in. Fame, not really the deal. Fortune? Well, if it gets me more time to attain everything necessary for full mind expansion. To get me where I am now."

"Sleeping?"

"Living. Experiencing within the brain, using the full capacity of the mind. H.P. Lovecraft opened his tale, *The Call of Cthulhu* with this tidbit: 'The most merciful thing in the world, I think, is the inability of the human mind to correlate all its contents. We live on a placid island of ignorance in the midst of black seas of infinity, and it was not meant that we should voyage far.' It goes on. Point being, he was wrong. The New England gent was afraid. Though the statement was for a piece of fiction and now, when you eventually get to talk to him, you'll see he's anything but afraid." Burroughs circled back to his point. "The mere sniff of an existence most humans can't imagine experiencing is a shit stain on tighty whities. Fear. Nothing more. So many people live afraid. That's not living. Society disapproves of a true life."

He seems to drift, losing focus. I worry something is wrong. I figure talking might eat the time, so I want to carry on, but then he stops, eyes shifting to an even darker shade—a void—and shuts down.

"Must let me work the blood properly now, kiddo. I've only tested this on lizards and insects. Their appreciation is magnified when I really work the blood."

With so many more questions I want to ask, I squeeze out one before he settles in to work the blood properly.

"Why me?"

"Why not?" Then, more precisely, "Luck of the draw."

"Nothing but chance?"

"Let me work the blood now. I know how you feel. You'll really learn to appreciate the sassiness of patience once I shut up."

He settles back, pulling the shadow fabric to his shoulders. Closes his eyes. Cats curl into every crevice of his silhouette. Immediately, the orbs speed into action beneath the lids. A stone skips across his still features, birthing ripples that threaten to devour the flesh.

I back away, to the stone block that houses the syringe. Slump against the cold hardness. Wrap my arms around myself, the chill more from within than ambient.

I am this close to experiencing the Centipede in all its miraculous glory.

All I have to do now is be patient.

CHAPTER 27

BLAKE

The Midwest bled the life from those more accustomed to the idiosyncrasies found on the outer edges of America. As Blake drove the rental toward 1927 Learnard Avenue, the landscape cried out for chaos. Lawrence, Kansas, could be anywhere in the Midwest, USA.

The only thing that distinguished their trek was familiarity. Even the sparse people outside of homogeneous homes seemed cut from the same white cloth. Their prying eyes and putty faces lacked personality. Nothing here inspired. Hence, there was often a sense of sleepwalking uniformity that made Blake uneasy, never wanting places like this to infect him. As if he had any better aspirations, perhaps settling into old age and becoming one with the architecture, the furniture—whatever—would be less grueling than the life he had undertaken. Yet despite his cheerless demeanor, the life he had chosen was better than this. At least he was still fighting. A losing battle in the end—it was for all of us—but he would not go down without bloodied knuckles and a sense that at least he got something out of his life.

Jane had found a shop with information, maps and more, where they found a slim pamphlet on Burroughs' home.

"It's been made a historic site, yet funds haven't followed up to make it a museum or even a tourist attraction."

"Burroughsland?" Blake raised a brow as he said this, looking askance at Jane.

"Sure. Admission is one soul."

"That's if you still have one."

Blake could see a laugh struggling to escape Jane's face, but she glanced away, not allowing it free reign, and got back to the pamphlet.

"Many don't see Burroughs as anything but a druggie who decided to die here and would prefer to leave this legacy and the possibility of fans, drifters, low-lifes" — she paused, taking it in — "it actually is written here, just like that, "low-lifes" — as if it's a warning." She harrumphed. "Druggie" as well, not even junky." She continued. "At this time, it is in limbo. The house is locked up and empty."

"Poor saps can't imagine anything shaking up their placid lot in God's country. I can understand the sentiment, some place to retire to. Most of the folks we've seen are far from that age."

"It's both a university town and one of the ten most popular retirement towns in America." Blake glanced at Jane as she tapped the pamphlet. "A wealth of information." Slim lips creased, smiling.

Blake glanced back to the road, the roll call of street signs. Time sighed, waiting...

"There. Learnard Avenue."

Turning down the road, he slowed to a snail's pace, and then realized the ridiculous nature of his move. Just look for a red cottage.

They saw it to their right, set back a bit, weeds in abundance, a sense of disarray on display. Not exactly a cottage, but cottage enough.

"I'd say the efforts to make this anything more than a dilapidated reminder housing ghosts without distinction —"

"The norm here," Jane said, reading Blake's thoughts.

"—have fallen deep into the well of negligence. A historic site. A sight to bruise eyes."

They parked in front of the red cottage. Blake's intuition ratcheted up a notch, yet his mind and eyes saw hope as lean. Still, intuition usually won out.

"Even the paint's faded. I'm not feeling too confident, Blake."

"What's confidence got to do with anything? My intuition says, let's get out and take a closer gander."

Jane gave him a look he could not read, somewhere between the whittled confidence she normally expressed, and a belief they'd gotten this far primarily because of his intuition.

They exited the rental car and walked to the front porch. An abundance of cats, most of them plump and furry, scurried about the yard, dallied toward them, yet kept their distance.

Blake took in the neighborhood, the blank slate awaiting inspiration: a charcoal line, a swipe of the paintbrush. He also noticed curtains from a house across the street ripple closed, and a man with a lawnmower, the engine praying loudly to the dimming blue sky, take notice of their trespass, but before he turned away, the man was back to cutting the grass to the perfect length. A white picket fence surrounded him, his cage as defined by the 1950s American standard of success.

It seemed such a time warp, this place.

Despite his regular relations with those who lived in the margins, the junkies, drifters and lowlifes, Blake found that splintered lifestyle more appealing than this.

He was a masochist for sure.

When they made the porch, their weight causing the wood to awaken, Blake said, "Tell me something about Burroughs."

"Why?" Jane brushed her hands together, as if cleansing herself, but she'd yet to touch anything.

A gray tabby cut the distance and coiled around her ankles. She rose on one heel and gently nudged it away. It protested, yet moved on.

"Amuse me."

"Well, the basics, he was a junky, heroin being his primary vice, who wrote some fascinating experimental novels dealing with—"

"No. Tell me something about him. The man. Interests. Not the patented wiki-bio shit." Blake tried the doorknob, getting the expected and receiving no success.

Jane paused, pursed her lips, then said, "Well, he believed in subverting the norm. Detested systems of control, authority and otherwise."

Blake stepped off the porch, circled around the house.

Jane followed in a rush, dancing around the dried weeds and more stray cats that followed them. She shielded her eyes against the sun's setting glare burnishing the windows with kisses goodnight.

"And…well, he lived the life of the outsider with conviction. He also had many deep interests: the occult, I've seen a clip on YouTube, just a snippet, of him performing some ritual related to something of this nature. And science. Information, in general. Varied."

Blake nodded his head, "Hmph," then stopped. He knelt down, touched a stone with a named etched into it.

"What's this?"

"Part of his pet cemetery, I expect. He loved cats—"

"Loved cats?"

"Yes. Seems they're still keeping watch over his humble abode," she said, hands outstretched to the growing feline audience. "I don't remember the quote, but he once noted he had no wherewithal when it came to love, yet with cats, that was all the love he needed." She put her hands on her hips, watching Blake.

"Science. The occult. A different thinker in general. Loved cats."

"I'm sure there's much more, but I'm also sure we did not come here to write his biography." Jane brushed her hands together again.

Two lizards raced across the side of the house. Blake peered in their direction and noticed the bustling insect life that scurried about at the base of the house. He stroked one of the cat grave markers again, thinking. He lifted the stone with Lone Joe etched into the hard surface.

"What in the world are you doing, desecrating the poor kitty graveyard?" Jane said.

"Looking for something," he said, setting the stone back in place, and picking up another one: Betsy. Then another, continuing the process.

"Do you think Marlon's hiding under one of those?"

Blake tilted his eyebrow her way, an aloof statement to the madness in progress, thinking about cats, all the strays here. Strays not chasing the lizards or messing with the insects. Just twitching their tails and licking themselves and purring gleefully. And watching them. Just here, as if all of the creepy elements are simpatico. As if this is home. As if…

"Ruskie. Russian slang, right?" Blake asked.

"Yes, he had many cats, but one of his faves was Ruskie, a Russian blue—"

"Blue? We're back to blue?" Blake's faced split into a smile. He teetered down to the large stone, touching it, with no results. Then:

"What, pray tell, are you doing? Have you lost your mind?"

"Just waking up my inner feline," Blake said, leaning forward, tongue stretching toward the stone. Like a cat, his intuition was inclined to take a licking…or give one.

The cats around the perimeter bounded into action, stomping and circling around them.

A sound like a roll-up door being cranked open struck him like a blow. They both stepped back, Jane practically stumbling, while Blake rose up, wary.

A rectangle opening near the house where the insects and lizards had scampered, opened up, a filthy maw. The dirt atop the hidden door piled at the edges.

"That...is some trippy shit," Blake said.

Jane was flummoxed. "What the...? How did you know?"

"I didn't. But with the info you gave me, well..." He shrugged his shoulders. Something in the information had led him to explore a bizarre avenue, one beyond Learnard Avenue. One not on a map, and leading to a hole in the ground large enough for a person to enter.

"We really need to find a way to package and market this intuition deal you've got going. We could make a fortune," Jane said, as they both approached the hole.

Stairs stretched down into a darkness. She shivered. Blake sighed, knowing what was next. He reached inside his trench coat to a zippered pocket, unzipped and pulled out a small but strong pen light.

He clicked it on and said, "We can look into that after we look into this." Nodding to the hole, the stairs, and the darkness.

CHAPTER 28

CHERNOBYL

The engine idled at a quick pace, running hot. Rudolf wondered if this had anything to do with his presence, with what he could inspire when his control was lax, distracted. Yet he did not feel he was lacking control, despite the hunger filling his belly and veins; his mind.

Perhaps it was just a sign of his impending meltdown, whether he wanted to admit it to himself or not.

None of this mattered as much as what he caught view of from his perch along the curb, two houses down from a fading red abode.

"Well, well, Cowboy," he said, his voice scratchy, bad reception on a dying radio. "So you're a part of this, too."

His focus narrowed, pulling away from the gong-rattle mayhem inspired by the internal homing device in his head, his bones, his being. When he'd barged into the dilapidated warehouse outside of Lafayette, Louisiana, spotting Marlon Teagarden just as he disappeared, the sound clutter had been a caterwauling din he'd never experienced before. Now, the decibels had fangs.

There was more going on with Teagarden than he'd ever conceived. This stealthy trip, bouncing between here and wherever, along a path leading to some sort of narcotic, perhaps hallucinogenic elixir of incomparable audacity, must be part of the reason he was zeroed in on Marlon with such intensity, but what of his own needs, his own obligations? He did not linger on how it would play out. His employer, riding in a van behind him, would get Teagarden, that's the gist of their deal. Rudolf was, if nothing else, a man of his word, no matter his questionable status as human. He would hand over Teagarden and worry about payment later. If his employer wanted the drug for himself, that would cost much more but, even at that, Rudolf wasn't too sure if he would give it up.

After all, his body and mind demanded more. Need coursed through him, a panther stalking a gazelle, waiting patiently. Sharing with a hyena was not necessarily a part of the bargain...and his employer was definitely a hyena.

Peering into the dying light, the sun shadowing the world in slivers of glare and obscurity, he watched as the man in black he'd met a couple days ago in Roswell, New Mexico—perhaps less a chance meeting, than an unfulfilled introduction, since his presence here meant he was in some way looking for the same thing Rudolf was looking for; which also meant Cowboy had followed up on Rudolf's handiwork on the woman in the hotel room—as he squatted along the side of the red house more like a cottage, touching stones, lifting some up, inspecting them. This curious display rendered Rudolf mute.

A woman he vaguely remembered from Roswell—a flashing snippet of memory put her on the street, near an indistinct rental car, yet also taking in the odd exchange—pretty in a sharpened knife way, stood next to Cowboy, her stance preparatory, not relaxed. Cowboy leaned down, face to the ground—to a large stone?—and abruptly, she stumbled backward, almost toppling to the ground. Cowboy was swift to rise and back away as well.

Rudolf was locked in, concentrating, uncertain of what the hell was going on, yet intent on finding out. He'd just let them finish whatever they were up to, then take them out and take over. It might help lead him to his prey, the gazelle.

A knock on his window did not draw his visual attention away from Cowboy and the woman, though Rudolf pressed the button and automatically lowered the window a few inches.

"Are we ready? He wants to know if we're ready." The man was wiry as beef jerky, tough. A scar along his jawline and the nervous tic in his left eye did not go well with the expensive dark gray Armani suit he draped over his frame: *brutta figura*. Rudolf wondered if the nervous tic and generally jittery stance were inspired by Rudolf's present, less than handsome appearance. What lived inside him had awakened, courtesy of the drug, even if just the frayed edges of the drug; the searing promise and the way it changed his appearance might inspire even the toughest grunt to question their own grit and rumble ideals.

Rudolf did not turn to face him, though the desire to smile through the corruption needled his sadistic streak. He continued to watch Cowboy and the woman converse. Cowboy reached into his trench coat and pulled something out. He expected a gun, but a bright light beamed from the end of the object. As he watched, he said, "When I say we are ready, I will let you know. Until then, do not disturb me. You won't like the repercussions of interrupting Rudolf Chernobyl again. Understood?" Rudolf said this casually, as if speaking about the weather. He peripherally gauged beef jerky's tough façade as it crumbled just a tad. Just enough to let him know his silence was confirmation of understanding as he walked back to the white van.

Then Rudolf saw something impossible. Cowboy and the woman walked toward the side of the red house. As they progressed, they seemed to shrink, sinking into the weeds grown rampant. Disappearing, not as Marlon had done, but in a way that left him perplexed.

"No," he said, bleating his disapproval, shoving the door open and breaking into a sprint. Only a handful of seconds passed as he ran to the side of the red house, yet that was quite long enough to give Cowboy and his woman their path to

Marlon—it had to be—or possibly an escape route from his piercing glare.

They hadn't seen him.

No way had they seen him.

Lizards and insects landscaped with curious intent. They manipulated dirt and weeds in front of the bleached red wood.

Rudolf clenched his hands, sparks crackling in the womb of each fist. He stepped back, closed his eyes, breathing deep to derail the fiery fury within, replaying all he had just witnessed. The internal homing device warranted attention as well. Such noise, less a sound and more a bulldozing force decimating his focus. He had to push it aside, battle within the cranial arena and pin it to the floor.

Instant replay left him unsatisfied, nothing to really hold on to. Something mysterious had happened here. Something he needed to figure out, and fast. He stopped the looped replay at the point when Cowboy and the woman had stumbled backward. Whatever had just happened was connected to whatever Cowboy had just done. Rudolf knew this, knew he was correct. But what had he done?

He leaned forward, his face masked by the weeds. Leaned forward...

Rudolf opened his eyes. An orange cat weaved between his legs. He kicked it hard with the tip of his white alligator skin boot. The cat hissed. More cats flitted about or luxuriated in the weeds.

Names were written on stones all around. He read them and figured this was a graveyard of sorts, for animals. Perhaps the cats were paying respects to their fallen relatives. He took in the names: Lone Joe. Betsy. Ruskie. A few more fading names he could not make out.

He fidgeted, anxious, knowing Marlon was near, yet uncertain of where. If the internal homing device was correct, he was very close. "If" being tendered only because of previous events. Rudolf already knew the house would be empty. If Cowboy and the woman hadn't gone in the house, there was no reason for him to even consider it a possibility.

Ruskie. Russian. The stone glimmered moistly as he stared at it. He rubbed his eyes. The stone still glimmered. Cowboy had leaned forward.

"No." Rudolf dropped to his hands and knees, not caring if he soiled his white pants. Again. An orange tabby and a calico friend approached him.

Rudolf barked, growled and bounced a bit on his hands and knees. A pit bull in angel's clothing. He'd really gotten in touch with his canine side the last few days.

He succeeded in scaring off the impending intruders as well as all the rest of the cats. They scurried around the back of the red house. Some hightailed toward a separate garage.

He let his tongue loll, panting as he did. He howled as the sun prepared to give way to the moon. The gloaming glimmered off the stone with *Ruskie* written on it. Rudolf leaned down to it, sniffing. He reached out. The stone was wet.

"Comrade," he said, nodding.

He let his tongue loll out, wagged it side to side before touching the stone; then, licking eagerly.

His reaction was contained, but he heard the sound of something unraveling—something metal—and a rectangle opened from the side of the red house.

A cat sprinted out of the hole.

Two cats scurried in, the orange tabby and the calico again, dashing from the side of the house. As if with a purpose.

(To warn Marlon of his presence? Did Marlon sense he was being followed? Tracked?)

He stood up and strolled toward the rectangular space. Stairs led down, losing visual solidity in the darkness. Rudolf had no flashlight, but this would not be a problem. He knew it would not be good for his already unstable condition, but he did not expect it would take long to find what he needed. Marlon.

His veins pulsed hot and furious.

He tilted his head, cracked his neck, and pulled from within. Tapping into the chaos.

His eyes pulsed in measured strobes, before settling as beams of twin lighthouses.

He peered deeper, but only saw stairs. Metal stairs.

This place was constructed with a purpose.

For the cats?

No matter, he knew what was next. He would descend the metal stairs to meet his destiny. If destiny meant the successful attainment of the drug.

He turned to the van, to beef jerky standing outside the driver's side door. He raised his hand and waved. *Come here.*

He watched beef jerky lean into the van. Watched a side door slide open. Watched as beef jerky rushed to the door and pulled out the ramp.

Watched as his employer was rolled down the ramp. The bumpy ride the stairs were going to be for his employer didn't matter the least to Rudolf. *Hurry up.*

As ugly as Rudolf knew he presently looked, his employer had all nightmares beat. As much as Rudolf only utilized the shell of being human for what mattered to him up to now—using his inherent strength and guile, along with the sadism that led him down this path, to acquire the things he loved: art; nothing else really mattered—his employer had beaten him to the punch when it came to embracing one's inhuman side…at least in appearance.

None of this made a dent in the measured beam of his focus, though. He had one thing in mind. One thing and only one thing.

It was a long way down, perhaps to Hell, for all he knew. But if shaking hands with the devil was the only way to get to Marlon and the drug, so be it. His grip was firm; he was ready.

CHAPTER 29

TEAGARDEN

Patience: gumming a steak, the ability to rip and tear rendered impotent. Waiting for teeth to fill the mouth, jut through with force, with anticipation, to encourage the primal pleasure.

I stroke a cat, one of Burroughs' many feline friends. Their presence altered perceptions, softened edges. This place, steeped in dismal trimmings, made bearable by their purring.

Addiction is the one truth of my life. Changing over time, as one drug runs its course, the influx needed of a more potent replacement. The expectations higher, scraping the soft bellies of clouds; higher still. Eviscerating everything I have known, the only path for me. Releasing me from the past, the life of comfort sandblasted by all father did to corrupt it. The past that shaped me, realizing this as I sit here with the ultimate experience so close. With my addiction eager to participate in the ultimate experience. This is my truth.

My thoughts meander to that past again. A past shaped by the cold knife of reality, yours and mine, my dear sister. The reality of simply being and getting by in a cruel world that truly does not care. A reality that just wants to devour souls and consume the fleshy remnants, use the bones as toothpicks.

That's why I choose a different reality...

I choose to grow similar teeth, to devour the soul of reality itself. Fight fire with fire? To swish reality in my mouth like fine wine, something I've only experienced when foraging in our parent's liquor cabinet. Mother's need for anything and everything alcohol made available without hesitation. She in her own forgetting mode, forgetting to even live. Filling space.

("Why are you being nostalgic, Marlon? You're so damn close to your heaven. Why dwell on the past? Bury the fucker and move forward." Marilyn again, always chiding me for my melancholic ways, my bending but not breaking. You'd think she'd find something there admirable. "Admirable is a petty conceit."

"Shut up, shut the fuck up. I'm not slipping into nostalgia. I am waiting. How the hell else am I supposed to wait?") Bitch.

Insects and lizards and the strange things that don't belong to either category skitter under the shadow cover of Burroughs. Cats circle around him, finding open space to feel his body against theirs. They snuggle and purr, lick his arm, the puncture wound their oasis. Warming him, maybe. Or siphoning from the outside a taste of my treat. I almost swat them away, but let it go.

I am weary.

I ache in ways inhuman. There is no other way to put it. I ache in ways I have never imagined. My skin looks like skin, but feels as I would imagine an exoskeleton would feel. Restricting the layers beneath. I can acclimate to the mechanics of breathing just fine, yet feel like I am suffocating.

My body has undergone many alterations, my exoskeleton suit made not to fit, but to change. I have a corset shaped I know not how. A carapace armor never to be removed. Perhaps I will know in time.

Perhaps not.

Time is hell. I need it to move more swiftly. With this thought Burroughs' stirs, the cats shuffle but do not leave him. His penis lengthens again, though no semen masked as insects is ejaculated. This time it swivels and coils, dancing as a snake to the unheard music of the charmer.

He props himself up with those bony elbows, and smiles as his head clears the shadows.

"You're gonna love this. It's time for you to Ride the Centipede, Marlon."

I stand so quickly my head spins, and realize my limbo state, the thoughts and designs and harsh geometry of being within me, is the last time I will ever have to go there. The past is almost officially gone. The moments before injection, gone.

I am ready.

I am ready to Ride the Centipede.

As I stride toward Burroughs, something echoes within this tight space. The space expands, stretches out, as if made of rubber, as if air is being blown into a balloon. I hear strange sounds, different sounds. Different than the sounds of insects and lizards and purring cats and Burroughs' monotone rumble. These sounds are more common, in a way. Of the world out there. Of the world I am leaving. My only question is, how did they get in here?

CHAPTER 30

BLAKE

"They seem to go on forever," Jane said, hand on Blake's bicep as they plunged deeper and deeper into darkness eternal. "I would say, 'You sure this is a good idea?' but I also know this is why we are here. Still...how much longer?"

"Only time will tell," Blake said, stepping down another stair and swiping at abundant cobwebs, hoping not to run into any of the architects, what with all he's seen of insects over the last few days. Another step, two, three, each one the tick on a clock that grinds patience and reality to gruel. Eaten by the darkness, digested as sustenance. Demanding the price of their descent...when they hit bottom.

The room was massive, warehouse large—*larger*—high ceilings kissing the weeds and the red cottage sitting atop it out of view, way up in a darkness the pen light could not penetrate. Cats slinked or scampered by. The odor was of a cat box, yet much more than that. The cold was hollow, empty, like a cave. A place the sun has never brightened.

Scanning left to right, Blake spied an odd disarray of stone blocks looking like prehistoric furniture. At about 1:00 o'clock, a dimness that couldn't be qualified as light, but of a different texture than the darkness, signaled which way to go.

About halfway to their destination, Blake pocketed the pen light. Jane's grip, having moved from his bicep to his aching right hand, grew firm. The deep chill of the place inspired protests from every joint. He almost did not mind, protecting this damsel in willful distress. Perhaps not willful, but necessary...

As they crossed the length of a football field, the light shimmered dully, no brighter, yet with their approach, more of it was visible.

A figure rose up from where it was scrunched down against one of the big stone blocks. Blake registered the person was in deep concentration. Something about the tilt of the head, the oblivious tint to the eyes.

The tapping of their footsteps hadn't echoed in the least, as though they had left them behind. Not signaling their progress but marking the path taken. Invisible breadcrumbs. Braille footprints.

"Marlon," Jane called out as she rushed past Blake. He had suspected as much, though the figure looked leaner, more ragged, much older than ten years would add to a person. A carnie with the gift of guessing one's age, if there be such a gift, would fail miserably with this poor man boy.

"Jane?" Then, recognition, all question marks left to the insects. "Jane! You finally made it."

Blake stepped forward, aware of being on edge. He watched as the long-lost brother and sister embraced, an awkward thing in many ways. As if they remembered only the people they were, strangers glimmering from the past, nothing more. Of course, time had passed, lives had changed, the brittle princess had become the steely queen. The frantic, mad man boy transformed into the man made of twigs and perseverance, yet still a boy.

"You've just made it, my dear sister," Marlon said, taking her hand in his. Blake registered Jane's desire to flinch, yet also her desire to hold on and never let him go. She seemed trapped in a tangle of emotions. The circumstances did not help alleviate her wary condition.

Insects sprinted between the ubiquitous cats. Many feline eyes peered out from the dark corners as if they were wary.

"You should have been with me the whole trip, Jane. What wonders await. It could have been ours."

"Only one at a time," a voice said, deep as though dipped in thick, black oil and full of glee. The shadows along a stone slab shuffled, the cats causing a commotion. A figure resided there.

Burroughs?

The walls bristled with life. Blake clenched his fists, the right one reminding him of the past.

"Come with me, Marlon. Let me help you. Let me help you out of this life and to one that will bring you...happiness."

"Happiness? What do you know of happiness? I want this. You know I have wanted the ultimate experience since before I left. Life unhinged. This is the real deal, the pure distillation of that quest. I want this."

"But it cannot lead to anywhere but deeper into the hole you've called home for so long, Marlon..." Jane stroked Marlon's arm.

Blake picked up on Marlon's under-the-radar reaction, a subtle shudder of discomfort. The arm bent oddly, all bones momentarily gone. He seemed elastic.

Blake took a half-step toward them, blinked hard, and the arm seemed normal again. Bones solid as bones again. He paused, giving the siblings space, not one to intrude until necessary, which kept him amped and mentally armed for action. He felt haste was their best move. A flitting thought about the parameters of normal made him shake his head and turn away.

"You used to believe," Marlon said, sounding hurt. Sounding fourteen years old, stubbing a toe into the concrete floor.

Blake decided against hesitation. Marlon gesticulated oddly, then twisted a tight knot into his hair.

"Who is this, Jane?" Marlon asked.

"He is a friend. He's helped me find you. Please, let's find our way out of here—"

"No. Don't you understand? I am so close. I'm about to Ride the Centipede. I'm about to live as few before me ever have."

Jane glanced to Blake, pleading, as if he had the answers to anything here.

Blake remained silent, observing, letting them work it out. The hackles on his neck bristled with unease. This place inspired dread but, more so, a sense that anything could happen at any time pervaded it all. He changed his strategy, turning to the stone block, the unsettled allegiance of the shadows as if concealment of this figure was unnecessary. Despite curiosity, he wanted the figure to remain within the womb of darkness.

"Burroughs?"

"Who were you expecting, Dr. Benway?"

He could see it in Jane's features, the scrubbing away of shadows across her always serious demeanor. This was Burroughs. Jane was enamored yet fearful.

Marlon simply smiled, relief and anticipation propping up the corners of his lips. He was captivated.

Blake wanted out of there ASAP. The vibe was making his skin crawl. Or perhaps it was the insects. He pawed at his sleeves, pulling at the cuffs.

The world was at a standstill. Here, time was irrelevant. He gauged the sensation, the tick-tock of footsteps only a suggestion of the passage of time as they made their way to Marlon, and Burroughs. This limbo state dominated. Blake couldn't escape the sense of being stuck, waiting because that was all he could do. Yet, he could leave, this much was true. He'd led Jane to Marlon, now it was up to her to finish the deal, lead him out. He could just walk away. There was no reason for him to linger here, waiting for nothing but to be a guide out. Out was behind him. Jane could make the trek, hand in hand or arm in arm with Marlon. She could do it. She could.

Why did he stay? But her eyes told a different story. This woman who seemed made of iron and grit, was made of flesh and blood, emotions and hope. Hope, a word used by the weak to make it to the next day, and to endure the torture of their meager existence. Hope, a word he hadn't thought of in years, not one to cater to his weaknesses. Not one to allow false idols or frivolous fodder to fill the headspace usually clogged with alcohol.

So why was he waiting?

Jane glanced at him as she held Marlon's hand.

He stayed to be lost with her, to be supportive in a situation that did not bode well for a positive outcome. He stayed because it was the human thing to do, even as he listened to Marlon ask Burroughs how much longer? And Burroughs replied, "Just about time." before he laughed, a tectonic rumble that made Blake's balls scrunch up into the cavity above his scrotum.

He stayed because in Jane's eyes he saw a little girl's desperation...

(*Claire, sweet Claire...*)

"Who's that?" Jane said, her eyes peering behind Blake.

Blake, always attentive, had allowed his concentration on Jane and Marlon (*and Claire*) to distract him from the bigger picture, though he'd sensed something he only qualified as not good ripple throughout his body.

The sound of footsteps, muffled yet approaching, welcomed him as he turned around. A squeaky, metallic sound as well. Four figures neared. Two silhouettes in suits, one of them pushing a wheelchair carrying a third figure of curiously indiscernible shape. But these figures seemed insubstantial in the presence of the fourth man. A man who's eyes lit their way. A big man, with lightning for hair, and a countenance to melt glaciers.

The big fella from Roswell.

Rudolf Chernobyl.

And he was not looking too good.

As the idiom goes: All bets were off.

Confirmation was attained with the first words to pass from Chernobyl's lips: "What brings you to these parts, Cowboy?"

CHAPTER 31

CHERNOBYL

Rudolf Chernobyl rubbed his hands together, the friction white hot, practically welding them as one. He did not need to look down to confirm this. He felt it. He was white hot everywhere.

He pulled his hands apart. A drooping web of light dripped to the floor, spattered and faded.

"Probably the same thing that brought you here, Chernobyl," Cowboy said, his stance one for action.

Rudolf Chernobyl thought him a fool for both the statement and the stance. But at least he did not need to introduce himself to Cowboy, whose name did not matter in the scope of what he was after.

It all came down to priorities.

"Who are these people, Jane?" a man said, a lean, praying mantis of a man. From his previous fleeting moment in his presence, Rudolf knew this was—

"Marlon. Son." The voice was thick and sticky, resonant as if spoken from within a barrel.

Rudolf turned to face the thing that called itself Mr. Smith, the mask slipping fast. Father or freak or remnant of fire, it disgusted even him to view it.

It. Warren Teagarden.

"Father?" Rudolf watched the woman take a hesitant step toward them, then halt as the wheelchair was rolled into view. "Oh, my…"

"Father? No, you cannot be here, *Father*. I buried you and your depraved desires, buried, never to be—"

"Marlon, stop." The woman, the sister, Jane was her name, if Rudolf remembered correctly from the news reports those many years ago. "Stop with the fantasy here, with the fantasy of what our father did to you. Of all of it, the lies. Stop, my brother. Come back with me and let me help you."

"A family reunion. How delightful. What do you make of that, Cowboy?"

"I don't make anything of it. It's not my place to judge."

"But if you were a wagering man, how would you see this playing out?"

Cowboy's face remained firm. A poker face set on bluff?

Rudolf smiled.

"Now, get the drug. The syringe. It must be here, somewhere." Warren Teagarden's voice made Rudolf's ears ache.

"No, Father. You've taken everything else, but not this. This is mine and mine alone." Marlon's fists clenched, ball peen knobs at the end of his long arms.

"Father, why didn't you tell me you had survived the fire? Why didn't—"

"Tell your brother to give me the syringe, Princess. Tell him his father needs it in order to…to get better." An undercurrent of something that itched at the cerebrum of all present infused the request with a sense of unwholesome need.

"No. The drug is mine," Rudolf said, arms folded over his chest. *Deny me and die.*

Warren Teagarden, in all his repulsive glory, turned to Rudolf and said, "I paid you to get—"

"To get you to Marlon. Which I have done. I expect the rest of my fee sent to my account promptly, as soon as we get out of here. But the drug...the drug is mine."

"No. Both of you. No. I've already injected my blood—*my blood*—into Burroughs. It's my ride on the Centipede. No others can experience—"

"No others?" Frustration from the mound of scarred, permanently melted flesh that was Warren Teagarden. "I want that syringe."

"Father, what are you doing?" Jane said, eyes glossy in the inconsistent light.

"Getting what I want, what I need, Princess. As I've always gotten from your brother." The statement prodded the truth from its hiding place, naked and ashamed. Marlon cowered, shaking. The look on Jane's face was priceless, no deposit, no return, just drained of hope.

Rudolf, though amused, remained firm.

"And I've told both of you, the drug is mine." The humidity in the cavernous room escalated to the edge of bearable, Rudolf's ire felt by everybody.

"Aren't you listening? It won't work for either of you. It will only work for me."

"Listen to the boy," Burroughs said, from the sheath of shadows. "This is his ride, amigos."

Defiant, Rudolf turned to Warren Teagarden, leaned in so close his Sahara warm breath dipped into the gristle-topped ridges and blackened crevices that defined the mottled, scarred flesh. "You wanted Marlon. You've got Marlon. I don't care about what else you want, especially if it's this wonder drug, this ultimate experience promised by it. No price will get that for you. Because it's mine now. Mine now that I am here and *it* is here. Anybody who stands in my way will meet the most unpleasant of repercussions. Do you understand?"

Warren Teagarden whined and sobbed. Quivered in anger, frustration. A multitude of curious sounds emanated from his mouth, even if Rudolf wasn't certain exactly where the mouth was placed on this bulbous blob.

"Did you...harm Marlon, Father?" Jane said, perhaps in need of confirmation of something else Rudolf didn't care about.

The sobbing hitched, a spike of laughter, a sign of sick perversion.

"Enough of this. You all should congregate at the homestead and hash over the fond or fouled memories. I've the Centipede to ride."

Rudolf started toward Burroughs, when Cowboy angled in front of him.

"You don't want to do that, Cowboy."

"I can't let you harm them on your way to the drug. Seems things are out of sorts and—"

With one swipe of his forearm, Cowboy was lifted with little effort and tossed against a stone block. He slumped there, out cold.

"Blake!" Jane said, two steps forward, into the path of Rudolf.

"I suggest you—"

Gunshots punctured Rudolf's back. The sound was a dead thump. The sensation burned within him. He turned.

Beef jerky grinned at him, as if bullets gave him any advantage.

"Shoot him again. I want the goddamned drug."

"You should pay attention, amigo. This ride is for Marlon and Marlon alone." Burroughs said. "You won't like what it does to you. It's Marlon's ride."

"I don't care. I've nothing left but pain."

Rudolf's eyes pulsed brightly. Shiny dark gray tears streaked down his unhealthy-looking face. Lead. The bullets did no harm.

"Shoot him again, goddamnit," Warren Teagarden said. His warbly inflection indicated conviction had been replaced by resignation. Or perhaps desperation. Rudolf didn't understand either.

"I don't think so," Rudolf said, stepping toward them.

Beef Jerky and the other goon spun and hightailed it into the darkness from whence they came. No matter where they ran or hid, Rudolf would deal with them later.

Warren Teagarden slumped in his wheelchair and seemed to crawl into himself.

Rudolf thrust a searing talon into that clump of malleable meat and squeezed. Teagarden burned, but it was so much more than the burn that had left its scorched signature in Warren Teagarden's flesh.

The man yelped, a gurgling mix of shock and anguish.

The woman, Jane, her confusion evident in her mixed allegiance, cried out.

Marlon grunted, satisfied in a way.

Even the Cowboy groaned from where he stood shaking and rubbing his head in Rudolf's peripheral vision.

Rudolf pulled his arm out of Warren Teagarden. A cauterized cavity yawned at him, still sizzling at his intrusion. It looked like a lumpy volcano. Steam wafted from the hole where Rudolf had reached in and squashed the heart into blackened pulp.

Turning back to Marlon and Jane, keeping Cowboy in his sights, he said, "Time to take a hike, or take a dive. Which will it be?"

Marlon ran into the strange shadows atop a stone block, speaking, but the words drifted past Rudolf's ears without understanding. Nonetheless, Marlon's urgency demanded Rudolf follow suit.

Jane was frozen in his path. Rudolf relished the possibility of distributing more pain as he raised his arm, eyes rimmed red with designs on slaughter. Cowboy entered stage left and shoved Jane from behind, pushing her out of Rudolf's path. He stood tall as he moved in front of her, protective. "Marlon, it's time to go," Cowboy said, cojones as big as cannon balls.

"It's mine. It's mine!" Marlon held up the syringe filled with a weird, iridescent fluid that promised so much. Not just blood, it was something else; something more.

Rudolf's attentions were realigned. Marlon. The syringe.

"Marlon, please, dear brother. Let it be."

"No. It's mine. If for no other reason than to blot out what that thing we knew as our father did to me. More so, the ultimate experience awaits."

"Like father, like son," Rudolf said, marching toward Marlon with mad intent.

CHAPTER 32

BLAKE

Blake teetered, still woozy. He pressed his right hand to his ribs. At least a couple were broken. Breathing hurt. He should have listened to Potters, but this lost woman inspired rare compassion amid a life drained of any.

Cats sprinted to and fro, agitated by the unaccustomed intrusion in their underworld paradise.

The acrid stench of whatever Chernobyl had done to Warren Teagarden brought tears. Blake's nose hairs twitched like the legs of surrendering spiders.

Jane seemed oblivious to it all. Her focus was on her brother's safety, which was in dire straits as Chernobyl bore down on him.

The grogginess sifted through Blake's head like a mist made of fluttering insect wings, distorting, the pixels rolling on a screen gone sideways.

Chernobyl's almost handsome yet ruthless countenance, though considerably scarred since their first encounter, started to bubble. Boils played a symphony of havoc, disfiguring him further. Mutilating from within. Blake sensed Chernobyl's heat, the aura skating over his flesh and clothing. Electric charges gone awry.

Blake would think it all impossible, yet with everything up to now, the impossible was most likely probable in this strange new world order.

Marlon's lean figure moved with insect agility, jittery, of a purpose, holding the syringe in his hand at the end of an arm that seemed too long, too long. Ready, or as ready as he could be, to engage in whatever was necessary—battle; *war*—with the Russian. As if he had a chance. Yet, as Blake observed as Marlon's knees bent backwards, maybe he did. With the general design of Marlon's body a mystery, Blake had no idea what to expect.

"Do something. That monster will kill Marlon."

"What can we do? You've seen what he can do."

"But...Marlon..."

He had to try something. Talk was their only hope, Chernobyl's strength too much for even Blake. Words might work, or words might fall to the concrete floor and join the insects drawn to Chernobyl's bright eyes. Blake watched them swarm, yet during approach, they snapped, crackled, and bounced off the invisible field around Chernobyl, landing in charred clumps at the monster's feet.

What choice did he have?

"Chernobyl. Let him go. Don't hurt him. Please." Blake did not know whether it was a plea to stop the inevitable or if Marlon really had a chance. The images filling his eyes only complicated the issue.

"He's lost. Please let us help him. Please, Mr. Chernobyl," Jane said, her voice like cool air passing through a crack in the world.

"I don't need your help, dear sister. I don't need anybody's help. You had your chance long ago to join me. You did not. Well, it's too late. I've got what I want, and it's time to inject this into—"

Chernobyl grabbed Marlon's too long arm.

Blake took a few steps toward them, palm to Jane's chest, making sure she stayed put.

"You already had a taste, Cowboy. You know you don't want to go there again."

Blake continued to approach them, then spoke again, uncertain of what action he could take that would make a difference. Something physical was out of the question, what with his broken ribs; more so, what with Chernobyl's obvious advantages.

"Marlon. You've seen what Chernobyl can do. There's no winning here. There's nothing but escape, and leaving this madman to his bounty."

"This is my ride. The Centipede is mine," Marlon said, as Blake watched antenna sprout from his forehead. Blake rubbed his eyes and Marlon was just a man again, but Chernobyl was not...

"I'm not one for patience, Cowboy. I'm not one to be denied. Marlon has made his choice. Like the rest of these infernal flying insects, he shall have his wings clipped," Chernobyl said. He clamped his large hands on Marlon's shoulders.

Steaming boils burst and dripped acid down Chernobyl's face. He smoldered, changed. Blake stood frozen as Rudolf Chernobyl tore Marlon's arms from the sockets Marlon wailed, a wordless cry.

Blake stumbled back, shocked, though he knew he shouldn't be, by the ease with which Chernobyl had maimed the insect, Marlon.

Chernobyl dropped the left arm, reached up to the still clenched fist of the right arm, and pried the syringe from the dead meat fingers.

Blood spattered blackly against the concrete as Marlon tripped over his own feet, landing dully on the floor. His head hit full force, no arms to impede his fall. The crack ricocheted through the vast space. Ricocheted from far away, but made its way back to Blake's ears.

Jane, her face shiny with tears, the dam broken, shielded her gasping mouth with the back of her hand. She'd made steps closer, wanting to help her brother, but Blake's raised palm was a stop signal she dared not cross.

Chernobyl tossed the severed limb in her direction. The bent elbow slammed hard into her belly. She gasped again, this time for stolen breath. Blood stained her clothes, her face. She clenched her eyes closed.

Blake figured she was praying to wake up from this nightmare. Because this nightmare, no matter how mad, felt like cement hardening in his bones.

This was the most awake he'd ever been.

"You think you're one mean fuck, don't you, Mr. Chernobyl? Trust me when I say, this was Marlon's experience to be had. Ah-Puch and his death starved cohorts will have their way with you in Mitnal, if the Centipede doesn't just eat you itself," Burroughs said from the darkness.

"Whoever you are, your words are accounted for and subtracted from recall. They mean nothing in my quest for the ultimate experience. Ah-Puch or any of his Mayan swine do not stand a chance against Rudolf Chernobyl."

Blake was at a loss for the vagaries of Ah-Puch or anything Mayan. Perhaps Jane could clue him in…if they made it out of here alive.

Chernobyl peered into the fluid shadows around the block of concrete. Cats hissed and scurried from his glaring lighthouse surveillance.

Blake backed away, sensing whatever was next was not something he wanted to experience, even if from the outside.

Jane moved past him, eyes on Marlon while Chernobyl and Burroughs verbally waltzed.

"In your case, Mr. Chernobyl, you will experience that which you have never experienced —"

"That is the point of this whole ordeal, is it not?"

Blake reached out and took Jane's left hand in his right. His damaged right.

She turned to him. "Perhaps I can drag him out of harm's way."

Blake glanced at the lifeless slug of a body that was Marlon and knew harm had already had its way with him.

He gripped her hand harder. The ache swelled.

"The Centipede is meant for one person.," Burroughs said. "Anybody else who interrupts, anybody else who takes the drug instead, goes for a ride into the darkest realm of themselves. Has nothing to do with the chosen one's experience. Would have more to do with the evil mix masturbating in your baking, black soul, handsome." Burroughs sniggered, a nasty sound accompanied by the taint of sulphur. "In your case..."

"In my case, it's time for the ultimate experience." Chernobyl said. "Dark or light or whatever awaits. It will be mine!"

"Quiet now. It's too late," Blake said. "Quiet now. And don't watch." He held onto Jane's hand as she teetered between here and there, where her brother lay motionless.

Rudolf Chernobyl thrust the needle into his arm and pressed down on the plunger until it was empty. Chernobyl's already chaotic appearance, as if being boiled alive, went viral.

He dropped to his knees and let out a wail that put Marlon's arms-torn-off wail to shame. Though his was accompanied by words.

"No. No. Father..." Chernobyl blurted, his mouth twisting and lips peeling.

Blake wondered about Chernobyl's father, as reported to him by Potters—"... *born the day of the Chernobyl disaster, crawled from the radiation and took shape as a man, lightning bolt hair, some kind of new breed of human and radiation, a blotch, an aberration, cancer with teeth.* "

"Yes, Mr. Chernobyl. You will experience that which you have never experienced. And being of obviously strange origin, one can only guess as to what that might be."

"No. Not *this*."

Blake squinted as Rudolf Chernobyl went supernova. Watched as the madman's, the mad-*thing's* flesh burned bright, the light within searing as lasers dissecting a dead frog. But Chernobyl was anything but dead. The process turned him inside out in a rolling, roiling, regurgitating mass of bones splintering and grinding to dust, while flesh melted and organs roasted in a broth of boiling blood. Tumors, dozens and more, with black razor teeth smiled and salivated and chomped down on the thing that was Rudolf Chernobyl, cannibalizing him as well as each other.

Eyes born of the deepest pit of Hell stared out at Blake as he stared back.

"Dear God," Blake said, his gorge rising but settling in the back of his throat.

Jane pressed herself closer to him as she glanced back, turned away, and glanced back again.

Chernobyl protested, the sound spiraling as an ambulance siren, but no help was to be had. The thing that was Rudolf Chernobyl mutated into a concentrated blob of raw, red meat in constant motion, as if caught in an invisible machine that pulled and teased him like taffy.

The smells crashed as a wave over him, entering his nostrils as well as his flesh. He gagged on the sickening scents of burned plastic and animal musk; damp, aged ruins and electrical currents. Blake found himself backing away as the invisible tentacles of intolerable heat reached out to him.

The core of the thing that was Rudolf Chernobyl glowed as sunlight kissing chrome. The glare spread outward.

Insects and lizards flew past Blake's head. A percussive rhythm grew spastic as they smacked into the glare and instantly turned to ash.

The thing that was Rudolf Chernobyl's tortured scream droned on.

Cats whisked past Blake and Jane, their claws tearing at their clothing, attempting to latch on to either of them. Scratching posts made of flesh, drawing blood. As if they noticed.

The amorphous mass of Chernobyl swelled. The vortex of light to rival the sun's became a vacuum.

It was feeding.

Marlon's broken body was sucked toward Chernobyl.

Broken, but not dead, Marlon mumbled something unintelligible.

"Marlon," Jane yelled as she shuffled swiftly around Blake just as Blake felt the pull at his back, the vacuum of the vortex demanding more sustenance. Her movement loosened his hold…and she was airborne.

One moment. One moment that meant everything. One moment to save a life. Blake reached out with his damaged right hand—it was nearest to her—and grabbed hold of her small right hand—

—*When Blake was twenty-three years old, he met a stripper, Leticia Conley, at a club at the tattered edge of Portland, Oregon, while on a case. During the three weeks he was there, he got to know her well enough to understand in life we are given gifts, and perhaps this woman whose aspirations were much like his, just wanting a normal life away from the grime and grit and streets covered in shit, was his gift.*

They professed their love and were married two months later.

Blake got a job doing construction, something he seemed made for. He liked the physicality of it, no matter the underlying aches and pains it weaved in his body.

Normal kicked into high gear when Leticia got pregnant three months into the marriage.

Nine months later, Claire was born. The light of his life, a reason to wake up in the morning…or the middle of the night. The couple embraced parenthood, even if they had no clue what they were doing.

At least Blake tried, while Leticia showed signs of post-partum depression.

Blake worked ten-hour shifts and come home to the small apartment with his daughter stinking of unchanged diapers and his wife dozing on the sofa, a liquor bottle or three dead and drained on the brown carpet.

Confrontation led to no good. She was slipping, and hard. Blake tried to garner the sympathy to care, but he could not do that and take care of their daughter as well. It was not something he was good at, not a part of his history, no matter how hard he tried.

When he got home on a Wednesday evening in early January, three weeks from Claire's first birthday, and found his daughter alone in the unlocked apartment, that was his breaking point.

How could Leticia leave this precious child alone. How could she not care?

It was the first time Blake ever remembered crying.

Shaking, he took the child in his arms, changed her diaper and gave her a bottle of milk while she muttered, "Dadda" and "Momma." He could not let her mother ruin her life. As much as he loved Leticia, she was a product of a hard upbringing that was ingrained in her soul. The empty syringe on the floor next to a pacifier was evidence enough that he had to save his daughter from her negligence.

Uncertain of what to do, he knew at the very least he had to take Claire away. The weather had pushed below freezing, and light snow flurries had commenced a couple hours previous, the reason he was sent home early from work. Negotiating the icy stairs, he made way to the car, put Claire in the car seat without strapping her in as he meant to clear the parking lot before her mother might show up. As if that really was a possibility. That was a confrontation he did not want to have. He was afraid of where his anger might take it.

So he drove, no plan but to be away. Made it to Interstate 84 east, when he realized driving in this weather was not safe, no matter his haste to be away. Remembered a co-worker who lived in Stevenson, Washington, just across the Bridge of the Gods, and took the exit to go there. Chill for the night. Think.

He only experienced black ice this once in his life, as he approached the bridge…and the car swerved off the road… and into the Columbia Gorge. And the nightmare that haunts his every sleeping hour.

…as the current pulled the child away, he reached toward her with his damaged right hand. The current pushed back: it wanted its prize. He yelled and water filled his mouth. He tried again, desperate to save the child, his daughter. The frothing tide pushed against his fingers, intent on bending them all the way back to his wrist, flattened out as a stump sculpted from futility. "Daddy," she said, not "Dadda," or "Momma," but "Daddy," clear and crisp. Her first and last true word. His curse forever. He watched his daughter's shocked expression as she lost the feeble grip on the car seat she should have been strapped into, the eyes moments ago full of joy, now nothing more than dull buttons on the rag doll that remained. He yelled again, a stream of bubbles flowing from the inside roof of the car and out the crack in the driver's side window. He pushed against the stick shift with strong legs, his shoulder shattering the window. The sound was a muffled explosion. He watched the rag doll fade to black beyond the car's beams. He closed his eyes, fighting back tears as he swam up, or somewhere, this watery oblivion his personal hell…

—and held on for dear life, even as he fell to the hard concrete floor. Even as he slid toward the force, luckily hooking his foot on one of the blocks of stone.

A moment of peace shimmered through Blake, an impossible nod to a past he could never change, but here, now, he could. And did.

Nothing else mattered but the straining muscles in Blake's arm, and the grip loosening at the force of the pull.

No!

Suddenly, he heard Burroughs exclaim, "Well, this is rather unexpected." Burroughs skin started to tear. From within him, a cut and paste collage of insects and syringes filled with multi-colored substances darted out from beneath his skin, before the skin turned to dust and he was sucked into the ball of light.

"Please hold on," Jane said, her voice tiny amid the tumultuous congregation of noises converging within the ball of light and the scream loud enough to shatter eardrums and the universe, Chernobyl's final soliloquy, before tentacles of electricity, radiation—Blake was not sure, he could only watch in awe and fear—lashed out from the ball of light that was Rudolf riding the centipede.

Blake held on.

Held on...

Rudolf Chernobyl reached for Jane.

The tentacles tried to wrap around her ankle and she screamed, kicking at them.

"Blake..."

Blake concentrated all his strength to his arm, his forever damaged hand.

"Blake," she cried.

The tentacles had taken a shoe.

Blake stared into Jane's eyes as she pleaded with him, but beyond her face, he caught a glimpse of the shoe bursting into flame and melting. The tentacle, like a child throwing a fit, smashed the concrete floor. Blake felt the earth quake and watched as cracks dissected the floor beneath them.

Blake pulled his focus completely back to her eyes, holding her in his sight as his arm beaded profusely, sweat coating the floor for an instant before evaporating amid the escalating heat.

If it didn't stop soon, it wouldn't matter if he held on or not, they'd be barbecued alive. Blake pushed this thought away and continued to stare into Jane's eyes and did the only thing he could do.

He held on.

Held on...

There was a moment when dozens of tentacles rose up from the churning ball of meat and light and death, for sure, and the white noise that filled the gaps between thoughts pierced with abandon, mutating into a howl, human and of such depth and agony Blake could not imagine. The tentacles arched as scorpion stingers ready to take them, now. Ready, but then the cry fell silent, momentarily erasing sound from the slate of present experience.

Rudolf Chernobyl was no more. He was a broadening throb of intensity…and gone.

Jane dropped leaden to the floor.

Blake's damaged hand refused to let go of her. He pulled her toward him.

"Jane. Jane." He ran his other hand through her hair, along the ridge of her cheekbone.

All he could do was hold her. It seemed the right thing.

After a time, the adrenaline settling into a bearable pace, Jane looked up at him and said, "He's gone?"

"Yes. Gone forever, I'm sure."

"Where?"

"Just gone."

Made as much sense as anything else, under the circumstances. As if answers were to be had right now. Exhaustion, perhaps, but no heavy thinking.

Minutes in silence. A sanctuary of sorts.

Jane started to sob, shaking her head as she gently hit Blake's chest.

Blake took her fist and broke open the fingers, wrapped her hand in his.

And held on some more.

CHAPTER 33

BLAKE

Terrance Blake did not know that when he was seventy-nine years old he would die in his sleep from a broken heart. A life lived. If someone had told him that would be how he would die, he would have laughed and said they were crazy.

He did not know that between this moment and then, he would build a true friendship with Jane Teagarden. He would end up heading security for her sprawling home in the hills outside of Los Angeles, as if she really needed security. But it was what they both needed.

He would perform the duties of a surrogate father and give Jane Teagarden away at her wedding twelve years after her brother and father had died.

He would meet an ageing actress, Miranda Salander, famous for being a Scream Queen, at the wedding. They would connect, much to Jane Teagarden's joy. "I've been trying to find you a woman for years," she would say afterwards.

Terrance Blake and Miranda Salander would be married less than a year later.

Jane Teagarden would have her only child a year and a half after her wedding. Her husband, Robert Weathers, an investment banker, would insist they give the boy his father's first name, William. Jane agreed, as long as she got to give him his middle name.

William Terrance Weathers.

When she told Blake this, he cried for only the second time in his life that he could remember, then smiled.

So this was happiness?

The moments big and small would all matter, because he had changed. He was not the same man he was before. That man was buried underneath a house in Lawrence, Kansas.

The night he knew he was leaving this earthly realm, he would call Jane and tell her as much.

"I just wanted to say knowing you has been the brightest joy of this man's journey, but it's time for me to go. I love you!"

"I love you, too, Terrance." She sniffled. She understood. "Without you, my life would never have made sense."

"Funny how it all works out, isn't it? Meeting as we did. Tracking a lost boy, losing the lost boy…and finding what we both needed to make sense of our lives. And finding out what he wanted was always within reach."

"What do you mean?"

"The ultimate experience."

"But what do you mean?" Jane asked, her voice cracking. Blake could tell she was sobbing, though she hid it pretty well.

"You know exactly what I mean." He smiled. He knew she could sense it in her heart.

"Yes," she said, the sobbing louder, but still contained.

"I'm going now. Time to sleep, sweet angel."

"Safe journey, my friend," Jane said, now crying.

"No tears, sweet angel. Time for me to hook up with my wonderful Miranda, and another sweet angel who I haven't seen for too long." Claire… "Or time for me to become a worm buffet," he said, and even through their tears—yes, he would be crying at this point, too—they would both laugh.

No matter the destination, it would not matter.

Because here, now, two months after watching a man who was not a man turn into a ball of soul-extinguishing light, and watching a man who was still a boy strive for something he could never understand, and holding on to a woman for dear life while reality took a vacation, he was standing at the vast bay window of Jane Teagarden's large house in the Los Angeles hills, looking out over the valley as the sun started to break through the cloud cover, uncertain of what she wanted from him. What more could she want from him?

When she said in an offhand way, dodging around the subject, finally getting to the point, she'd like him to head her security for the house, which really didn't need security, but came with an adjacent cottage—room and board and considerable wages—he surprised himself and blurted, "Yes," before she'd even laid out all the details.

It wasn't security either of them needed. It was friendship with one who understood as no other would, what they had gone through.

Perhaps it was the view that inspired his immediate reaction, taking in the most astonishing rainbow he had ever seen. Red and orange and yellowgreenblueindigoviolet, more brilliant than any painting, than anything imagination could create. This was the world before him, nature sending him signs. A pot at the end of the rainbow...

He would move in the following day, to the apartment next to the house.

They would celebrate Thanksgiving for the first time together a little over a month later, the two of them eating pizza delivery—sausage, artichoke hearts, green olives; damn good—and talking about everything but what they experienced. Bonding.

It was, in a way, the beginning of something neither of them had truly embraced until now, dealing with their demons for so long.

All Terrance Blake knew right now was this: The ultimate experience awaited their participation.

The ultimate experience was always there, it just depended on both of them to come around and join in, please.

The ultimate experience, every second precious, no matter the pain of loss, the participation of chaos, or the passion of love, all part of the deal. No longer a drifter, he was now a participant in the grand scheme of things called Life.

Either that or he was a fool to be taken on this ride any longer, but his instincts were keen on the possibilities otherwise…

Afterword

The Birth of the Centipede

I'm in Italy. Summer of 2013. My girlfriend, Alessandra, lives there. It's July and it's hot already. Alessandra gets August off, as does much of Italy, so I'm left to my own warped devices during the days as she takes her son to school and heads off to work. My mindset is to figure out what Big Project will follow up my previous book, the mini-collection, *Autumn in the Abyss*. I'm thinking it will be a novel, of which I've completed two: *The Corner of His Mind*, more magic realism than horror (unpublished), and *The Wilderness Within*, a trippy, psychological affair amidst a sinister, living forest (published in 2018 by Trepidatio/Journalstone).

I'm thinking it will be a novel...but I am in need of an idea. That's when I start to go through files containing snippets of ideas and openings, of which there are dozens, seeing if anything grabs my attention, when I run into this:

William S. Burroughs sits across from me and Kiddo and says, "More," so I take the needle from my arm and hand it to him. He puts it in the cellophane clear skin of his arm, barely covering the bone beneath, yet filling out ever slightly as he injects the blood I've just drawn, just as we've heard it's done.

For what purpose? Curiosity—we had to follow up on the rumors.

That's why we're sitting in this dank mausoleum outside of Kansas City, unmarked and more a gray bunker, but it works for those like us who want a taste of one of the true masters, as well as the promised deathball hybrid drug infusion we've heard can lead to some wild, hallucinatory imagery worthy of Naked Lunch. The deathball hybrid drug mix being one's blood injected into Burroughs' long dead body—dead but not dead, something lingers, this soiled spirit—and after it runs through his system for an hour or two, and he's riffing big time about the usual Burroughs subject matters of drugs, homosexual sex, subversion of many forms, that's when you're supposed to pop the needle into your arm again, press the plunger and open your mind's eye to the Burroughs acid trip of your wildest dreams.

Too bad Kiddo wasn't of the proper mindset to really enjoy the rainbowtastic melting monsters and bulbous beauties—or extra [ ] cocks, for those like Burroughs in that respect as well— heck, we didn't have a clue yet, so it could go anywhere— because he was afraid of letting go.

We'd had the conversation on the way here, after getting directions from Matteo, a dread-locked, mouth full of silver, slang end of slang spitting Italian living in the states, floating about, as a permanent location might trigger suspicion, something Burroughs doesn't need—hence, we met him in Lafayette, Louisiana, checking out the crocodiles, when he finally came to us, after we had mentioned our deep interest and understanding of how things were done, then forgotten.

What happens in a gray concrete mausoleum in Kansas City, stays in a gray concrete mausoleum in Kansas City.

But only I understood, and in order for things not to go so south Satan's spreading your cheeks and getting behind some inspiration and anal sex you might not want to indulge in, well, Kiddo had to come around.

Anyway, long story red-penned, I am sitting here about ready to ask for the needle and the ride, just as Kiddo should be doing—Burroughs is a duel-armed dealer—when Burroughs catches the vibe and says,

That's it, raw and spat out in one shot, brackets for the missing word included. It ends with a cliffhanger, more likely me uncertain of what the hell is going on, so I let it be. But this weird snippet sets my brain to contemplating something more, a fuller picture, a potential Big Project aligning itself in my head.

As it percolates, I know there will be a detective, family with money, and an addict seeking to do *something* as he searches for what that snippet suggests. The ultimate high, courtesy of William S. Burroughs.

As I begin the writing process, I'm still piecing things together. I get it rolling with the detective, a call, a mission. I know, for reasons only the writer's brain ever understands, that I want the novel to be a kind of road trip, very David Lynch circa *Wild at Heart*, but the trip is through the use of a special drug, an extension of what's known as *Riding the Centipede*, which will lead to the destination noted above, with a transfer of blood from the addict to Burroughs, and then back to the addict. Burroughs who is not dead, just dreaming, much like Cthulhu...

As I mentally map out the pit stops along the way, the bizarre characters I want to meet, the first one to strike my interest is called Chernobyl Bob, along with his radioactive, metallic dogs, the ratchet hounds. As I start to build elements of this pit stop, the character starts nudging himself deeper into my psyche. He wants more room to play.

At this point, I've started writing the novel, and as I reach the end of chapter one, detective Terrance Blake is set on a path by Jane Teagarden, a rich socialite, to find her brother, Marlon Teagarden, whose drug addiction is begging him to go to mysterious places...but then, a wrench is thrown into the mix.

Chernobyl Bob has become Rudolf Chernobyl, and he's got big plans. He is that special spark that will give the novel direction, a broader scope, and some genuinely horrific sequences.

At this point, the novel begins to pour out with real intention, real force. It's where I want to be every day. It takes over my brainspace.

An amusing aside: I don't usually listen to music while writing, and I still don't, despite what I will write here. Alessandra picked up a four-disc set—the first four albums—of Echo and the Bunnymen for me when I got to Rome. As I wrote, I played those CDs on a loop, especially the first two. But it's not as if I was listening to them. I distinctly remember locking in with writing as the music would play and eventually stopping, tilting my head up and thinking, What song is this? And realizing in most cases it was six or eight songs into an album…and I hadn't heard anything! When I am locked in, distractions or music do not matter. It's the characters who are talking to me, and that is all I am hearing.

Upon completion a few months later, early 2014, I sent *Riding the Centipede* off to my now sadly shuttered publisher, Omnium Gatherum, and Kate Jonez. We had worked on my previous book, *Autumn in the Abyss*, and it was a wonderful learning experience for me. Working with Kate was a lesson in editing, clarity, and how to get a story right; it was a masterclass. She is a wonder as an editor!

I patiently waited for a response and after some time messaged her to see how it was going, if she had started reading it or if she had, if she had any thoughts she could pass my way. She informed me, oh yes, though she's still reading it, she will be publishing the novel. She said after she read chapter 8, she knew as much. I smiled. I knew why: it was the fully immersive quality of that chapter (as with much of the novel) that had gripped her, stolen her attention from the real world. The Centipede had crawled inside her head…

Riding the Centipede became a finalist for a Bram Stoker Award for Superiority in a Debut Novel. Those who read it commented privately or in reviews quite a favorably. This pleased me immensely, as I'd had so much fun getting it all down on paper. One never knows what to expect, but with *Riding the Centipede,* no matter the bizarre subject matter, I knew I'd gotten it right.

And here it is for you or was as you've probably just completed reading it…and I hope you've enjoyed your ride on the centipede…

– John Claude Smith
March 2025

About the Author

John Claude Smith has had three collections, four chapbooks, and two novels published, along with tales and/or poems in Vastarien, Pluto in Furs, and more magazines and anthologies. His debut novel, *Riding the Centipede*, was a Bram Stoker Award Finalist. His novel, *Our Savage Anatomies*, will be published by Hybrid Sequence Media in 2026. He splits his time between the East Bay across from San Francisco, and Rome, Italy, where his heart resides always.

Curious about other Crossroad Press books? Stop by our
website: http://crossroadpress.com
We offer quality writing
in digital, audio, and print formats.

Subscribe to our newsletter on the website homepage and
receive a free eBook.